Death Calling… Please Hold.

A Comic Novel

George Berkin

ISBN 979-8-9854324-0-4

Available as an electronic book. ISBN 979-8-9854324-1-1

Death Calling…

Please Hold.

ONE: HARRY

It is a truth universally acknowledged that a bereaved family in possession of a recently deceased relative must be in want of an undertaker.

It was a Tuesday afternoon, and everything seemed to be proceeding with nary a problem on the horizon. I had laid out Mr. Garrison Hopkins with my usual attention to the smallest of details. His red tie was perfectly knotted, set off smartly atop the stark white shirt and night sky blue jacket. His longish brown hair, with just a hint of gray around the edges, was perfectly combed.

Mr. Hopkins' open casket, white silk interior trimmed in gold, held him like a flower in an outstretched palm.

As is ordinary practice, the deceased's family stood next to the open casket. His wife, Allison, was still in shock since Mr. Hopkins, still in his 40s, had suddenly dropped dead of a heart attack. She was crying inconsolably as others gently held her as the line moved toward the coffin.

Their two young sons, both not yet teenagers, stood next to her, silent in their disbelief.

Mr. Hopkins' sudden demise, during an otherwise routine Saturday morning run not far from his suburban home, had shocked both staff and students at Eleanor Roosevelt Elementary, where he had worked for the past 14 years. The school's principal had made the announcement of his death during Monday morning homeroom, but few students had not already heard the news. Still, hearing the words echo over the loudspeaker was, to students and faculty, a second punch in the gut.

And now, the line to pay respects continued for hundreds of feet behind Mrs. Hopkins. Not far behind was Mr. Lloyd, the gym teacher, who looked perfectly formal in coat-and-tie, except for his ratty-looking gym shoes. Mrs. Anders, the music teacher, was walking bowed slightly forward, causing her glasses, on a chain, to sway back and forth with each step. Mr. Donaldson, the school's vice principal, kept pulling a handkerchief from his back pocket to wipe away tears.

The room was a near-silent sea of whispers when all present heard a sudden rat-tat-tat coming from the far end of the room. The abrupt series of knocks caused heads to pivot toward the noise and eyes to aim gazes at the explosive interruption.

There, striding swiftly toward the open casket, was a woman, a youngish-looking woman. A quick appraisal made her out to be, I would guess, early or middle 20s. Her hair, long and trailing her like the tail on a kite, was bright blond and streaked with pink. Her tight-fitting dress, funeral black and pressed up against lanky thighs, was so short that it made those legs seem, if possible, even longer. The legs were sarcophagus white.

What stood out, though, was her lipstick. If her lipstick was fire engine red, it was a mighty big fire.

And then, bending over the open casket, the young woman's face came straight down upon the defenseless face of Mr. Hopkins. With a noise that made even her just completed strides sound muted by comparison, the young woman planted a lip-smacking mouth-to-mouth kiss on Mr. Hopkins.

The room, in those few seconds, went silent, too shocked to immediately respond.

And then, the young woman, once again upright, announced with the clarity of a church bell at midnight:

"Mr. Hopkins was my sixth-grade teacher," she said, in a loud and defiant voice, speaking from side to side to address her audience. "I've been in love with him ever since I was in the sixth grade, but he never suspected a thing. I've been wanting to do this for ten years, and now I can."

The young woman turned once again toward the open casket. "Mr. Hopkins, I'm so sorry. We could have made a great couple. And now it's too late."

Bursting into tears, the young woman strode out of the room. No way to chase her down. She was gone in a flash, as quickly as she had entered.

"Did you see that?" said Mr. Lloyd.

"What was that all about?" said Mrs. Anders, not quite processing.

"Who was that?" cried Mr. Donaldson.

Mrs. Hopkins was too stunned to say anything.

"Mom!" said her oldest son.

"Mom!" echoed the younger.

Me, I just stood there kind of stunned. Viewings are supposed to be sedate affairs, nothing like this. Heart struck, I approached the grieving widow.

"Mrs. Hopkins, I am so sorry," I said. "I had no idea she was going to do that."

Mrs. Hopkins quietly nodded.

Dear reader, let's pull a curtain over that scene so that the family can grieve in private. That done, let me introduce myself.

Call me Harry, Harry O'Toole.

By way of introduction, recall the famous opening line of a celebrated British author's bestselling novel. The novelist, perhaps especially popular in Austin, Texas, announced the essential need of every young man lucky enough to have a stack of ready cash. He is in want, our scribe tells us, of a wife.

And maybe that's true enough. The pursuit of marriage certainly makes for good bedtime reading.

But let's face it. Love and marriage, as they say, go together like a horse and carriage. But not everyone needs a horse, and not everybody is in want of a carriage.

Death, my friend, that's different.

Death (and taxes, alas), you can't avoid them. There are bachelors in the world, but no one escapes death forever. (Taxes, maybe.)

And so, everybody needs me, or somebody like me. Everyone in possession of a recently deceased relative is in want of an undertaker. In that troubled time when the grim reaper makes his unwanted visit, you will call upon me, your friendly, neighborhood, undertaker, or another representative of our noble profession.

By the way, please don't call me or any of my fellow laborers in the end of life business by that commonly used but unfortunate designation: funeral director. Oh, how "funeral director" stings! Privately, to ease our hurt, we joke. No "fun" in funeral. And we're not "directing" anything. We are simply trying to follow your precise instructions during this difficult time.

So, please, undertakers. We are undertakers, undertaking a noble and often less than fully appreciated service to honor your deceased relative. But, as you might imagine, things don't always go smoothly. Shortly after Mr. Hopkins' wannabe paramour made her dramatic appearance, my assistant walked in and told me that some guy straight out of GQ magazine had marched into my office.

"He was waving a handful of Benjamins."

"What does he want?"

"Not sure, but he did not seem very patient."

Friend, this undertaker profession is a strange business indeed. In most normal professions, life and happiness make the rounds. For us undertakers, death and sorrow are constant companions.

That simple fact, the fact that I am surrounded with death, with everything that accompanies death, is something I've long struggled with. I know that the Reaper walks the hallways of my chosen profession, but that doesn't make death any less frightening.

Truth be told, that fear of death began stalking me when I was yet a child. And so, some time ago, effecting a casual tone, I mentioned that fear to a friend of mine. He suggested a novel solution. Literally.

"You should write a novel, or a memoir," Tom said.

I told him I thought memoirs were only written by former gangsters and mafia types, or by out-of-office politicians seeking to settle scores.

Nah, he said. "You've got a couple of great stories. Maybe you could dig them up and bury them in some sort of book." My friend likes to make undertaker jokes.

And so I tried. I wrote up a few chapters, and even joined a writing club. You know, where they meet once a month and the would-be scribes comment on each other's submissions.

I tried to keep things lighthearted, telling the story of some of the funny things that go on during funerals. Alas, it didn't work. My fellow writers were utterly grossed out by my chosen topic.

"Your writing's ... interesting," they said. "But might we suggest that you may want to try a more delicate topic."

And so, I punted on the writing club. Instead, I'm going to tell you my story. The ups and the downs. How folks respond when their loved ones pass. How I came to cope with that fear of death I suspect I may have in common with many outside the profession. You can judge for yourself how "delicate" my account might be.

But first, I've got to attend to that decked-out man waiting in my office.

TWO: ANTOINETTE

When I closed my office door behind me, I discovered that there was not just one man waiting for me, but two.

The guy in front was a skinny guy, a bit shorter than me, and dressed casually. Tan slacks. Informal button down shirt. Wingtips. Introducing himself as Mr. Melkov, he extended both hands and clasped my right hand in greeting.

The second man, towering more than a full head above me, stood to Melkov's right and slightly behind him. This guy had the packed meat build of a professional bodybuilder. Unlike the first gentleman, this guy was clad in an expensively tailored three-piece suit, as my assistant had noticed. But the suit was about two sizes too small, fitting over the man's massive frame like an undersized glove.

Mr. Melkov did not introduce the second man, and indeed, the second man never said a word aloud during our entire meeting.

"I want to order funeral," Melkov started out. "Tomorrow afternoon."

"We're happy to provide our excellent services," I replied. "Let me check my schedule."

"Tomorrow afternoon," Melkov repeated. I detected a slight, an ever so slight, Slavic word crunch.

Three quick raps from outside interrupted our opening conversation. The door opened and the love of my life burst in through the door.

Gabriella Antoinette, who went simply by Antoinette, my wife since college – more on that later – was dressed in tight-fitting jeans, a blue blouse with white ruffles along the collar, and heels that highlighted her slender build. Her jet black hair was pulled back, accentuating her high cheekbones.

"Hey, babe," she said.

"Hi there, sweetheart," I said.

For a moment, there was, for me, no one else in the room.

"Sorry to interrupt," Antoinette said, "but I want to ask a huge favor."

"Ask away," I said. Then, turning to my guests, I said, "This will only take a minute."

"The girls and I are planning a Halloween party," Antoinette said. "We want to get dressed up as ghosts and skeletons."

"Nothing unusual about that," I said.

"It's just that we're planning to hold the party at the community center, and we want to make a grand entrance, a splash," Antoinette said. "We'd like to show up in our family hearse for the occasion."

"Your idea?"

"Babe," Antoinette said, breaking out in a wide grin.

"On one condition," I said.

"Babe," Antoinette said, pretending to pout.

"That I get to drive."

"You're hired," Antoinette said. Then, in a silky voice, she added, "A hearse is a hearse, of curse of curse, and no one need walk if there's a hearse of curse."

At this, the big guy in the undersized suit leaned over to the little guy and mumbled some garbled words. In response, the little guy carefully pronounced "hearse," twice, followed by some words in a language I didn't understand.

As my two visitors were conversing, Antoinette walked across the room to a vase holding a half dozen roses. She picked out a rose, placed it horizontally between her teeth, and walked back toward me. She inserted the rose into a button hole on my left collar and then put both her hands on my throat in mock execution style. A moment later, she released my throat, placed her hands on both my cheeks, and planted a fat kiss on my lips.

My casually dressed visitor let out a whistle.

"One more request, babe," Antoinette said.

"Yes?"

"A butterfly?" Antoinette said.

"A butterfly?"

"A butterfly," Antoinette repeated.

"You want a butterfly?"

"Not a real butterfly," Antoinette said. "The kind that makes you more beautiful."

"Huh?"

"Any ink-ling of what I'm asking?"

It dawned on me. "Oh," I said.

"Okay?"

"Okay, where?" I said.

"In that special place," Antoinette said.

"That special place?"

"Cheek to cheek, they were dancing cheek to cheek," Antoinette sang. She also ever so slightly wiggled her behind.

At this, the skinny man in casual attire tilted his head to eyeball Antoinette more closely. The big goon in the too-small suit involuntarily turned his head slightly.

I nodded.

"Excuse me," the skinny man spoke up. "Our funeral?"

"Right," I said, turning in his direction. "Let me solve this. It will only take a minute."

Smiling, I bowed toward Antoinette and gloriously addressed her. "Pharaoh's daughter, the pride of Egypt, and my beloved main squeeze, desires a royal chariot to lead her bejeweled entourage on a tour to inspect her thousands of desert-addled slaves. Thousands of roses, lilacs and chrysanthemums will sacrifice their oh-so-brief lives as they give homage to her beauty."

Antoinette returned my smile, gave me a quick peck on the cheek, and bounded to the wall where a menagerie of vehicle keys was hanging. Examining the collection closely, she selected one set of keys, waved it back and forth until I nodded, and dashed out the door.

The skinny man in casual dress whistled a second time, this time just a bit longer, if quieter, than the first go round.

"To business," he began. "Cost no object."

With that, Melkov opened a leather-bound folder, pulled out a wad of bills, and placed them on the table. The stack of Benjamins, many inches high, slouched to one side. Using the palms of both hands, he straightened up the leaning tower.

Why no envelope, or even a box? I wondered. Even checks, you keep for safekeeping in a box.

"Mr. Kovchenko had two sets of friends," Melkov continued, for the first time revealing the deceased's name. "Very important to keep them apart."

"I understand perfectly," I replied, thinking hard.

"We also expect some uninvited guests," Melkov continued. "You need to ask them," he said, before stretching out his next words, "very politely, to leave."

"Oh."

The funeral was held, as Mr. Melkov had instructed, on the morrow. It went off much better than I might have expected. The men were dressed in suits that fairly shouted money. The women attending were, on average, some two decades younger than their male escorts.

A crowd of uninvited guests did show up, parking several BMWs and other high-end vehicles near the front entrance to my funeral home. Fortunately, I had taken the precaution of alerting the police to possible trouble, and the cops posted a squad of armed officers outside my door. (I later made a generous contribution to their union's annual charity drive.)

The drinking was mostly kept under control. Toward the end of the viewing, a few men challenged each other as to who could most quickly consume an entire shot glass with one motion of hand to lips. Cheers celebrated the winners.

Inebriated, some of the men began to sob loudly.

Yes, being your friendly neighborhood undertaker does have its moments. Still, unlike the guy who always wanted to be a newspaper reporter ever since junior high when he got that part-time job delivering papers, or the elementary school girl who fell in love with science when she won first place in a science fair, undertaking wasn't my first choice of calling.

If my childhood would have had anything to do with the matter, undertaking would have been my very last choice of profession. So let me start my story there, before moving quickly to the present.

But first, briefly an epilogue to the funeral service for those Russians. After the eulogies were spoken, a middle-aged guy, cheered on by his comrades, sauntered up to the open casket. After holding aloft a Benjamin so that everyone could see, the guy slipped the bill into the coffin, placing it in the right hand of the deceased.

"Here, give this to Saint Vladimir," the man said. "Tell him you want a word with the Big Guy."

THREE: GRANDFATHER

And so, from the beginning.

Back when I was in the fifth grade, in the summer, my grandfather would take me fishing. He would show up every Saturday morning, like clockwork. Sometimes, if my parents had to call me from the backyard, he would sit in his favorite chair as he and my parents caught up on his latest doings.

And as I ran into the living room, Pop-Pop would rise from his chair, turn around to face me, and announce in a loud voice:

"The men got some serious business to attend to! Fishes, watch out!"

With that, we would head off to the garage. There, we would rummage through the piled-up stuff and pull out a couple of poles, tackle boxes, and a huge dark blue plastic pouch with "Macy's" written on it. Then we would make a quick trip to the backyard, and we would dig out a handful of worms. Every Saturday, my parents would point to a different spot where it was "possible" that we could find some worms. I never suspected how it was that my parents were so clued in to where the worms were hiding.

Our gear gathered up, we would climb into Pop-Pop's beat-up Chevy, which he always parked in the grass just off the driveway. Pop-Pop would always let me sit on his lap and let me hold the steering wheel as we drove out of the driveway and onto the street.

"Would the gentleman agree to relinquish his place to his fellow Musketeer?" Pop-Pop would ask in an aristocratic tone, just as we reached the street.

"Aye, aye, Captain," I would always reply before sliding off his lap and onto the passenger seat.

Our lake, a short drive away, was a special place. It was always nearly deserted, with just a few fishermen scattered around its edges. When mosquitos or other insects showed up, we would hold a contest as to who could swat the most in a morning. Whenever either one of us caught a bug, we would hold it out in an upright palm so that the other one could see it.

"Lunch, my friend?" the successful swatter would offer.

"Oh, gross," we would say in unison, just before the successful swatter would flick the tiny carcass into the wind.

I know you're supposed to zip the lip when you fish, but we would talk. Not a steady stream of conversation, but snatches here and there.

It wasn't long before I would tell Pop-Pop a lot of things, things I would never dream of telling my parents. Like the time I peed in my pants during gym class. Or the time I pocketed a candy bar when my parents took me shopping. Pop-Pop made me tell my parents on that one, but the spanking made me feel better, even though I screamed a lot while it was going on. For all that, it was only a minor spanking, because, as my father told me, I had "fessed up" before I was found out.

And then there was the time that Pop-Pop let me in on something, something that was, in my mind, a home run.

"Did I ever tell you how I met Grandma?" Pop-Pop asked. My ears perked up even more than usual. Grandma lived in a nursing home, and my parents had taken me to visit her several times.

"She was the most beautiful creature I had ever seen," he began. "Red hair, the color of fire. Freckles, like tiny red rubies. And a smile from here to Cincinnati."

That Grandma once had red hair was a true revelation to me. I had never seen Grandma with anything but whitish hair. It almost didn't occur to me that she wasn't born that way. And so, with Pop-Pop trusting me with this top secret information, how could I not breathe out my own secret?

"Pop-Pop," I began, with the steely determination of a spy who is about to reveal a state secret. "I am in love with a girl in Mrs. Solomon's class. She has red hair just like Grandma. Freckles, too!"

Pop-Pop chuckled that smile of two young men who know what it's like when each has been bitten by the love bug.

"Freckles, too," he said, in a longing kind of way.

We sat silent for a moment.

"Them's good fish," Pop-Pop added, capping off our time of mutual confession and bringing us back to the task at hand. That day was perfect in every way. Love confirmed, and a healthy catch of fish besides. To top it off, Pop-Pop promised me a special treat next week.

Next week, Pop-Pop promised, he would give me some wonderful details concerning how he had won Grandma's heart.

The next day, Sunday, it was my turn to take out the trash, and I did so without my usual complaining.

Monday, I flunked an in-class quiz because, in all the excitement over the weekend, I had forgotten that our teacher had told us to prepare some special homework. Tuesday and Wednesday and Thursday were each a bust, for similar homework reasons. On Friday, that Special Someone smiled at me, pumping me up even more to hear Pop-Pop's encounter with his Special Someone so long ago.

Fishing was never so much fun.

From my room, I could hear Pop-Pop arriving a little early, so I began to change out of my sleeping clothes. I spent a few minutes making my bed, wanting it to be perfect. Mom always complained when it wasn't perfect, and I didn't want to upset her today.

My books and notebooks were scattered on the floor and some were even under my bed. So I crawled halfway under the bed to pull them out. Remembering last Monday's homework fiasco, I opened my assignment notebook to get a quick look at this Monday's assignment. But I had a hard time reading my own handwriting, so I shut the notebook and stuffed it in my book bag. "That's for later," I said, half out loud.

My friend, Jimmy, yelled at me from the field in back of our house, and I could hear him through my half-opened bedroom window. I ran over to the window, climbed up onto a desk and pushed the window frame fully open. I jumped outside, threw a few balls back and forth with Jimmy. As I ran back toward the open window, I heard screaming inside, but ignored it as I ran into the living room.

Running toward the sofa, I could see the back of Pop-Pop's bald head just above the long stretch of furniture. Ignoring the commotion in the room, I ran up to him, threw both hands over his eyes and yelled, "Guess who?"

There was no response. Pop-Pop's head was strangely heavy, like when you grab a bowling ball with both hands.

It was then that I noticed my mother off to the left, a stricken look on her face. Wailing, she leapt toward me, moving behind the sofa. She pulled me backward without ever turning me around. With a steady grip on both my shoulders, she escorted me back into my room. She planted me on my bed and then pulled me toward her.

She went silent for a full ten minutes.

"Pop-Pop won't go fishing with you today," she began.

After another pause, my mother began speaking, slowly and in a quiet voice. She must have spoken for about twenty minutes or so. But I didn't hear a thing she said, and I certainly can't remember anything of it now. I only remember balling my eyes out during the ceremony that my family held a week later, and that the preacher man said something about God and Pop-Pop.

One other thing. A few weeks earlier, a neighbor had come by, and had invited me to what they called vacation church school, something like that. Children, they told my parents, would hear stuff about feeding thousands of people at a "Jesus picnic," dividing a baby in two, and stuffing a bunch of animals onto a boat. As an extra treat, kids could pretend to be those animals, and crowd into a special boat built just for the occasion.

It was all for helping young children "get to know God," these neighbors told my parents. My parents weren't particularly religious. We never went to church, and they never talked about God or anything like that.

But they figured, what the heck, let's get the kids off our hands for a few weeks, and give them something to do this summer.

"Maybe God will give them something good," my father quipped as he sent us off.

But now, weeks later, with my head in my mother's arms, it all became suddenly clear. God took Pop-Pop. I decided, then and there, that any talk about a good God was mere fairy tale. The fairy tale wasn't true, and I wanted nothing to do with it.

And on that day, death, God's partner, planted a terrible seed, an abiding terror, deep in my heart.

FOUR: ONE MORNING

As the years began to stretch out, it was not easy for me to come to terms with my grandfather's abrupt death. And then, to my further dismay, death, ever resourceful, knocked yet again. As before, close to home.

Just weeks after I began my freshman year in high school, tragedy struck my school. On a Wednesday morning, a bus transporting my fellow students was minutes from school when it was struck by an oncoming 18-wheeler that had edged over the center line.

Four students died almost instantaneously and another two students were pronounced dead at a local hospital. More than a dozen other students were critically injured.

The news spread instantly throughout our campus, by word of mouth and via social media. The next morning, newspapers dutifully reported whatever details they discovered, from biographies of the dead, the arrest of the truck driver and speculation concerning road conditions. But, frankly, nearly every student knew almost everything by lunchtime.

I asked to be excused from classes, saying I was not feeling well. Dozens of other students were likewise excused. Those who remained in the building attended a schoolwide assembly called in an attempt to make whatever sense could be made of the tragedy. Teachers and counselors met one-on-one with dozens of students.

When my mother came to pick me up, around lunchtime, her eyes were glistening. "Harry, I'm so sorry," she said, barely above a whisper.

Once at home, I retreated to my room and crawled into my bed. I pulled the covers up over my head and pulled out my smartphone. Photos of the deceased students were already posted on a local newspaper's website.

In the weeks since school had started, I had already made friends with several of those students. One was a friend from junior high. They were all my age, each one just barely a teenager. The hair, the glasses, the smiles, all seemed versions of myself. It was almost like I was looking into a mirror.

Staring at each face, I slowly whispered the names of the deceased, one by one. "Jonathan. Sarah, Isaac. Judith. Carmen. Jose."

And they were dead. Dead. Their lives suddenly snuffed out long before any reasonable schedule might call for their departure.

I stared at their faces. Everything they and I so passionately enjoyed had suddenly vanished. Their lives, a vapor, as momentary as a puff of smoke. That promise of a lunchtime flirtation, cancelled. The after-school pickup basketball game, gone forever. Chomping down on apple pie after supper, thrust into a black hole.

The more I thought about what had just happened, the more it unnerved me, angered me, terrorized me. Death, you took my friends. You stole my friends. How unfair you are. You snatched away my friends. You kidnapped my friends – without warning, without notice, without even the slightest chance to pack up their things. Without a chance to even say goodbye.

"Death, you monster." I spit out the words.

I tried to call upon whatever mental resources I might possess to think "rationally" about what had just happened, somehow to make death less terrifying. Tapping my fingers, I counted the reasons why death was not after me personally. School bus accidents, fatal ones, are extremely rare. Death is mostly for old people. I'm healthy.

But death took my friends. My friends. Death did not play by the rules.

My feeble attempt to make sense of death was just that, a feeble attempt amounting to nothing. My terror at death, my terror at death's unpredictable and sudden arrival, welled up inside me. It wasn't just death's untimely arrival that spooked me. There was also the sheer unknown of what followed death.

I had never bought into the old wives' tale of when you're dead, you're dead. That's what they try to tell you in biology class. To me, that never made sense. It just wasn't how things worked. When you stop being awake, you don't just go into a nothing state, where you don't exist. No, you go into a dream state. Why would death be any different?

Besides, nobody minds going to sleep. But I don't know anybody who wants to die. "Nobody wants you," I whispered. Then I thought, "How stupid I am. Death doesn't listen."

Nor did I ever believe the opposite fairy tale. You know, ask most people what happens after death, and you get a lunchtime serving of warm and fuzzy mush. You go to heaven, and get to play harps forever. Only mental idiots and small children believe that fantasy.

No. After death, the great unknowable black hole. Some place you never escape from. But, what WOULD death be like? There, in silence and darkness, I thought long and hard. Maybe death is something like falling. Falling, falling, falling forever. Falling unprotected into a vast abyss. Try to escape upward, and an invisible hand pulls you back down.

Or, maybe, something even worse. Maybe, just as you pass out of this world, somebody, not a god, but somebody, will be there at the edge of that black night. That somebody will be there just waiting to point out all the nasty things you did in life. The things you know about, but nobody else does. And suddenly, time to pay up.

There, under the covers, the terror again welled up in me. First, my grandfather. Now, my friends. Next, me.

That wasn't all. Unlike maybe a lot of other people, my conscience has never been an easygoing imp I could brush off with a wave of the hand. No, my conscience has always been a thug, bat in hand, waiting on a street corner of my mind, waiting to beat the tar out of me.

Even before I got to high school, I could always remember bad stuff I had done from years earlier. Picking a fight with somebody. Mouthing off to my parents. Lying about why I didn't do my homework. Trivial stuff, but my thug would use it to beat up on me. To remind me that he would be waiting for me when death tapped on my shoulder. And after beating me up, the thug would lock me up.

I began to shake uncontrollably. "Harry," I said, loud enough to be embarrassed if anybody heard me, "You're being irrational. Death is a long way away." Only it wasn't. The vivid photos I had just stared at on my smartphone did away with that too-easy answer.

To try to calm myself, I shut off my smartphone and pushed it down near my feet. That didn't help much. I looked around. Still dark. I lay there, quiet, the room silent.

Suddenly, my mother's voice pierced the stillness. "Harry, supper's ready. Wash up and come and eat."

It took a full half hour to calm myself before I could come to the dinner table.

By then, hours after she had picked me up from school, my mother was back to her even-tempered self. She, my father, me, the three of us, discussed the morning's tragedy for more than an hour. Each of us spoke our concern for the families of the students. My father, who ran a funeral business, said he would not be handling any of the arrangements.

"If you need to talk about it some more, we're always available," my mother said.

"Thanks," I said. "I think I'm okay."

But I wasn't. The fear of death, planted long ago when I came upon my stricken grandfather, had fully ripened deep within me.

FIVE: FROSH

I don't know much history, but I do know that George Washington was not the lover of the British monarchy that I suspect his father was.

Nor did Neil Armstrong follow the earthbound career his father pursued. Nor did Shakespeare follow his father into the glover's trade.

As with most funeral homes across America, the place where my father earned his livelihood was family owned. And that family ownership was more than a single-generation phenomenon. Before my father took over, the O'Toole Funeral Home was owned by his father, and his father's uncle before that.

"The O'Toole Funeral Home," said the sign posted outside its modest quarters, "Helping You Celebrate Your Loved One's Life. Family Owned and Operated Since 1947."

The family business was located about two hours northeast of Harrisburg, the Pennsylvania state capital. My parents seemed to know everyone in the surrounding area, and everyone seemed to assume that I would follow in the family footsteps.

But by the time I hit eighteen, I had resolved that I was not going to go into the family business. I had already made death's very personal acquaintance, twice, and had decided to stay as far away from him as possible.

So, for me, no future in the funeral business. No way. No how. Not ever.

"I'd like to explore other possibilities," I told my parents, masking my determination with soft speech.

By the time I reached college age, I had more than a little taste of the family business. My father, whom I respected enormously, encouraged me on several occasions to try my hand at preparing a face in advance of an open casket viewing. I could never get it quite right, and he always had to fix my amateur attempts. On other occasions, he let me ride along as we picked up bodies from a morgue.

At times, he instructed me to get dressed up so that I could hand out programs as families arrived for a viewing.

In between those times when I would help out, I fantasized about how children in other out of the ordinary family professions would help their parents carry out their respective trades. Perhaps some of the Corleone children pitched in as their elders carried out a necessary hit here or received a drug mule package there.

My family business seemed in many ways no less strange, and it just wasn't for me. Death all around. Death surrounding me, nibbling everywhere at the edges. With death so omnipresent, maybe it would sneak up on me, even upon me, unannounced. Follow in the family footsteps? No, thank you.

I didn't share these reasons with my parents. I just repeated a line that could be understood as youth beginning to explore the world.

"I just want to keep my options open."

My high school grades were not bad, considering that I didn't study much, and I benefitted from a short-term fascination with calculus. I did do a weekend down-and-dirty course on how to improve your SAT score, and that provided just the boost to my record I needed. And so, the fall after I finished slouching through my senior year in high school, I enrolled at Penn State, less than a four-hour drive from our house.

At last, I was a college freshman in a school with a big-name reputation. After the close quarters of my rather small high school and the cramped space of a family-run funeral home, arriving here was like a forever Saturday afternoon with everybody for blocks around having a yard sale. Four years of rummaging through this and that alluring knickknack.

At freshman orientation, booths were set up to help incoming students make sense of the vast number of academic possibilities.

At the pre-med table, the older students manning the booth were friendly enough. But looking at them, as they spoke of their calling to help a medically afflicted clientele, their white coats kept whispering to me. "Hospitals. Emergency rooms. Operating rooms. Failed operations. Morgues. Death." It was too close to home.

"Thanks, but no thanks," I said, politely taking and pocketing their literature. Pre-med was not for me.

The pre-law booth was more intriguing. In the back of my mind, in a vague sort of way, I had occasionally thought about becoming a lawyer. The clean and tidy environment of courtrooms I had seen on Netflix, plus the chance to match argumentative skills with a worthy opponent, had always somewhat attracted me.

And so I picked up some of their paperwork, paperwork that was designed to spark a budding interest in a legal career. I flipped through some pages, and read at random.

"… some number authorizes no direct appeal to this Court from the grant or denial of declaratory relief alone … there must be an open, notorious, and pervasive violation of the statute for a long period before desuetude will take hold … there is no doubt that a conspicuous policy of non-enforcement exists …"

No, pre-law and law school were not for me.

The English booth was next. Who wouldn't want to be an English major? After all, I may not be able to speak that gobbledygook at the lawyer table, but I have no trouble with normal sounding English.

Unlike the other tables, this table was manned by a real professor, if I could judge by the apparent age of the man attending the booth. I introduced myself in what I took to be a normal fashion, expressing how grateful I was to be attending his honored institution.

Shaking my hand, the professor sought to introduce his department and its mission. "We are committed to making an epistemological investigation into the aggregate origins and systematic inculcations of white privilege and the conscious and unconscious manifestations of minority oppression," the professor began. "Inculcating our students with an appreciation of the inveterate nature of racism is an existential imperative of the university faculty."

If I want a foreign language, I thought, I'll head over to the Spanish table. When the professor took a breath, which seemed an eternity in arriving, I politely thanked him and moved on.

I didn't sign up for any of the majors represented by the tables I visited that afternoon. After about ninety minutes of going table to table, I put the rest of the day's project on the "later this afternoon" shelf and headed off to the school cafeteria.

The food wasn't bad, and there were a lot of choices, and I made some new friends while moving table to table. I never returned to the majors tables set up outside.

In the end, I "opted" for a psychology major. I was interested in how people think, and the requirements didn't seem that rigorous. It was my kind of major. I didn't do a lot of studying, but I picked up enough of the "psych" lingo to impress my parents on my trips home.

My less than rigorous schedule also left time to pursue the pleasures of the brew in a way I had not experienced before. My close working with my parents in cramped quarters had made it impossible for me to try out what most teenagers in less restricted environments get an opportunity to experiment with.

"Never got loaded?" Daniel, my roommate, said, his eyes wide.

"No, never," I replied.

"Then let me," he said, "invite you into the gustatory gusto of Guinness."

And so he did.

College life wasn't all books, broads and booze, of course. I wasn't much for doing all my assigned homework, but if I discovered a topic or author with the help of some friends, I was not averse to doing a little out of the classroom study. After reading aloud some of H. L. Mencken's satirical essays, me and three buddies decided to motorbike down to the Sage of Baltimore's house, reportedly made into a museum.

Leading the bike brigade was Charlie, who kept chanting "Born to Be Wild" at the top of his voice. Franklin, whose name we abbreviated to Frankie, was next in line. Following him was Bruce the Moose, whose large size distinguished him in any crowd. I rode shotgun.

I never mentioned the trip to my parents, for reasons I'll explain later.

Also going unmentioned to my parents was my participation in our dorm's special "water sports." My dorm, all male, had rooms on both sides of a long hallway. That hallway's floor was simple linoleum, and it wasn't long before the residents on our end of the hallway got the great idea of challenging our rivals on the far end of the hallway to a water fight.

Buckets were brought out. Studying for Monday morning exams could wait. Even those not facing a Monday morning exam were invited to attend. The sheer joy of water combat made the stern lecture we received afterward seem a small price to pay.

When I did study, I often hit the books while sitting on benches in the outdoor Quad. For me, the still silence of the library was like a sleep-inducing drug.

For the most part, college was a blast. The time between visits home got longer and longer as the semester progressed, and I felt more and more that my freedom from the family business had been extended indefinitely. Not wanting to upset my parents, I avoided any talk concerning my feelings about the family business.

I also avoided mentioning several other episodes that disturbed me greatly during my first year at the university.

SIX: INVITATION

I was enjoying a Wednesday afternoon looking at internet porn on my computer in my dorm room when I got a knock at the door.

I was pissed off at the interruption because the blond girl and the redhead were just getting to the good part. But, not wanting to advertise my hobby, I minimized the screen to attend to the presumably more important business not far away.

"Can I help you?" I said, trying to hide the irritation in my voice.

"You're Harry, aren't you?" the guy at the door said.

"Yeah, who are you?"

"I'm Stan, and I live down the hall, room 506. I just wanted to invite you ..."

"I'm rather busy at the moment," I broke him off.

"No, not for right now, for tonight."

"What's the big occasion?" I said. "Is your frat having a party?"

"No, we'd like to invite you to our church," he said. "It's youth night, and we'd like you to come."

"I'm not really interested," I said, my youthful episode with church vacation week flashing into my head.

"It's not as bad as you think,' the guy said, strangely insistent. "We really have a lot of fun. Lots of other students will be there, and you may know some of them."

It was at the "we" that I first noticed that the guy was accompanied by two girls, one on the left and one on the right. The one on the right was a blond, a bottle blond as evidenced by the fact that blond didn't reach all the way to her scalp. The other was a light-skinned Black woman with spiky hair and hoop earrings the size of china tea saucers. Both were drop dead gorgeous. I was in the presence of living and breathing female flesh.

"I really don't care for that sort of thing," I said. "I'm a homebody."

But glancing at their eager eyes, I could feel myself weakening. Babes is babes.

"We'd really like you to be there," said the woman to my left. "We'll both be there, and we'd really like to get to know you better," added the one to my right.

I felt myself weakening still more. "Okay," I said. "What time should I expect you to pick me up?"

I wasn't religious, and aside from my week at children's church whatever, I had never set foot inside a church. I was expecting stained glass windows and priests in top hats, the kind you occasionally see in the movies and in pictures of medieval cathedrals. I figured I could put up with The History Channel for a shot at Madonna and Beyoncé.

The first surprise was that our destination wasn't a church at all. Instead, we stepped into what looked like an office flanked on both sides by a bunch of stores. A row home shopping mall.

The trip's payoff, I soon discovered, came right up front. Madonna didn't pay me much attention, but I got some good face time with Beyoncé. Over sodas and cake, we engaged in ways that no mere internet flirting can achieve.

"You've got cute ears," she said.

"Yours aren't so bad either," I replied.

"So what are you studying?" she inquired.

"I'm a psychology major," I said. I usually told people "psych" major, but "psychology" sounded more impressive under the circumstances.

After my all-too-short flirtation with Miss Earrings the Size of China Tea Saucers ended, we each went our separate ways. After snack time came music time. I went to sit in the back row, steeled and ready to pay my dues for the pleasure of her brief company.

The music wasn't bad, considering. Folk music, a handful of guitars and a drummer paddling a box in place of a drum set. They even had a flute player. Canned Heat, I wondered, or Woody Guthrie? I couldn't understand what they were singing about, although obviously something about Jesus. The words were projected onto a wall up front, but to my mind they didn't make much sense.

After a few minutes, I found the tunes so catchy, and the guitar, flute and drums harmonies so soothing, that I moved from the back of the room to sit up front.

The lights went dim and a guy in a Hawaiian shirt got up to speak. He started out with some pleasantries, greeting some visitors, who briefly rose to applause. In the midst of those shout-outs, he called out my name, but I remained seated and merely turned around and waved.

Pleasantries taken care, the man got down to business.

"Open your Bibles to the book of Revelation."

Oh, good, I thought, space aliens, flying saucers and plenty of thunder and lightning. Maybe what I was going to hear was going to be the makings of a good movie script.

Unfortunately, like a pitcher throwing fastballs, the preacher man began to fire in my direction. People who don't buy into this Jesus thing, he said, "would be cast into the lake of fire." Amidst the flames, unbelievers would be tormented, "day and night, forever and forever."

The extreme language seemed to me funny at first, the way you might regard a raving lunatic chained safely to his bed or a roaring tiger safely behind steel bars at a zoo. But after a few minutes, his ravings began to make my skin crawl.

This man was no fool, and no mere showman. "The devil with a pitchfork and a funny tail, is that what your friends tell you?" he said. "That's for children."

I remembered that the pitchfork and pointed tail was exactly what a buddy of mine had told me some years ago. We had laughed at the humor of it. I smiled the briefest of smiles, but was then once again struck dumb as the man continued.

"No, hell is deadly serious," he continued. "Someplace where you don't want to end up."

Gazing out over the audience, the preacher man pronounced a triple curse.

"Where their worm does not die and the fire is not quenched."

"Where their worm does not die and the fire is not quenched."

"Where their worm does not die and the fire is not quenched."

At this, I just plain wanted out of there. Casting all politeness to the wind, I rose from my seat, marched through multiple extended knees to get to the end of the row, and strode purposefully to the door and outside.

An unpleasant episode from a high school history class came to mind. "Fire and brimstone is fine for Puritans and sinners in the hands of an angry God," I said in a defiant voice to no one in particular. "But not for me, not for me."

No one was in sight, and my words, it seemed, just bounced off the pavement.

I cursed myself for letting myself get seduced into coming to this horrible, horrible place. "My Lady with Earrings the Size of China Tea Saucers, how could you be so cruel?" I muttered, once I had cooled down somewhat.

I vowed, never again, never again would I ever set foot in any kind of church. "Mental note," I added. "Sometimes those churches don't even look like churches, so watch out. And watch out for good-looking girls with Earrings the Size of China Tea Saucers."

I took a cab home.

Just weeks later, another blow struck.

I was sitting in the cafeteria near the end of the lunchtime when my friend, Frankie, one of the guys I took the motorbike road trip to Baltimore with, sat down next to me. We started off talking about sports. But after a while, the conversations turned, as it so often does in college, to the "meaning of life."

"What's it all about, Alfie?" Frankie asked. It turns out that's a famous song lyric. I think he really wanted to know, but I was no help.

"I dunno," I said with all the seriousness I could muster.

A week later, Frankie was killed in a motorcycle accident. He was showing off a little, and the bike scooted out from under him, throwing him into a tree. He was killed instantly.

Several dozen members of the freshman class attended his funeral, which was arranged by a funeral home not far from campus. I left the service just as it ended, skipped the reception afterward, went to my dorm, and threw up in the bathroom.

SEVEN: FALLING IN

Despite the hell fire and brimstone spooking and the tragic death of my friend, college wasn't entirely a downer. The hallowed halls of the university was where I met Antoinette, the love of my life.

At college, I quite literally fell for her. Thus began a whirlwind romance.

On that fateful day, I was taking my time in the school cafeteria, finishing up a long lunch hour with a handful of my buddies. Unlike in high school, university lunches often touched on gourmet. Breaded tilapia, meat lover's pizza and deep dish lasagna made not infrequent visits.

The place was about half full when I decided, with much reluctance, to quit the dining hall for a much delayed appearance at some quiet study corner. I rose to put away my tray when one of my buddies stuck out his leg to trip me.

I went horizontal and my tray went flying, scattering orange juice, a half-eaten cheeseburger, several butter patties, a few tomato slices and a nearly untouched peach cobbler like pellets from a shotgun. The unwitting target of the airborne repast were students sitting two tables away.

The peach cobbler struck someone I was not yet acquainted with. But in the days, weeks, months and years that followed, I always remembered that it was the peach cobbler that struck that special target.

"Hey, guys, watch what you're aiming at," the Peach Cobbler girl shouted, brushing off the pale yellow slices from the shoulders of her "Fire Up the Revolution" tee-shirt. "I'm not the Bastille."

Then she broke into a smile as bright as a summer sunrise.

I didn't realize it at the time, but I was goner from that moment. I was still sprawled out on the floor, the continuing subject of guffaws all round. But as Cobbler Girl strode out of the cafeteria, I did get a worm's eye view of her shapely legs, tightly tucked into her jeans.

It was about a week later that I ran into Cobbler Girl, quite by accident. My buddies and I had decided to make a list of the first lines of famous novels. This was to be a strategy to impress whatever "lit chicks" we might want to date. We had found these first lines on the Internet. My assignment was to go the library, foreign territory for me, and find the actual novels.

I was standing at the help counter when a seated bookish looking girl with glasses raised her head.

"Hey, I know you," she said.

I didn't immediately recognize her. Her glasses made her look, well, so studious.

"Yeah, it's nice to see you," I said, scouring my brain for clues.

"It's not often that guys fall for me."

"And it's not often that I fall for young ladies as attractive as you," I replied, finally catching on.

She was indeed quite the looker. Jet black hair gave her the glamour of a 1940s movie star. High cheekbones underlined her bright blue eyes. An engaging smile that promised mischief, a promise no red-blooded male can resist.

I decided to not tell Antoinette exactly why my friends and I wanted the famous novels. Better to pretend that we were trying to better ourselves thorough the riches of western literature and culture. Antoinette eagerly suggested some additional authors and their iconic works.

It turned out that Antoinette, despite her "Revolution" tee-shirt, was a voracious reader of the classics. She could pull titles, and often first lines, off the top of her head.

"First lines have many current day applications," Antoinette said. "For example, in college, you're going to have good days and bad days. It will be the best of times, it will be the worst of times."

Fire and brimstone and the death of my friend flashed through my mind as Antoinette gave a takeaway two minutes on Dickens and the French Revolution. But as she continued, her voice, sultry perhaps without intending to be so, was a soothing jazz melody. The best of times, I thought, my good fortune at being tripped in the cafeteria.

At the end of Antoinette's library work shift, we moved to two chairs in the library foyer, and talked into the wee hours. Thank goodness that school libraries stay open late.

Our first official "date," if you can call it that, was almost a bust. We had planned to meet late at a far off-campus café, far off-campus and late at night so that there was no chance of inquisitive friends happening by. Various chores demanded the attention of each of us and we were both late. So most of our conversation was by way of back and forth texts.

When we finally got to the café, about ten minutes apart, the place was about to close. We were also too exhausted to talk. But gathering up my courage, I reached over and gave her a peck on the cheek.

Antoinette burst out into laughter that must have lasted ten minutes. When she finally got control of herself, she said in a loud voice.

"You little devil!"

Her voice was so loud that several patrons who were lined up to pay their bills looked in our direction. Antoinette flashed them a brief smile before returning her attention to me. Then she kissed me.

Antoinette did weekly volunteer work at a nearby nursing home, and she invited me along. "How's our angel of mercy?" the residents would greet her as she hugged each one in turn. With everyone in wheelchairs lined up, Antoinette would play the piano and sing popular music songs from a half century ago.

Antoinette and I spent Saturday afternoons walking in a nearby park. Near the end of one of those days, it began to cloud over. As it began to rain, we took shelter under a rock ledge overhang. The ground under the rock was muddy, the space cramped, and we crouched down at first. After about fifteen minutes, though, we surrendered to our aching muscles and plain sat down in the mud.

"So what are you going to do when you graduate?" Antoinette said.

"Not sure," I said. "Graduation is still pretty far off."

Antoinette was a year ahead of me, but after only a year and a half of school, I was still facing two plus years before donning the cap and gown. My grades resembled the Titanic headed for an icy encounter, and I had neglected to tell Antoinette of the meeting I had recently had with my college dean.

"But whatever you do," Antoinette said, "we're going to do it together, aren't we, babe?"

"I got you, babe," I sang, donning my best Sonny voice.

"I got you, babe," my Cher replied.

It was the best of times.

We only had one argument, and it was, as most lovers' quarrels are, over nothing.

I was about twenty minutes late for our meeting at the Quad, and we were going to do a road trip to a fish-and-chips place with special barbecue sauce about an hour from campus.

"Sorry I'm late," I said, giving Antoinette a peck on the cheek.

"You should have texted," she said.

"Don't get all snippy," I replied, moving my index and middle fingers together and apart in what I thought was a "scissors" joke.

"I'm not getting snippy," Antoinette said. "And you're the one who's late. And you didn't even apologize."

"Okay, I'm sorry," I said. "Did you like my fingers' joke?"

"It was okay."

The rest of the afternoon almost went south. I had a headache, which didn't help any. She, in her turn, was irritated at her roommate. "She keeps invading my side of the room," Antoinette said.

"Not nice," I said.

Toward the end of the afternoon, Antoinette got practical. "You need to think a little more about what you're going to do after you graduate," she said.

"Don't worry about it."

"I am worried about it," she said. "And you should be, too."

As we drove back to campus, a thunderstorm kept approaching and the clouds kept getting darker and darker. "I hope that's not us," I said.

"Babe, it's not us."

"I got you, babe," I sang.

"I got you, babe," she sang.

As I pulled into student parking, the clouds burst. For more than an hour, the rain kept coming down, making it impossible to leave the car. We got to know each other a little better.

About six weeks later, Antoinette popped the question.

"Hey, babe, if I were preggers, would you marry me?"

"Are you pregnant?"

I thought of saying, how did that happen, but this was no time for joking around.

Antoinette was silent, so I asked a second time.

"Are you pregnant? Are you sure? When did you find out?"

"I'm not saying that I am, and I'm not saying that I'm not," Antoinette said. "I'm just asking, would you marry me if I was pregnant?"

"I guess so," I said. "It would be the honorable thing to do."

"Well," Antoinette continued, "Do I have to get pregnant to get you to marry me?"

"Uh, no, I guess not."

"Well, then, why don't you ask me?"

"Right now?"

"Right now."

With that, I got down on one knee, and did the asking deed. Not having a ring, I pulled my keys off the key holder, a circular device about an inch in diameter, and offered it to Antoinette as an engagement ring.

About twenty minutes later, walking her to her dorm, I piped up.

"So you're pregnant?"

"No, not really. But we're still on, right?"

I thought a moment.

"Yeah, babe," I said. "We're still on."

EIGHT: NEW NUPTIALS

"I found the perfect venue for our wedding," Antoinette told me shortly after we had gotten engaged.

The location was a beach on the Jersey shore. In the weeks leading up to the ceremony, Antoinette was a flurry of activity, inviting the guests, ordering the food and liquid refreshments and otherwise making all the necessary arrangements.

Unlike many couples, we decided not to wait until after the end of the school year before tying the knot. "Strike while the iron is hot," as Antoinette put it. Needless to say, as I took part in the wedding preparations, my studies got even less than their usual lackadaisical attention.

And so, less than a month later, I, plus Bruce, my best man, and a dozen of my friends arrived on location to witness Antoinette and myself exchange our nuptial vows.

As we approached the open-air pavilion, Bruce asked, "Do we really have to do this with nothing on?"

"Technically, it's clothing optional," I replied. "But nobody will be wearing anything, and if you do, you'll stick out like a sore thumb."

"That's not the only thing that's going to stick out," Bruce said.

We confiscated everybody's smartphone to make sure that there was no unauthorized recording of events. Still, the clothing optional practice produced some remarkable observations. We discovered that Joe, a fellow classmate, had a "Make America Great Again" slogan tattooed across his suddenly exposed posterior.

"I thought you were a Bernie supporter," I said.

"I am," Joe said. "But the tattoo lets me express my contempt for the Orange Man every time I sit down to eat."

Another friend, Charlie, told me he was reluctant to expose himself in public for a very personal reason. "I know I'm fat, very fat," he said. "But with my layers of clothing, I can hide it, at least a little bit. Naked, though, I'm really fat, and everybody can see it."

Some of the girls took advantage of a first-time modesty exemption, and showed up in two-piece swim suits. "I've got to hide nature's miserliness in the boobs department," one of Antoinette's friends told others.

As for Antoinette and me, each of got a special "fig leaf" to cover up our privates and mammary protrusions.

"Got to keep at least some surprises for the wedding night," Antoinette told the assembled guests.

My parents were offered a special exemption, suggesting that they might attend without shedding any clothing. They declined to attend, saying they would not feel comfortable, given the general atmosphere.

Still, my parents were careful to express that they really liked Antoinette as a person and daughter-in-law. "She's a bit over the top, but she's a treasure," my father told me after one of several days we all spent together. "She has an enthusiasm and get-go that will be good for the both of you."

The Most Right Reverend Doctor Martha McMuffet officiated, and she was given a special clergy pass so that he could wear her clerical collar, miniskirt and fishnet stockings. And, in a concession to the shifting sand, tennis shoes.

"As the wind and waves join in blissful embrace, and the sun and clouds complement each other in joyous harmony," McMuffet said, "so, too, today we celebrate the union of Antoinette and Harry, united forever in body, soul and spirit."

Not a religious man, I still managed to utter an "amen" after that affirmation.

Despite our unconventional setting, the highlight of the wedding was a very traditional exchange of wedding vows.

"Do you take Antoinette as your lawful wedded wife?" the right reverend asked.

"You bet I do," I replied, prompting the pastor lady to focus her eyes on me. "Sorry," I added, "I do."

"As do I," Antoinette said when called upon to make her commitment to me.

For all its strangeness, the ceremony went off quite smoothly, with a few minor exceptions. A nasty insect bit one of my buddies at a location where the sun don't ordinarily shine. The itch bothered him for weeks afterward. A bird overhead dropped a calling card on one of the female guests at a most inopportune time and place.

Several of my college hall mates, energized by the on-display appearance of numerous nubile females, got on their knees and asked for their hands in marriage. The women, being of a more sensible disposition, turned down each and every one.

"But I'd be happy to see more of you, and perhaps less of you, at a later date," several young ladies quipped.

In one surprise, it turned out that the local newspaper had gotten wind of the unorthodox wedding. I suspected one of my college buddies had tipped them off, even though none of them would fess up afterward. And so, a reporter and photographer, both female and both fully clothed for the occasion, showed up to record the festivities.

"Most of the time, nobody wants to cover silly things like weddings," the reporter told me. "But as you might imagine, the newsroom jocks fought over this one. We got the assignment because we were the only ones who weren't salivating like a bunch of out of control hound dogs."

The write-up for the newspaper's "Lifestyle" section a week later was tastefully done. The reporting was straightforward, with any possibly salacious language edited out. The photos were likewise tasteful, showing that it was a clothing optional wedding but leaving any unduly exposed body parts out of the picture.

Several attendees mentioned to me that one of those airplanes that routinely fly over the Jersey shore, ostensibly to carry a banner advertising this or that product, seemed to fly back and forth several times during our ceremony.

The news about our open air wedding, open air in all senses of the word, spread far and wide. In the weeks after the wedding, Antoinette and I received numerous "special offers" from various clothing-optional resorts around the country, offering "slashed" rates should we desire to spend vacation time and money at their facilities.

"Once is enough," Antoinette said, each time tossing out the proffered material. "One husband, one ceremony, one splash."

"One bride," I replied, "One special bride."

In the weeks following the ceremony, my college buddies could not stop talking about the most unusual wedding. To be more precise, they could not stop joking about it.

"I read the nudes today, oh boy," said one, misquoting an old Beatles song. "About a lucky man who made the grade."

After a weekend honeymoon in the Poconos, Antoinette and I held a second wedding ceremony at my parents' house. A repeat of the ceremony was only fitting. It gave those too embarrassed to take part in the first ceremony an opportunity to witness our nuptials.

"She really is a gorgeous girl," said my mother, gazing upon Antoinette, this time dressed in a dazzling white wedding gown.

My parents were quite kind in not forever razzing us over our unconventional wedding. About the only gentle dig was a beverage prominently displayed on the refreshments table: "Naked" brand iced tea.

"I couldn't resist," my father said.

Three weeks after the wedding, an assistant dean called me into his office. Like a sniper taking precise aim at a target, Dr. Waverly fired off a series of complaints concerning my academic performance.

"According to your professor, your attendance at Shakespeare 101, a distribution requirement, has been rather spotty."

"Non-existent," I said. "Professor Dollop hates men, and she sees everything in bizarre feminist woke speak."

"You've also been failing to attend Philosophy 102, which is not a requirement, but which you voluntarily signed up for," the assistant dean said.

"I thought I would like the class, what with Plato and Aristotle and all," I said. "But for the life of me, I can't understand a thing the professor says. The meta-whatever and epista-this-and-that is killing me."

"Maybe you should withdraw from the university, with the option to return in six months, at the start of the fall semester," the assistant dean said. "Otherwise, we're going to have to permanently drop you from the student roster," he said.

"How about I just drop myself," I said.

"That sounds like a wise decision."

As I left his office, I noticed something. Over the past few weeks, I was so accustomed to everybody talking about Antoinette's and my unusual wedding, ribbing us or simply asking prurient questions. But from this assistant dean, no mention.

Neither Antoinette nor my parents were surprised about my withdrawal from school. My new bride decided to follow suit. "After all the real Romeo and Juliet," Antoinette said, "Shakespeare classes seem like just so much playacting."

NINE: WAFER

The morning after Antoinette and I got married, I woke up, walked into the bathroom of our Poconos motel room, placed my hands on my hips, and growled at the mirror.

"Harry," I said, "you are the luckiest guy this side of Pluto."

A minute earlier, Antoinette appeared to be asleep, so I did not expect that she would have heard me. But now, from the bedroom, came her distinctive voice. That voice sounded like that of a tiger.

"Harry, do you really think so? Let's make some music together."

About ninety minutes later, both of us were getting dressed before heading out for breakfast at a nearby pancake place.

As usual, Antoinette, a month shy of 22, looked stunning. Tall and slender, her naturally curly jet-black hair formed ringlets that nicely framed her high cheekbones. Her lips wee bright red, even without lipstick. Her delicate nose curved slightly upward. Her tee-shirt, perhaps one size too small, accentuated her firm breasts. A two-inch black-and-red rose tattoo just above her left ankle added just the right artistic touch.

As we were driving to the restaurant, I remembered something Antoinette once told me about how she dealt with boys in high school.

Always fabulous to look at, Antoinette had garnered her share of male attention. Teenage boys were constantly asking her out. And so, she would agree to a Saturday snack on many occasions.

"But the boys were all boring," Antoinette had told me. And so, whenever she went on a date, she always insisted that she take a smartphone photo of the boy. Afterward, at home, she would print out the photo, hang it up in her bedroom, and throw darts at it. Then she would toss the punctured photo in her bedroom's wastepaper basket.

"It was wonderful target practice," she had told me. "You, Harry," she reassured me, "never got the photo treatment."

"Did you ever tell the boys about your hobby?" I had asked Antoinette.

"No, of course not," Antoinette said. "But they never got a second date."

Driving to the restaurant, I thought, this is exactly what I love about this woman. Harry, you are one lucky puppy.

Sitting down, waiting for breakfast, our conversation turned to a topic that always fired up Antoinette's engines.

"The time when I dropped the wafer."

Antoinette had told me this story during our courtship, but I loved hearing it again. Telling me the story both before and after we got married reassured me that it wasn't just a tale told to impress a new boyfriend.

Both of her parents, though now divorced, were staunch followers of the Roman faith. "I was a good Catholic girl, from a good Catholic family," Antoinette said. The youngest of six siblings, Antoinette had gone through CCD class, the training all young people go through before taking their first communion. In the Eucharist, Catholics believe that they eat the actual body of Christ and drink his blood.

"Everything was okay until Father O'Malley handed me the wafer," Antoinette said.

"The wafer."

"I was so nervous, my parents watching and all," Antoinette continued. "And all of a sudden, just as the priest placed the wafer on my tongue, my nose began to itch, so I reached up to scratch it. That's when I accidentally knocked the wafer off my tongue, and it fluttered to the floor."

"And then?"

"And then, when I went to pick it up, I tripped on my dress," Antoinette said.   "So I fell forward and accidentally stepped on the wafer."

"A double whammy," I said.

"A double whammy," Antoinette agreed. "Father O'Malley was in shock. I had both dropped Jesus on the floor and stepped on him."

The priest began to yell at her, Antoinette said. So did her father. "He shouted, "Saints have mercy.' Then he yelled some things I don't need to repeat here."

Antoinette said she returned vocal fire. "And then I stormed out of the church."

Unfortunately, Antoinette explained, she was not able to leave the church grounds because she had not yet gotten her driver's license, and so she had to get a ride home with her parents.

"The air was so thick you could cut it with a knife," Antoinette said.

The conflict continued into the next day, Antoinette added. "I told them I was going to join the Baptist church down the street. I wasn't really going to do that, of course, but I knew that telling them that would really piss them off."

"Did it?"

Antoinette merely smiled.

After a pause, she continued. "About a week later, I announced that I had become an atheist," Antoinette said. "I didn't really know much about what atheists thought, but it seemed like a fun thing to say."

At this point, a waitress brought us our food. A meat lover's omelet for me, waffles for Antoinette. Antoinette reached over and picked out the few pieces of bacon in my omelet and set those pieces to the side.

"Bad luck to eat bacon for breakfast," she said.

Digging into my omelet, I picked up the conversation where Antoinette had left off. "So what did your father say when you announced that you were an atheist?" I already knew the answer, but I always enjoyed hearing Antoinette tell me the story.

"He said he already knew that," Antoinette said. "He said those Baptists down the street were already atheists."

"And then?"

"You know, I had to stick to my newly announced principles," Antoinette said. "I did a little bit of research, and discovered Sacco and Vanzetti."

"Remind me again who they were."

"From a hundred years ago, Italian immigrants, and anarchists and atheists to boot," Antoinette said. "They were convicted, falsely, of murder after a robbery."

"I remember that from high school history class," I said.

"I wasn't really an anarchist, but their passion lit my fire," Antoinette said. "They were into workers' rights, so

I joined up with some labor union brothers and sisters. That's when I marched in that strike I told you about."

"So what did your parents think about that?"

"They thought I had gone off the deep end," Antoinette said. "It didn't help that I wore my Sacco and Vanzetti tee-shirt around the house. My father told me to take it off and wear something else, but my mother overruled him and said I could keep it on."

Just watching Antoinette's facial expressions as she related this history held me spellbound. I was so taken that I simply put down my fork and stopped eating.

"How did this flurry of revolutionary activity play out?" I said.

"Alas, I was not able to fully escape the capitalist grasp," Antoinette said, smiling. "I got that job in a grocery store stacking shelves two nights a week."

"You joined the proletariat."

"I joined the proletariat."

"But even as a member of the working class," I said, "you've always aspired to higher things. The call of the artist, for example."

"I really would like to work on my art," Antoinette said. "Remember those paintings back at college?" Antoinette said. "Did you like them?"

"How could I forget?" I said. When we were dating, Antoinette had shown me some pretty remarkable oil canvases she had painted and hung up in her dorm room. "When it comes to a passion for painting, I've always assumed you were related to Rembrandt."

"Not Rembrandt, Harry," Antoinette said, punching me gently in the arm. "More like Andy Warhol."

"So, you want to be the next Andy Warhol? The next high priest of pop culture?"

"No, not exactly Andy Warhol," Antoinette said. "Andrea Warhol. The high priestess of pop culture."

TEN: HOME PLATE

Every marriage must pass a first milestone: the newlywed couple's first argument and its resolution. Ours happened thus. Shortly after we moved into our own apartment, we had a spat over who would do the dishes.

Okay, we had a few disagreements before and afterward, as do most couples. But none quite like the one focused on the contents of the sink.

As Antoinette and I began to live together as husband and wife, we discovered that we had very different approaches to neatness and putting things in order.

When socks were taken out of the dryer, for example, I insisted that each sock be matched with its partner and the pair be placed together in the appropriate drawer.

"This isn't the army, Harry," Antoinette said. "Let's give them, and us, some freedom."

Or take the bed, scene of our nighttime and morning adventures. For me, what could be so difficult about taking two minutes to straighten up the covers afterward? Wasn't there some admiral who wrote a book about how making your bed can change your life … and maybe the world?

"Some admiral wants us to make our bed?" Antoinette said. At this, Antoinette did a two-step and sang out, "You're in the army now. You're not behind the plow."

"Admiral, that's navy, Antoinette, not army," I said.

"Whatever," Antoinette said. "We're civilians."

One crazy disagreement was over the coffee spoon, the placement and use of the coffee spoon. To me, it made sense to put one spoon we would use for making coffee in a special china spoon holder set atop the microwave. Use the same spoon over and over, and you wouldn't have to wash extra silverware all the time.

Then, when you use that spoon to scoop coffee granules out of the instant coffee jar, bring that utensil, along with the coffee jar, over to the counter. Only then, I explained to Antoinette, would you scoop out the coffee granules and dump them into your waiting coffee mug.

"Otherwise," I explained to Antoinette, "you spill some of the coffee granules on the shelf under the microwave. Mice will come out at night to eat up the coffee particles. We'll never be rid of the mice."

"Sorry, I can't do that," Antoinette said. "Before I get coffee into my system, I'm simply not conscious enough to follow your rocket science instructions."

It dawned on me that one of the things that was tremendously attractive about Antoinette during our courtship, her free-spirited nature, was going to express itself even in how she made coffee. I would have to give up my bachelor way of doing things.

"Besides, what's a few extra spoons?" Antoinette said. "And the mice, we have lots of room. A few mice to share our lovely quarters, how can we not share our creature comforts with other creatures?"

Antoinette always had that counterintuitive way of looking at things. Besides, who could be a monster when it came to a little kindness toward those cute little critters? Creatures who left calling cards commemorating their nocturnal visits?

Elsewhere, Antoinette's approach to closets reminded me of a roommate during my first semester at college. His name was Rick, and I don't think that he had ever held a clothes hanger in his hand. Rick's clothes, from socks to jeans to shirts, were always spread out all over his bed, next to his bed, under his bed and on the counter next to the sink.

"Hey, Rick," I would razz him, "I know you like horizontal closets. Ever want to try expanding them in a vertical direction?" In response, Rick would simply brush his clothes off the sink counter and kick his clothes further under his bed.

I thought it would be tacky to repeat that line to Antoinette. To do so would seem like copyright infringement.

One thing Antoinette was good at, and this surprised me, was basic car maintenance. My habit was to ask the guy putting gas in my car to check the oil. If the engine oil was low, I would simply ask him to put in a quart. A few bucks. No big deal.

"Are we incapacitated?" Antoinette asked one day as the gas jockey put in a quart of oil. "We don't have to pay him to do that. We can put in the oil ourselves."

"But why should we bother with that?" I said. "It's only a couple of bucks. We don't fix our teeth, we let the dentist do that. Besides, this guy likes putting in the oil. Putting in oil is part of his job."

We agreed to disagree. When Antoinette wasn't looking, I had the guy put in the oil. Otherwise, Antoinette did her thing.

A few days later, Antoinette and I were getting out of bed when I picked up some of her socks scattered all over the bedroom floor. Examining the socks to bring together matched pairs, I folded matched socks together, opened a dresser drawer, and carefully laid each pair in neat rows.

Antoinette began vocalizing a slightly familiar tune. Not sounding out the words, just singing the tune. Suddenly, where it came from struck me. The theme song from The Odd Couple.

"Hi, Oscar," I said.

"Hi, Felix," Antoinette replied.

"Loved that TV show," I said.

"So did I," Antoinette replied.

But then, our first argument, if you can call it that, came about a week later. It started over who would wash the dishes. To be more precise, who would get to wash the dishes?

Strange as it may seem, I have always loved to wash dishes. There is just something deeply satisfying, okay, maybe not deeply, but certainly satisfying, about the very tactile sense involved in washing dishes.

Imagine. I enjoyed dipping a plate into the warm soapy water and rubbing a sponge over the dinner plate's front and back surfaces. Dropping the sponge into the soapy water, I would once again rub the plate's front and back surfaces, only this time with my bare hands under running water. Mission accomplished, I would place the dish in a waiting tray.

As a young boy, I would always ask, no, beg, to be allowed to wash the dishes. Shocked by my eagerness for the ordinarily despised chore, my parents would often excuse me from other household duties.

"It's the Felix in you," Antoinette told me when I explained the pleasure I experienced.

Despite our polar opposite personalities, when it came to washing dishes, Antoinette and I were of the same spirit. She, like me, loved to wash dishes. Only hers were a different set of emotions that accompanied the work at the kitchen sink.

For Antoinette, it was the sense of freedom she felt as she washed the dishes. No deliberate rubbing the back and underbelly of dishes as she washed them. No, for Antoinette, the dishes were escorted through the running water like so many convicts escaping from a long imprisonment. She flung the dishes into the waiting tray. It goes without saying that Antoinette washed the same number of dishes as I might in a fraction of the time.

And so, there came that day when we had our first argument.

I had gotten home a little earlier than expected, and Antoinette was still out shopping. There was a pile of dishes in the sink. I had promised Antoinette that she could wash those dishes. It was her turn, I told her, and I would not step on her toes.

But then, I was a little hungry and thirsty, and I needed a cup and a plate to serve myself some food. I looked in the cupboard. Okay, there were some cups and plates there, but not many. Besides, even though I was hungry, I was not quite ready to sit down.

In a moment of weakness, I surrendered to temptation. I don't know what came over me. My sin lasted less than ten minutes.

I washed the dishes.

"Harry, how could you?" Antoinette said as she came into the kitchen and saw my betrayal. "It was my turn."

"I'm so sorry," I said. "I just couldn't resist."

"You promised," Antoinette said. "You washed the dishes yesterday, and now, this."

"I'm so sorry, babe, but I'll make it up to you," I said. "Tomorrow, you get to wash, breakfast, lunch, dinner. Okay?"

"Okay," Antoinette said. "But only if you throw in snack time, too.

ELEVEN: YOU TURN

A month after Antoinette and I got married, my father passed away in his sleep.

The coroner ruled it a massive heart attack. My father had been referred to a cardiologist, and that visit had been scheduled for three days after his fatal attack. My mother was too distraught to cancel the appointment, and so I made the call.

The O'Toole Funeral Home did my father's service, of course. He would not have had it any other way. Had we "farmed out" his service, the local association of funeral providers would have taken such an unorthodox move as a sign of professional irresponsibility.

Still, doing the service for one of our own, the patriarch of our undertaking family, was surreal. To say nothing of the grief, personal this time. Add to that the professional disconnect. Imagine a doctor doing surgery on himself, or a police officer putting himself in handcuffs. Still, honor dictated that we do the service.

Holding our grief in check, we pushed on through. My father's assistants lovingly prepared his body. We carefully selected a mix of the classical, patriotic and rockabilly music my father so loved.

The eulogies were well-paced and thoughtful. My new bride had met my father fewer than half a dozen times, but her words perfectly fit our sad occasion.

"I didn't know him that long," she said. "But his eyes were the soul of kindness."

My mother, obviously still deep in grief, remained the perfectionist.

"His face doesn't seem quite right."

With all respect, it was perfect.

"He told me he didn't like that song."

In truth, "Danny Boy" was one of my father's favorites.

"The tie doesn't match his suit."

We had employed a red tie and blue jacket at more previous funerals than I could count.

What followed the funeral was a series of receptions. I say receptions, plural, because, unlike what follows many funerals, my family believed in the practice of the more eating and socializing, the better.

This gave me the chance to introduce my new bride to my extended family, young and old alike. Members of the older generation were unfailingly polite, and they asked about school, hobbies, interests, and the like.

Not so the younger generation.

"So how did you get that no-borders tan?" asked one particularly snotty nephew.

"Was there lots of boobs, I mean, booze, at your reception," snickered another.

Antoinette took it all in stride.

"Wanna see?" she said, before shaking her head at the eager response. "Sorry, boys, too late."

It was after the series of receptions petered out that it came time to think seriously about what kind of work I might do. I had some money saved up, but the cash was disappearing fast. And in all the excitement of the wedding and the sorrow at my father's passing, my attempts at finding steady employment had been half-hearted.

Several weeks after my father's funeral, my uncle brought down the hammer. "You need to find a job," Sean said.

"I don't want to rush into things," I replied, ignoring, as it were, my recent marital history.

"There's always the family business," he said. "I know you haven't always been so keen on the family business, but it's an honorable profession, and you've had quite the head start toward carrying on the family tradition."

My head wasn't quite with him, and the main thing I noticed about his speech was his use of the word "keen." Did adults really use that word?

"Let me think about it," I said. "I've got some other possibilities I'm exploring."

This was a lie, because, with the back-to-back upheavals of marriage and my father's death, I hadn't much thought about work or earning a living. I suspect my uncle didn't buy the other options rhetoric.

"Give me a few weeks to explore," I said.

"Okay, three weeks and I want a report," he said. "Serious."

"Serious," I replied.

I didn't lift a finger toward exploring opportunities or finding work over the following three weeks. Even Antoinette's gentle reminders did little to move me. Sure as clockwork, my uncle spoke to me on the morning of the twenty-second day.

"Time's up," he said.

"Okay, okay, what do you suggest?" I replied.

"Same as before." Then, softening his tone, he said, 'Listen, Harry, the funeral business is an honorable profession. Steady work, and you serve your friends and neighbors in ways they appreciate for years afterward. It's a noble calling, your calling. You're a natural. You're kind, thoughtful and gentle with people."

"And way too young to handle a funeral home."

"Nonsense," Uncle Sean said. "Your father was quite young himself when he took over."

"But ..."

"But nothing. Let me sign you up for mortuary school. With an accelerated program, you can obtain a professional license in a year. You'll run the family home, and you'll make your father proud. How about it?"

"Okay."

And so, I found myself, hemmed in by circumstances and my own lack of a competing vision, on track to take up the family business. To put on, as it were, the family mantle. The O'Toole family business continued, with my father's assistants doing the work, awaiting the completion of my training. To earn some cash, I did some shift work at a local grocery store.

Mortuary school, in hindsight, wasn't as bad as I expected. The learning how to prepare the deceased for viewing, which I dubbed "laboratory work," wasn't that difficult. My informal training since childhood helped buckets.

"So how's our future funeral director working out at learning his new trade?" my college buddies asked when we finally got together several weeks into my coursework. "Are any of your customers complaining?"

As if I had never heard that joke before.

"Hey, guys, I'm working on my bodybuilding skills," I replied. "If you ever need my services, just ask."

For all my uncle's encouragement, I wasn't the best of students. Bad study habits die hard. Fortunately, in funeral work, it's not where you put the No. 2 pencil on a final exam paper that counts. It's much more hands on and practical.

Time walked its steady pace, and I graduated. Not at the top of my class, but, surprisingly, not at the bottom, either.

"What do you call somebody who graduates from medical school last in his class?" I would ask my friends.

"Doctor," they would shout in unison.

"What do you call somebody who graduates last in his class from mortuary school?" I would ask.

"Mortician?" they asked.

"No," I said with conviction. "Your friendly, neighborhood, undertaker."

"I like mortician better," Seth said.

"Remember Khrushchev?" I said.

"Yeah, Khrushchev, what's he got to do with anything?"

"What did Khrushchev say?"

"I dunno," Seth offered.

"Remember when Khrushchev pounded his shoe on the desk at the U.N.? He pounded his shoe and promised the capitalists, 'We will bury you.'"

"Yeah?"

"Well," I said with a grin. ""That's what we at the O'Toole Funeral Home are going to do. We will bury you."

For all my bravado, however, I wasn't entirely comfortable with my newly chosen, or chosen for me, profession.

Even though I managed to slog my way through mortuary school, and even though I had seen dead bodies all my life, or perhaps because I had seen dead bodies all my life, the business still gave me the creeps.

The heebie-jeebies, at the oddest moments. A sudden memory of my grandfather's death. An unexpected reminder of the school bus accident in high school. Like an unwanted guest showing up unannounced, my longstanding fear of death kept tapping me on the shoulder.

The bite stung more when I recalled just how much partying I had done at the state university. Might a bit less beer and a tad more books have landed me in a different occupation, I wondered at odd times.

Help, at least some help, arrived quite unexpectedly when Antoinette and I attended a theater performance at a community playhouse near my parents' home.

"Do you ever get nervous just before going out on stage?" a young man in his twenties asked the lead actor of "Antony and Cleopatra" during a Q&A following the opening night performance.

"All the time," the actor confessed. "But if I don't tell anybody, they will never know."

The actor warmed to his answer. "Acting is show. But all of us, in all our professions, are actors. All the world's a stage, and we are merely players," he added. "Alone in my dressing room, before I go on stage, I'm terrified. But when I step onto that stage, before you my audience, I act. I perform. I act courageous, and I am courageous."

"This, he added with a great flourish, "is the great lesson of life."

"That, I thought to myself, is how I will handle constant attacks: Pop-Pop, the high school tragedy, Frankie, and even that betrayal by the Girl with Earrings the Size of China Tea Saucers. I'm an actor now, a consummate professional actor, and my funeral families need never know what's going on inside."

"Are you okay, babe?" Antoinette said as we exited the theater. "Your expression seems a little unusual."

"Never been better."

TWELVE: SERVANT

At my first funeral after mortuary school, everyone was perfectly attired. Except for me.

Following procedure, I dressed the deceased in standard issue white shirt, blue coat, red tie. His tie was smartly knotted. His button-down shirt collar was deftly fastened. His cuff links were placed at exactly the right angle.

When I dressed myself to greet the visitors at the viewing, I got the part about the white shirt right. Unfortunately, in my haste to do my first viewing as an official mortuary school graduate, I had neglected to purchase a new suit for the occasion.

And so, when I went to dress up, all I had in my closet were items I had picked up at the local re-uzit store. Yikes, I thought, but this will have to do, at least this once. I donned the blue checkered coat and a red and white striped tie.

"Quite the fashion statement you're making there," Antoinette told me after the guests had left the viewing.

"I hope nobody noticed."

"They noticed."

This funeral business was going to be a fashion change from college, where I was partial to torn jeans and ragamuffin football jerseys. Frankly, I was not in the habit of changing my underwear more than once or twice a week.

"Whether I needed to or not," I told Antoinette, only half kidding.

She put me on a different schedule. "Adult male diapers should be changed daily."

Being on call twenty-four seven was also an adjustment. It was bad enough having to be ready for an exam on a schedule you knew beforehand. But being ready for a "pop quiz" at all hours of the day or night was something altogether different.

Working my new profession also wrought a change in what came out of my mouth. It wasn't that I was unaware that the f-bomb wasn't appropriate in a funeral setting. It was that I had to put an extra guard on my mouth to prevent the sudden emergence of untoward vocabulary at a most inappropriate moment.

A few funerals in, my assistant motioned me to the open casket just as the grieving family had arrived to view their relative. The family had complained to my assistant that the deceased's face had shifted slightly, making it look not quite right.

"What the ...," I exclaimed, inadvertently dropping the f-bomb. Instantly realizing my mistake, I apologized profusely. Not very professional, I chastised myself.

Learning to curb my language was reasonable enough. But what was really a sea change from college days was just how linguistically placid a life of funeral services is.

"So what's the meaning of life?" my dorm mates would challenge me. We would debate this, passionately, long into the night.

"Who was the most influential man of the twentieth century?" one of the guys threw out on another occasion.

"Dostoyevsky or Tolstoy?" challenged one guy on our hall after coming back from his Russian lit class.

Or when things really got heated, "Can the Dodgers ever be forgiven for leaving Brooklyn?"

I get nostalgic even mentioning these things to you. Sure, mort school was mostly a focus on learning the trade. But even then, on some evenings, my fellow students and I would get together over burgers and beer, and the conversation would occasionally turn lively.

But now, everything was as bland as vanilla pudding.

"My condolences."

"I'm so sorry for your loss."

"He's in a better place now."

Not that my new manner of speaking was, from a larger perspective, a moral improvement. As the months and years went on, I learned to be perfectly smooth and polite, perfectly agreeable, and perfectly in agreement with whatever religious sentiment was expressed.

"He's in a better place," I would suggest.

"He's joined the angels in heaven," I would reassure family members. A confirmed religious skeptic, I didn't believe any of it.

"God has his purposes," I would agree with other family members, with a practiced sincerity that surprised even me.

I was becoming, as I noticed at quiet, inconvenient times, the perfect religious hypocrite.

But in other ways, I blossomed.

There was, for example, my exposure to many more cultures than I had experienced in college. In college and among my dorm mates, I got to know guys from a variety of cultural and ethnic backgrounds. Jackson, from

Zambia, an African who did not share many of the "African-American" viewpoints of my Black classmates.

Sergei, my Russian friend who spoke great English, with good grammar, except that he could never get the hang of the English definite and indefinite articles. "I am a freshman" always remained "I am freshman."

But as a funeral director, I got to experience true cultural diversity. Brazilian religious hymns, enthusiastic with a Latin American rhythm. Slow and methodical Dutch reformed hymns, played on a portable organ brought in for the occasion. During one Lutheran service, an older gentleman, seated at what looked like a hundred-year-old keyboard, wrung out "A Mighty Fortress is our God." I wasn't religious, but I was so impressed with the rendition that I later called it up on Spotify.

The toughest part of the job was something that soon dawned on me, something that would have been absolutely incomprehensible to me as a college student. Just this. As a college student, you are the one being served. The professors prepare your syllabus, teach your class, and hold office hours. Sure, you do the homework, sometimes, and you take the exams. But the entire enterprise is about you, your learning, your growth.

Now, the whole world was topsy-turvy. It's never about you. You're the servant. It's not about you.

I began to learn that one morning.

Antoinette was sitting on a sofa in our living room and plowing through "The Brothers Karamazov." She had nothing else on her schedule for that day, but I was off to check up on the preparation for a viewing later that afternoon.

"Can you get me a cup of coffee?" she said, looking up from her book.

"Hey, sweetheart," I said, "I'm really in a hurry."

"Hey, babe," she said, "Do you love me?"

"You know I love you."

"So, can you make me a cup of coffee?"

And so I did. The lesson of it all didn't occur to me until later that afternoon. But, thick headed as I am, it did occur to me.

But then, there remained the problem of inappropriately dressed female funeral attendees.

As a newly married man, I took great pains to not get enticed by the wildfire of female flesh that often shows itself at funerals. You would think that funeral services are supposed to be modest affairs, but it often just isn't so. Black is the color of mourning. Unfortunately, oftentimes a twenty-something female shows up in a black dress way too short.

Even with death as the "featured speaker" at a funeral, those dresses did a lot of talking, and I had to learn to tune them out.

Making matters worse, near the end of many funerals, the half-dressed women and the rest of the family would announce that they were off to a "let's get drunk 'cause tomorrow we die" party. Occasionally they would even invite me.

Given my "party hardy" memories of my college days, this was especially painful. Because, of course, I had to refuse.

And so, I was delighted when an appropriately dressed middle-aged woman showed up at my office one afternoon, asking that I prepare a viewing and funeral for her special someone.

THIRTEEN: A SPECIAL FRIEND

When I walked into my office, the woman was already awash in tears. "I need a funeral service for my dear family member," she said.

"You've come to the right place, ma'am," I said in my best undertaker voice. "Make yourself comfortable, and we'll see how we can help you."

The middle-aged woman was slightly heavy and dressed in what I took to be gardening attire. Loose-fitting blue jeans, a checkered shirt and comfortable tennis shoes. Her hair was pushed back from her forehead. A pair of sunglasses sat atop her head. She was carrying a handbag nearly the size of airline checked luggage.

Once seated in my office, the woman, through tears, outlined her wishes for the upcoming service.

"Flowers, plenty of flowers," the woman said. "He loved flowers."

"We are able to provide a fine assortment of everything from chrysanthemums and roses to lilacs and black-eyed Susans."

"Music," the woman continued. "He loved music, especially country music, Merle Haggard, George Strait and Willie Nelson, that sort of thing."

"We can provide that," I said.

"'On the Road Again,' that was his favorite song," she added, helpfully.

"I'll make a special note of that," I said, pulling out my pen and notebook.

"And pictures, I've got lots of pictures," she said.

"We can post pictures on special boards for display at the viewing."

"Baby pictures."

"Check."

"Grown-up pictures."

"Okay."

"Pictures with him and his whole family."

At this point, the woman burst out in renewed tears, and was unable to speak for five minutes. Toward the end of those tears, she pulled a dish towel out of her handbag, blew her nose, and resumed speaking.

"Visitors," she said. "He had more friends than you or I put together, and we're expecting they're all going to want to come by to express their final goodbyes."

"We have more than adequate seating," I said. "And what might be the name of the recently deceased?"

"Sam."

"Sam?"

"Sam."

At this, the woman pulled a large framed glass portrait out of her handbag. The size was about twelve by eighteen inches. At first, I could only see the backside, where a large pull-out tab would make it possible to stand the portrait upright on any coffee table.

As my guest flipped the glass enclosed picture over so that I could see the portrait, everything became clear. There, smartly dressed in a fashionable cloth handkerchief collar, was a bright-eyed dog.

Catching sight of the dog, the woman began once again to tear up. Her renewed expression of sorrow, perhaps two minutes long, gave me a chance to compose myself.

"Madam, I'm so sorry for your loss," I said. Feeling bold, I added, "He's in a better place now."

The woman's "Sam," to be sure, was one handsome pup. As I found out later, Sam was a chow collie mix. That diverse pedigree gave the dog an orange-brown coat, a black-and-red tongue and perked-up ears that gave him the appearance of an eager student.

Truth be told, the dog was movie star handsome. "That's one good-looking dog," I said.

"Don't tell him that," the woman said, covering the dog's ears in the photograph. "He was awfully vain, always wanted his way in everything. But he was a good dog, a good dog."

"He looks just like a fox," I said.

"You're right, that's what people would tell us," she said. "We'd take him for walks in the park near our house, and people would always stop us to tell us what a good-looking dog he was."

"A good-looking dog, for sure."

"They'd never tell us how good looking we were, me or my husband," she added, wistfully. "Just Sammy."

I was just about to share the bad news, that we don't do dog funerals, when my assistant burst in.

"Excuse me, Harry, got a minute? We've got a small problem. It's rather confidential."

Leaving my grieving guest, I followed my assistant into the hallway.

"You know Mr. Arthur Castleton senior, I'm prepping him for the viewing tomorrow. Everything was going okay until his son, Arthur junior, suddenly shows up. The son is a huge dog enthusiast, and he's got his so-called Lassie with him."

"Doesn't sound good."

"Not good, indeed. I've got Arthur senior on the table, but I bumped the table and his right arm slid off. Ordinarily, no problem, I'd just move it back. But in a flash the dog jumps forward."

"Let me guess."

"You'll never guess."

"That bad?"

"Worse than that. Lassie jumps up and bites off the dead man's finger, and swallows the whole thing like a piece of hot dog."

"That's a problem," I said. "What did the son do?"

"Well, he's in shock, almost beside himself," my assistant said. "He says we've got to do something, and fast."

I instructed my assistant that he should go back and keep Arthur junior calm while I dealt with the woman in my office.

"I'll figure out something," I told him.

Sam's owner had calmed down by the time I returned to her.

"I'm so sorry for the interruption," I said. "And I'm so sorry we don't do dog funerals. Perhaps you could go to your local vet."

"But Sammy was special," she pleaded. "He's a member of the family. We loved him, we still do."

"I can tell he was special," I said.

"Then please, please, give him that special send-off he deserves. You said he's in a better place. Those who repay the special love we have for Sammy will find themselves, when they pass, in that same better place."

In the end, I could not resist Mrs. Keller's pleas. We put Sammy in a special casket reserved, alas, for children who pass. In preparing the body, I gave Sammy a special shave from head to tail, giving his coat a smooth silky feel, soft as velvet. Because dogs, unlike humans, have a long snout, it was a challenge to position the face. A wooden cradle under the back of the head kept Sammy's face looking forward and not to one side.

"He's gorgeous," said Mrs. Keller as she stood by the coffin. Every member of her gardening and readers groups attended.

As for the senior Mr. Castleton, we simply replaced the missing finger with a wax substitute so realistic looking that you could hardly tell the difference.

"Don't ever tell my sister about this," Arthur junior pleaded. "She'd kill me if she ever finds out."

At the viewing, a slight imperfection raised the sister's curiosity.

"What happened to Dad's finger?" Arthur junior's sister, Sarah, said as she looked into the open casket.

Her brother shrugged. "Looks okay to me."

FOURTEEN: OH BROTHER

Six months after I took over the family funeral business, Antoinette and I were enjoying waffles with my older brother, Randy, and his wife, Mattie, at a posh seaside resort in Virginia Beach.

Fully astride his favorite hobby horse, Randy was touting the virtues of the Second Amendment.

"When every second counts," Randy told us for what seemed the hundredth time, "the police are just minutes away."

But here we were in a wealthy environment with no lack of security, I said. Surely, I suggested, there was no need to pack heat here.

"So, Randy," I said. "Are you packing now?"

Randy, until then a geyser of words, found no need to continue his oration. Instead, he merely lifted the edge of his polo shirt. There, peeking out from under the shirt, was a holstered handgun.

"A Glock," Randy said. "A trusty companion serving both police and ordinary Americans."

After the waitress took our orders, Randy, Mattie, and Antoinette headed off to the bathrooms to freshen up while I stayed behind to keep tabs on our table.

Five years older than me, Randy was almost everything I was not. Years earlier, when I dithered away my school years, unsure of what I wanted to do in life, Randy had set a steady course. His chosen field was medicine, and he pursued it from a very young age.

When I was busy scoping out girls in school, Randy was completing science fair projects. His exhibit on the incidence of Tay-Sachs disease in various populations won him a blue ribbon in eighth grade.

In cub scouting, Randy outdid me, his ne'er-do-well younger brother. Both of us were only Scouts for a few years apiece, and scouting never caught fire in our family as it often did in other households. But again, Randy shone while I exhibited only a dull shine. Randy attained the rank of Cub Scout, First Class. I did not progress beyond that of Cub Scout, Second Class.

After skipping a grade in high school, Randy was just 17 when he was admitted to the University of Virginia to study pre-med. After completing his bachelor's degree in four years, he went on to become a physician's assistant. He had no trouble landing a job in the emergency department of a Virginia hospital.

Our father respected Randy's career choice, and made no effort to recruit him to take over the family business. "The kid knows what he wants to do," my father would always declare. "So who am I to interfere?"

Randy's take on the family business was clear-headed. "I want to help people before they die," he would say. "Not after, when it's too late."

Like my father, I respected Randy's sure sense of calling. I envied, at times, the fact that he had such certainty concerning what he wanted to do in life. I often wondered why I had not been gifted with a similar sense of certainty.

Randy had met his wife, the former Matilda Collins, on a blind date. She was in training to be a nurse at a nearby university. They married shortly after he graduated, one year after she did. Their first child was born exactly ten months after the wedding.

"But who's counting?" we ribbed Randy after the quick pop-out child was born.

"Friends and family who count, don't," he always replied.

About a year after the child was born, Randy and Mattie moved into a spacious house in Charlottesville. A large marble table sat in the center of an enormous kitchen. A grand piano sat in the large living room, even though neither of them could play. The garage had room for three cars, with plenty of room to spare.

Shelves were Randy's passion, and he had placed them everywhere. As the months and years marched on, it became more and more difficult to find an overlooked wall without the requisite shelf.

Often, the only reason why a shelf was lacking was to make room for a framed and glass-enclosed diploma. The size of medieval coats of arms, diplomas celebrated everything from university graduations to faithful volunteer work.

During my first tour of their house some years ago, I was overwhelmed by the many diplomas and the large roomy spaces. "How can I ever compete with this?" I thought.

My mind returned to the present as Randy returned to our table, with Mattie and Antoinette not far behind. The conversation moved to the last time we four had gotten together, a few weeks earlier.

"How did you like the service?" Mattie said.

A longtime member of the Episcopalian Church that Randy and Mattie occasionally attended had died, prompting my brother and his wife to invite Antoinette and me to the funeral service. "We were wondering if you wanted to see how other funeral services operate," Randy said. "We hoped to cater to your professional curiosity."

The funeral service had been held at St. Andrew's, about a half hour drive from their house. As we had entered the church, a line of about two dozen people had lined up to walk past the casket, located just in front of the elevated pulpit.

What had struck me right away was the music. A trio of musicians in one corner of the sanctuary were playing a violin piece that I guessed was composed by Mozart. The steady pace of the music had given me the sense of looking out upon a lake with no waves. Much later, after we all went home, it had dawned on me. The musicians, it seemed, had not played a single religious song.

"What did you think?" Randy said. "Did you like the service? Did you like our church?"

"I was surprised by the message from your Most Reverend Smith," I said. "I had thought that there would have been some sort of Bible message, but all I heard was what a good guy your friend Vincent was."

"Actually, we didn't know him that well," Mattie said. "And the Good Reverend doesn't usually talk about the Bible very much, at least not directly. Mostly, he starts with a Bible verse and then goes off on his own tangent."

"He's careful not to bore anybody," Randy said. "He tells some great stories. To be honest, he does do a good job of keeping everybody's attention."

"Just curious," I said, "do you believe in that religious stuff? I've never found it very interesting."

"Of course, I believe it," Randy said. "Everybody knows it's true."

"They do?" I said. "I don't think it true, at least most of it. So tell me, Randy, do you read the Bible?"

"No, not really," Randy said, "I usually just let the Reverend explain it."

At that point, the waitress brought out our food. Waffles. Pancakes. Eggs. Sausages. Hash browns. Bananas. Orange juice. Apple juice. Our family has always liked to eat. Famished, pausing for nothing, we dug right in.

The conversation turned to politics. As usual, there was not much subtlety in Randy's views. Republicans? Good. "Libs?" Bad.

"The libs just want to take away your guns," Randy said.

Just before our day at the beach ended, the four of us walked out of the third-floor restaurant and into an elevator. I noticed that there were already a half-dozen people in the elevator, all strangers to us.

I addressed Randy. "You know, Vinnie, we really need to get rid of that body in the trunk of your car. The cops are getting suspicious, and the body is starting to smell."

Our fellow passengers gave me a strange glance, but Randy didn't miss a beat.

"Don't worry about it, Meatball Mario," Randy said. "I've already chopped up the body and placed the pieces in special garbage bags, ready for disposal." My brother then turned to our elevator audience and placed his outstretched index finger over his lips.

"Shush!" he whispered to the startled onlookers. "Not a word!"

And then, turning to me, he said magic words.

  "Let's go talk to Don Corleone, the cook. He'll make you an omelet you can't refuse."

FIFTEEN: TOENAIL

When I woke up one morning, the big toe on my left foot was asking for my attention. No, not asking. Demanding. And so, putting aside my phobia about all things medical, I arranged to see my podiatrist, Dr. Mark Frederickson, later that afternoon.

Even I could see that I could no longer avoid doing something about an ingrown toenail.

"When the yellowish green pus started coming out," I said, sitting down on his examination table. "That's when I knew I had to make an appointment to see you."

"Better late than never," the doctor replied, turning my foot from side to side.

When it comes to my own body parts, I am a coward's coward. Most of the time, that attitude serves me well.

For example, for the most part, big toes mostly go about their job without complaint, prompting me to mostly ignore them. On the infrequent occasions when I might stub them, they usually require just a minute or two of massage and they're back to normal. And thus I ignore toes until the next, brief, crisis.

But now, and over the last three days, the crisis had arrived. My big toe was not playing by the rules. Slowly but steadily, my toenail had left its assigned place and invaded the flesh bordering both sides of that rock-solid material.

"Does it hurt much?" Dr. Frederickson said.

"Was Babe Ruth a great ballplayer?" I said.

Dr. Frederickson cracked a brief smile.

To divert my attention from the crisis at hand, I glanced around my temporary cage. Dr. Frederickson's examination room was a veritable temple to the medical profession. Taking pride of place was a large photo showing Dr. Frederickson and his two brothers, also physicians. Under the photo was a large caption, "Three Physicians, Brothers in Arms."

Next to the photo was a full-sized ink drawing of the human skeleton, replete with the names of all two hundred plus bones in the human frame. Off to its right was a detailed chart showing the evolution of Homo sapiens from various ape-like ancestors.

And next to that chart was a set of drawings detailing the evolution of feet from pre-human ancestors walking on all fours to fully modern human feet.

Last but hardly least, to the left and to the right, were portraits of Charles Darwin and Voltaire.

"I think we've caught this in time," the good doctor said. "A few snips of the toenail, some antibiotics, and you should be as good as new."

"Do I need to make an appointment for the toenail cutting?" I said. I suspected that the doctor had in mind cutting the toenail right now, but the prospect of immediate additional pain had me scrambling for an avoidance strategy.

"No, I think we can solve this right here and now," the doctor said, a cheerful demeanor in his voice.

The doctor opened the exam room door and called out to a nurse. A few minutes later, the nurse brought in a tray covered with a cotton cloth. The doctor unveiled the tray, exposing several scalpels, tweezers, needles and other instruments of various sizes.

"This won't hurt much," Dr. Frederickson said.

"Much?" I said.

"Okay, not so very much," the doctor said, too cheerful for my taste.

I was not persuaded.

Dr. Frederickson began his work on my toenail. First, a careful and thorough wiping of the target area with an antiseptic. Next, a needle to insert something to deaden the pain. Then, a few minutes wait.

Back to work, Dr. Frederickson gently pulled apart the swollen flesh from the imbedded toenail.

"You might not want to look," he said.

"You may be right," I said, turning my head.

As the doctor's cold steel approached my flesh, I flinched. "Steady," he said. The good doctor then proceeded to cut away the offending portion of toenail.

A few minutes went by. "We're done," the doctor said in a cheerful voice.

I turned my head back toward my feet. What struck me was just how thin the remaining toenail looked. I also noticed some bloody gauze in a nearby wastebasket. For good measure, Dr. Frederickson had also clipped a few too-long toenails on both feet, giving me, in effect, a pedicure free of charge.

"So how's the funeral business?" Dr. Frederickson said, setting side his instrument tray and washing his hands. "I understand you're pretty busy these days."

Unlike most doctors, Dr. Frederickson was one to ask the "warm-up" questions mostly after his work was completed rather than before. I think he employed that approach so that his patients would have a few minutes to calm down after his cutting into their toes.

"Yeah, pretty busy," I said as the doctor settled into his chair for a short intermission before his next patient. "But let me ask you a question, a question that occurred to me as you were digging into my toenail."

"All sorts of strange questions occur to my patients as I dig into their toenails, usually having to do with fame, fortune, or beach trips," Dr. Frederickson said. "But go ahead."

"So tell me," I said. "Which is worse, pain or death?"

"That's a new one on me," the doctor said. "What made you think of that?"

"Well, I help people deal with death, and you help people deal with pain."

"Let me get a little personal with you," Dr. Frederickson said. "Death, and pain, is exactly why both my brothers and I became physicians."

"I did notice that all three of you chose the profession," I said.

"Yes, Matthew went into emergency medicine and Nathan is a cardiac surgeon," Dr. Frederickson said. "For a bunch of reasons, I chose a less demanding specialty, but a still fascinating expression of the medical calling."

"Medicine is a noble calling," I said.

"It is that, and more," the doctor said. "As you know, as especially you know, the world is filled with death. It marches to and fro, taking down old and young alike. It's a take-no-prisoners enemy."

"That it is."

"But who's the real enemy?"

"What do you mean?"

"Who's the real enemy?" Dr. Frederickson said. "The real enemy? The universe around us. It's the universe that mocks us, watches as we get old, gives us cancer, or, in your case, merely teases us with an ingrown toenail. And then, in a final act of sadistic humor, the universe sends death to our door."

"It does seem that way."

"Oh, yes," the doctor continued. "Sometimes, the universe laughs at us, sending incurable pain, or, in the case of you and your toenail, delivers just a small taste of things to come."

"Ouch."

"And that, Harry, is why I became a doctor. It was my way of extending a defiant middle finger to the universe."

The doctor fell silent, and I paused to consider his words.

"So why the portraits of Darwin and Voltaire?" I said.

"Polar opposites, but both dead-on right," Dr. Frederickson said. "Voltaire, a very courageous man. He had the courage to say what everybody knew, that there is no God. In 'Candide,' he showed that the idea that God exists, that we live in the best of all possible worlds, was sheer nonsense."

"And Darwin?"

"Darwin is the answer to Voltaire," Dr. Frederickson said. "If Voltaire is the pessimist, Darwin is the optimist. As the chart shows, we, mankind, we're getting better."

"Slowly but surely."

"Yes, slowly but surely," Dr. Frederickson said. "It has taken a long time, and it will take still more a long time. But we're getting better."

"A hope for today and tomorrow?" I said.

"A hope for today," the doctor said. "And tomorrow."

SIXTEEN: A NEW OUTFIT

"How do you like my new outfit?" Antoinette asked.

Antoinette always dressed with a sharp fashion sense, so I was a little surprised by the unremarkable appearance of today's outfit. The sides of her dull gray jacket fell down past her waist. The collar extended up toward her neck. And overall, the jacket seemed two sizes too large for her slender frame.

"It looks great, you always look great, but isn't it a bit large for you?" I said.

"A bit large, because it holds a surprise," Antoinette said.

"You're pregnant?" I said.

"No, not that," Antoinette said. "This."

With that, Antoinette lifted the bottom left edge of her jacket. There, sitting snugly in a holster, was a handgun of some sort.

"A Glock," Antoinette announced.

"A Glock?" I said. "What do you have a Glock for?"

"And this," Antoinette said, lifting her jacket's bottom right side. "A Taser."

"Yikes," I said.

"And this," Antoinette said, now unzipping her jacket. "A bullet-proof vest."

"Holy moly," I said. "Mrs. Harry O'Toole has morphed into Mrs. Harry Callahan."

"It's my new job, Harry," Antoinette said. "I've gotten a job as a bounty hunter!"

I knew that Antoinette was looking for a job, and I certainly knew that Antoinette would never be content with a run-of-the-mill assignment as an office clerk or something like that. But this choice of occupation threw even me for a loop.

"Are you sure you want to do that?" I said. "Isn't it rather dangerous?"

As soon as the words came out of my mouth, I realized that I had just vanquished any possible objection to Antoinette's newly chosen profession.

"Danger? Harry?" Antoinette said. "Danger is exactly why it's the perfect job. Nabbing bad guys on the run and collecting a hefty paycheck at the same time!"

Antoinette told me that she had gotten the inspiration for signing up as a bounty hunter after borrowing the movie "Domino" from the library. The popular movie of some years back tells the story of a former British actress turned bounty hunter.

"Is bounty hunting actually legal?" I said. "I know it is in the movies, but is it actually something they can hire you to do? Can't you get into trouble trying to kidnap people who don't want to be captured?"

"In the U.S., they're legal, at least in most states," Antoinette said. "Overseas, not so much. Harry, we are patriotic Americans. Bounty hunting is in our blood."

"In some of our blood."

"In all our blood," Antoinette said. "Our red, white and blue blood."

I did not know that Antoinette had such a patriotic streak.

"Don't you need a license, or some training, to do that sort of thing?" I said.

"Some places you do, but not in our state," Antoinette said. "I looked it up. I don't even need a license. You just sign up with a bail bondsman. Then you go after a guy who got arrested, but then skipped town before the scheduled trial, leaving the bail bondsman out a ton of money."

"So, you try and catch the fugitive."

"We nab the skip."

Antoinette's use of the first-person pronoun and bounty hunter jargon did not escape my notice.

"Somehow, Antoinette, come to think of it, I think this is the perfect job for you. Adventure?"

"Check," Antoinette said.

"A ballsy approach to a wily opponent?"

"Check."

"The thrill of the chase?"

"Double check."

"Perfect," I said.

"You know, Harry," Antoinette said, poking me in the ribs with her elbow. "You could have been one of my targets."

"Me, a skip, how?"

"Oh, if our wedding plans would have given you cold feet," Antoinette said. "I would have bounty hunted you to the ends of the earth."

"And I would have surrendered willingly, Taser or no Taser." I stuck out my hands in a mock gesture of surrendering to handcuffs.

A few weeks later, I accompanied Antoinette on her first assignment. The prey was a man named David

Garrison, 27, a local who had been arrested on an assault charge following a bar fight. At his court appearance, Mr. Garrison, pony-tailed and covered with tattoos, was released on payment of a $20,000 bond. "I ain't gonna show up for no kangaroo court hearing," Mr. Garrison allegedly muttered as he left the courtroom, according to several people waiting in the hallway outside.

Catching a fugitive wasn't as glamorous, or perhaps as dangerous, as it first appeared, Antoinette and I discovered to our slight disappointment. Antoinette made the rounds of Mr. Garrison's numerous friends, trying to gather clues as to his possible whereabouts.

"Ain't seen hide nor hair of him," his mother, thrice divorced and living in a ramshackle apartment, told us. The highlight of our visit, so to speak, was the rat that scurried across the room about twenty minutes into our interview. "Pay it no mind," Mr. Garrison's mother advised us.

Mr. Garrison's girlfriend, perhaps former and perhaps current, was similarly unhelpful. "He did this to me a month ago," she said, rubbing her stomach, "but I ain't seen him since. Let me know if you find my Prince Charming."

The bar owner, a grossly overweight gentleman with an overly long handlebar mustache, was long on stories but short on helpful information. "Dave's a good bloke, but he has a temper," Sherwood said. "It gets him into trouble." The slight British accent gave Sherwood's account the feel of Masterpiece Theater.

"When did you last see him?" Antoinette said.

"When the cops came to arrest him."

"How often does he visit his mother?"

"Not much, far as I can tell."

"And his girlfriend, how often does he go to visit?"

"Which girlfriend?"

"The one who's pregnant."

"Which one who's pregnant?"

Antoinette and I thanked our English friend, and headed for the car. "Time for a quick coffee and donut stop," I suggested.

After parking at a Dunkin' Donuts at a nearby strip mall, I got out of the car while Antoinette waited in the passenger seat. But then I noticed that a dozen or so people were waiting in line. And so I walked a few doors down to the 7-11. And there, to my astonishment, was our long sought after "skip."

Without a word, I walked out of the store and returned to our car.

"Antoinette, babe, he's in the 7-11, browsing the shelves at the back of the store," I said.

"He? Our guy?"

"Yes, he. Our guy. Our skip."

"Let me handle this," Antoinette said.

We both got out of the car, and casually walked into the store. "Hey, gorgeous," Antoinette said, approaching the man. "Want to have a good time?"

Our skip, seemingly thrown off his game by the unexpected proposal in a most unexpected place, managed only to mutter, "Maybe."

"You busy today?" Antoinette said, flashing a broad smile and wiggling her rear end. "Got time for some fun?"

At this, the man relaxed, totally.

"A deal?" Antoinette said, holding out her hand to shake his. He responded by extending his hand and grasping Antoinette's proffered hand.

At this, quick as lightning, Antoinette pulled a ready-and-waiting pair of handcuffs from the back of her belt and snapped them on both the man's wrists. He let out a string of curse words. He tried to run but tripped and fell, knocking over a boxed display of various candies, peanuts and other snacks.

"Merry Christmas and a Happy New Year," Antoinette said brightly to the man.

Several store employees stood around the man, still down on the ground, as Antoinette showed her authorization to take the man into custody. I called 911, and police arrived minutes later.

Looking at Antoinette, I could not help but marvel. I wasn't the only male that Antoinette could sweet talk into abject surrender. Me, she had captured me for the high calling of true love, passion and marital bliss. These other guys, Antoinette captured in the pursuit of justice. Over the next months and years, Antoinette added to a remarkable roster of captured bail jumpers, scofflaws and other assorted fugitives from the law.

"Skips," no more.

SEVENTEEN: TO SNEEZE AT

Perhaps the most important part of preparing for a viewing is something completely unnoticed by most families unless it goes wrong.

The face.

That is, the face of the deceased. Fixing that face to make it presentable to grieving relatives.

When we're alive, every component of our face -- the bones, the nerves, the facial muscles -- all work together to present a pleasing and well-coordinated performance. The actors, as it were, that make up the face may move stage left, stage right, up or down, or any of the vast number of possibilities in between as we speak, smile, frown, laugh or grimace.

Working in unison, they act out a drama, a coherent story, for family, friends, or even casual acquaintances.

At death, all that cooperation goes out the window. The deceased's forehead, once honorably upright, slouches to the left. His cheek muscles no longer stand guard over his cheekbones. They get lazy and slouch down this way or that. The skin under his chin, once faithfully clinging to throat muscles and bones, takes a well-deserved rest. That skin has been on duty for decades, after all.

From ear to ear, and from bald spot to breathing pipe, skin and muscles abandon all pretense of helping to maintain the countenance we have experienced in life, and expect, unreasonably, to maintain in death.

And so, before every funeral, that was my nearly impossible task. Making the face resemble, at least passably well, the appearance it proudly displayed in life.

Not an easy task. Move this portion of skin to the place it once held, and two other pieces of skin abandon their posts elsewhere on the face. Tuck here, and this untucks there. Rotate this, and not far away something else unwinds when it's not supposed to.

Preparing a face is somewhat like the task facing those police sketch artists trying recreate what the armed robber looked like after the perp has fled and the crime victim is trying to recall the particulars of his appearance. Sure, we undertakers may have a photograph, and that may help. Unfortunately, the photograph is often not a recent one.

Unfortunately, when families come to view their now-dead relatives, those families understand none of this. They're paying Michelangelo prices and they're expecting Sistine Chapel perfection.

And so, when Mr. Huckleberry's family came in for the double feature (my slang for a back-to-back viewing and funeral), the first thing Mr. Huckleberry's son did was complain loudly.

"Where's my father?" Thomas Huckleberry demanded, looking dead-on at his father's best-I-could-arrange face.

"That's him," I gently suggested. With a slight pause, I added, "He looks so peaceful."

"Peaceful, nothing," the son replied. "It ain't looking nothing like him."

Thomas Huckleberry's widow was next in line. She looked slightly older than her husband. She was of average weight, but with a large midsection that clung to her like an inflated inner tube. They had been married longer than she could remember. She briefly looked at her husband's face as she passed the open casket. Once she filed past, she simply shook her head.

Following them, a gaggle of assorted relatives ambled slowly past the laid out Mr. Huckleberry. The not-yet-adult members of the extended family shushed each other as they approached the honored relative.

By this time, I had discreetly moved away from the open casket so as to not disturb the family's privacy. It had been a tough morning, what with me spending several hours trying to get the face right, and family members not much appreciating my best efforts. Okay, the face probably wasn't quite right. Life, I mean, death, is like that. I did my best. Nobody's perfect.

I would never mention this in public, but I've always thought that a family lining up to view their deceased relative resembles, after a fashion, high school students lining up in the cafeteria lunch line. Everyone wants to be there, sort of, but it's far from everyone's favorite activity. Everyone gazes at the deceased relative's face with a certain amount of trepidation, much like students look at the "mystery meat" being served.

Enough of those irreverent thoughts. My eyes meandered over to the family viewing line, a line that was now noticeably nearing its end, with just a few stragglers.

Dead last, the deceased man's nephew approached the open casket. I had been introduced to this gentleman, Mr. McCabe if I remembered his name right. He stuck in my mind mostly because of his slicked back and greased hair. He was wearing black khaki trousers, slightly frayed at the cuffs, a black shirt with white buttons, and brown shoes with perforated leather.

Careful to act so that no one would notice, the guy pulled off his dead uncle's Rolex watch. During the consultations a few days before today's funeral service, several family members had insisted that the deceased's expensive watch be buried with him. The watch, with its bells and whistles, was a family heirloom, they explained. It would bring their dead relative good luck as he traveled to his new home.

This nephew, it seems, did not believe his uncle needed to keep track of time in the great beyond.

After removing the expensive timepiece, Mr. McCabe pocketed his prize. And in a motion that seemed a practiced ballet, he removed a watch from his other pocket and slipped it on the same wrist where the original had once been.

The whole motion, if I were to time it, could not have taken more than ten seconds. Aside from me, no one noticed.

By now, the viewing was winding down, and Mr. Huckleberry's other son, Mark, approached me.

"Can I ask you something?" he said, somewhat hesitatingly.

"Sure."

"The tux."

"What tux?"

"My father's tuxedo," he said. "The one he's wearing."

"What about the tuxedo he's wearing?" I said. Then, realizing I sounded somewhat defensive, I added, in a softer voice, "Was there anything wrong with the tuxedo your father was wearing? I believe your brother gave it to me, and asked that your father wear it for the viewing."

"Yes, I believe he did. It's just that I rented it for this occasion, and I've got to return it by tonight. Otherwise, there's an additional charge."

"Oh."

"Don't worry," Mr. Huckleberry's son added. "I can get you a regular suit, and you can bury my father in that. With the viewing over, and a closed casket, it won't make any difference."

"Oh. Okay."

I was just about this time that the sneezing began.

I've always had misgivings about our common practice of setting out dozens and dozens of flowers at both viewings and funerals. Roses. Daffodils. Chrysanthemums. Marigolds. All gorgeous, brightening an otherwise somber day. All perfuming the air with a mightily peasant aroma.

All, I might add, reminding us of the brevity of life.

But all, for the histamine unbalanced among us, a spark certain to set off explosions at a most inconvenient time.

The first sneeze came from the left side of the room. A big man, I wasn't sure how he was related to Mr. Huckleberry, let out a sneeze that turned a dozen heads in that direction. Those who missed the initial nasal outburst were just in time to catch the guy rubbing an eight-inch-long gooey liquid into a coat jacket, obviously hoping to make it disappear.

That noise was followed seconds later by an echo from the opposite side of the room. That man's face, wet with tears, melted first into a sheepish grin, and then morphed into a broad smile. His product was deposited not on a sleeve, but into a cupped hand. But he, too, worked to dissipate the nasal product into clothing, this time unto trousers, between the hip and thigh.

Not to be outdone, the first man responded with an encore sneeze, less mighty than the first but, pardon the pun, nothing to sneeze at. He, too, broke into a wide grin.

Taking up the challenge, the second man attempted to once again sneeze, but unsuccessfully. But everyone could see that he was trying, and everyone stood in rapt attention. Alas, at the moment, all that he could accomplish was watery eyes. But then, suddenly, his effort was rewarded with a new sneeze.

"I'll see your sneeze and raise you one," the first man responded.

"Challenge accepted," the second man replied.

The second man held his head, his response not yet available. And then, after a pause that would make the best dramatic actor proud, the sneeze arrived, a shotgun blast so wide that the man's cupped hand was not able to catch the entire fusillade.

As the two men continued to exchange sneezes, family members burst into applause, some cheering one man, some the other, and many both men. High fives were exchanged all around. A half dozen kids started cheering.

After the viewing, with the guests leaving, I privately summoned the nephew. Sheepishly, he surrendered the expensive watch. Mr. Huckleberry traveled to worlds beyond with two timepieces on his wrist. But not clad in an expensive tuxedo.

EIGHTEEN: FAMILY TALK

One Friday morning, I was in the funeral parlor when in strode what looked like a Johnny Cash wannabe.

The man, in a black suit, a black shirt and black wing-tip shoes, burst into the room where I had set up an open casket in anticipation of the day's viewing and funeral. A woman, also dressed in black, and several teenagers, formally but somewhat less somberly attired, followed close behind.

The man, breathing hard, took big steps as he bolted up to the open casket.

"Sorry I'm late," he announced to no one in particular. Reaching his target, the man bent forward and peered into the uncovered box holding the deceased.

"It's not Richard!" the man in black cried out in alarm. "What have they done with Richard?"

I quickly made my way from the back of the room, where I had been putting the final touches on arranging several dozen chairs for today's viewing.

"Can I help you?"

"We're here for Richard Smith's service," the man said. "I'm his brother, Robert Smith."

Like most people, this relative studiously avoided the word "funeral" in describing the upcoming event. It was always simply "service."

"I'm sorry, Richard Smith's service is scheduled for one o'clock this afternoon," I began. "I thought everyone in the family had been notified about the time. It's now only a little before eleven o'clock. This man's family is coming in a few minutes."

"Oh," the man said.

"Robbie, check your piece of paper," his wife piped up. "See what time it says."

Mr. Smith thrust his hand into his trousers, reaching for the verdict. His hand appeared unaccustomed to reaching into such narrow spaces.

Unwrapping up the crumpled paper, he held it up close to his face.

"Oh," he said, just before his wife snatched the evidentiary document from his hand.

"You," she said, just before clearly restraining the rest of her sentence.

"What now?" the teenagers piped up. "Do we have to stay suited up for two whole hours before this thing starts? I'm starved already."

The following joke, a classic, flashed through my mind in much less time than it will take to tell you. A beloved grandfather is on his deathbed, and his extended family has gathered around, waiting to say goodbye before he passes. The grandfather asks his young grandson to go into the kitchen to ask his mother, who is preparing a family meal, to bring him some of his mother's famous apple strudel so that he can enjoy it before he breathes his last.

The boy returns minutes later.

"Did you bring me some of your mother's famous apple strudel?" the grandfather asks.

"Sorry, Grandpa, I didn't," the boy, hanging his head, replies.

"Why not?" the grandfather says, his disappointment evident.

"Mom says the apple strudel is for AFTER the funeral."

Yes, this shopworn bit of humor flashed through my brain at the speed of thought. Hunger, it seems, waits for no man, dead or alive.

"What'll it be, Pizza Hut or Chinese buffet," one teenager challenged the other. Quick as a flash, the pair engaged in Rock Scissors Paper to determine a winner.

"Sorry guys, we're doing Denny's," their father interjected. "We can't afford to be stuffed when we come back for the viewing."

His wife gave him a "whatever" look. Then, after quickly glancing around, the four walked out. One of the teenagers tapped three times on the room's doorframe as he exited. Not sure why he did that.

Minutes later, family members for the funeral scheduled for eleven o'clock began to arrive. That funeral went off without a hitch.

Nobody inappropriately attired.

Nobody too demonstrative.

Nobody too long-winded.

Nobody visibly intoxicated.

Good for business. But boring, boring, boring.

Most of the time, we like boring. But my friends told me to leave out the boring parts when I penned my memoir. So I'm just going to skip over how the eleven o'clock family conducted their viewing and funeral service.

Then, like clockwork, the Smith family began showing up for their one o'clock viewing. The irregularities began when a cousin, Jesse Mumford, got up to give his contribution to the family album of remembrances.

Mumford was dressed to the nines, seemingly every hair in place.

Richard was not only family, but also a dear friend to me," the young man began. "Especially when I needed help when I got into trouble in college. It all began when I ..."

This cousin wasn't long into his speech when the tittering began. He tried to ignore it at first, but found it increasingly difficult to do so as the whispering spread like a fast moving wildfire in a dry California forest.

At last, a young member of the Smith family spoke up.

"Your fly's open," she volunteered.

Looking down, the speaker acknowledged what was evident to all. "So it is," he said, zipping up the offending article. As family lore had it long afterward, this cousin "zipped his lip" shortly afterward.

The next speaker, likewise a young man, drew a deep breath and likewise began to praise Mr. Smith's character.

"Like that time I thought I got that girl knocked up," Fred began. "It was a false alarm, thank goodness, but Richard was a real help in explaining things to the girl's parents, who were really pissed."

"More details! More details!" some in the crowd chanted as Fred broke off early and sat down.

It was a Trump-loving crowd, and there was no shortage of encomiums to the now former President, a man beloved by Richard Smith. One speaker, taking it still further, pronounced the names of various infamous "fake news" outlets.

"CNN!"

Boos rang out.

"The New York Times!"

Boo, hiss.

"The Washington Post!"

"Fish wrap!"

Not to be outdone, a smaller group of Democrats shouted their response.

"FOX NEWS, it's a snooze. If you watch FOX NEWS, you're sure to lose."

"Everybody stand up," the next speaker intoned at the end of one particularly raucous riff. "God bless America," the speaker began, in a deep baritone. The crowd, picking up the cue, joined in with mighty voices.

There were calls for an encore in the form of repeat choruses, so I figured this was going to last for some time longer. Moreover, I was a little politicked out, so I stepped outside and onto the sidewalk for a little breather.

And then, disaster struck.

NINETEEN: ON THE STREET

When I walked outside, I had to squint as sunshine flooded my face.

A warm spring breeze prompted me to loosen my tie. I took off my jacket and slung it over my right shoulder. Looking across the street, I noticed a dozen or so red-tailed birds perched together atop a power line that stretched across the horizon.

Like an actor resting in a dressing room during intermission between Acts Two and Three, I took a break from the on-stage personality I routinely adopted during viewings.

In the distance, I could hear children running, jumping and screaming as they played tag, swung on swing sets and climbed up onto jungle gyms.

"You're it!"

"No I'm not!"

"Yes you are!"

In front of me, a young couple holding hands flirted with each other as they strolled past.

My eye caught a middle-aged woman walking a dog from my right to left across the street.

"Puddles, now, behave," she said. "Remember, now, you're a good dog." The dog yapped and pulled at the leash.

Baggy jeans, an oversized tee-shirt, and nondescript shoes, the woman's outfit did not seem much out of the ordinary. But she did seem utterly enchanted with her dog.

The dog, a mixed breed the size of a small mailbox, had the baby face of a puppy beginning to grow into a mature dog. The owner alternately looked down to exhort the dog to good behavior and looked around to enjoy her surroundings.

Apropos of nothing, I watched as the woman greeted another woman, likewise middle aged, coming from the opposite direction.

"Harriet, my dear, what a pleasure to see you," the woman said.

"Gladys, I thought you were in Jersey, babysitting your new grandchild," her friend replied.

"I was, but I got home yesterday."

"How was it? And how was the little bugger?"

"Oh it was nice, just as I expected," the first woman said. "And Gus is as cute as a button. And he eats like a vacuum cleaner."

"Did you spoil him?"

"Of course I spoiled him," her friend said. "It's Grandma's revenge."

Life is good, I thought. Casting my glance away from the obvious friends, I looked down the street at the Art Deco shop a few door down. As usual, the display window was a smorgasbord of bright psychedelic colors.

Suddenly, close in front of me, there was a sharp smack, like a tree snapping in a windstorm, followed instantly by an ear-piercing scream.

My eyes turned abruptly to the scene in front of me. There, a dozen feet distant, a dog was sprawled on the asphalt. The grandmother was screaming.

The horrible truth seemed instantly clear. In a moment of inattention, the grandmother had briefly let loose of her dog's leash, and the dog had run out between two parked cars and onto the street.

It was obvious what had prompted the dog's tragic escape. A dog on my side of the street, several feet to my left, was pulling at a leash and letting out a torrent of barking. The inadvertently released dog from across the street had bounded toward its newly discovered friend or foe.

And then, in the twinkling of an eye, a mid-sized car had struck the running dog, tossing it two car lengths.

The wounded dog, down on asphalt, twitched uncontrollably. Its full-throated bark turned into a piercing yelp. Blood colored its fur and formed a pool of liquid under its body.

"Puddles," the woman cried, dashing after her beloved pet.

"Puddles, Puddles," she repeated, over and over. "What have they done to you?"

The dog twitched this way and that, painting the asphalt red on all sides. Its cry, piercing the air like stabs from a knife, continued for a few minutes before it fell silent.

The driver pulled to the side of the street, and ran up to the dog. I likewise sprinted to the poor animal to see if there was any way I could help. But no, the unfortunate animal was already clearly dead.

The woman, on her knees, cradled the dog in her arms. Tears ran down her face, producing colored streams of too heavy eye makeup. "Puddles, Puddles, I'm so sorry," she said.

The driver just stood and stared. "I'm so sorry, ma'am," he said, barely audible.

The children running after each other on the playground, their distant shouts still faintly audible, continued undisturbed, blissfully unaware of the tragedy on the street.

In the distance, I could hear the wailing of police sirens closing in on the scene. A few passers-by tried to comfort the dog's owner, but she was inconsolable. The driver backed away from the woman and stood quietly, leaning against his car.

What struck me was the sheer incongruity of it all.

Just minutes earlier, I had been in the presence of a family marking the death of a loved one, a fellow human being. There was a deep sadness in the air, but also a certain joy in the memory of that special someone. There was also a measure of laughter as family members egged each other on with this anecdote or that.

There, in that moment, as a professional undertaker, I supervised those funeral proceedings. There, I wore my on-the-job mask. Somber, sympathetic, compassionate. Sharing in their sense of loss, in my most professional manner, but with my emotions well under control.

But now, having just seen a dog -- a common, ordinary dog – get suddenly struck down, my emotions got the better of me. Uncontrollably, I began to cry. Not a body-shaking weeping, as was the manner of the owner of the poor dog. But a genuine tearing up nonetheless.

Embarrassed, I wiped my tears on first my right sleeve and then my left. When the police arrived, I walked back to the sidewalk.

I looked at my watch. Some twenty minutes had passed, and I figured it was time to return to the funeral service. The fatally injured dog had been wrapped in a blanket, and the owner's friend was holding the sobbing grandmother in her arms.

I turned around to take a final look at the scene. My eyes were now dry. But now, without warning, I was angry. Not so much angry at the driver who, by any reasonable measure, was not culpable for killing the dog. After all, the dog had run out between cars, giving the driver no warning of the sudden impact.

Nor was the owner, despite her pleas of "Puddles, I'm sorry," at fault. Who would be cruel enough heap that extra measure of guilt upon that poor woman? Surely she could be forgiven for her momentary inattention to her dog's leash.

No, I was angry at death. Death, the silent assassin. Death, the monster that silently, unobtrusively, stalks the street on a perfectly gorgeous afternoon. An afternoon in which children play tag, and friends serendipitously greet one another.

An ordinary afternoon, full of bright cheer and human happiness, before death suddenly and without warning pulls out its knife and stabs its victim.

"Death, you son of a bitch," I said, just loud enough that I, but no one else, could hear.

But then, without warning, a wave of terror washed over me. Coward that I am, I suddenly felt frightened. Why had I permitted myself to vocalize my anger at death?

It was almost as though I had, in a moment of outrage, insulted a terrorist holding me at gunpoint. And suddenly, fearing for my life, I instantly regretted pissing off the one who had life and death control over me. The terrorist who could harm me, fatally and without any measure of remorse, at any moment.

In that moment, I didn't apologize for poking death in the eye. But I almost did.

Turning back to the funeral home, I steadied my nerves and adopted my professional mask. The eulogies were winding down, and it was time to close things out and prepare for transport to the gravesite.

"You seem awful quiet today," my assistant remarked as we were headed for the cemetery. "Anything wrong?"

"No, I'm just a little tired," I said.

Minutes later, I had a private moment.

"Harry," I said, under my breath, "Harry, you need to be better at cranking up your professional undertaker mask."

TWENTY: FRIENDLY RIVALS

"Two point eight million plus people from coast to coast kicked the bucket last year," Sal said, looking up from his notes.

"Heart disease, nearly six hundred sixty-five thousand," he added.

"Cancer, just under six hundred thousand. Accidents almost a hundred seventy thousand. Strokes, a hundred forty-six thousand."

"Suicides," Sal ended with a flourish, "a paltry forty-six thousand and change."

Salvatore Gustav Balsam, my good friend and master statistician, was at it again. Just when I needed cheering up, or even when I didn't, he was there to dazzle me with all the numbers.

Death stats.

I had met Sal, the owner and operator of the across town Balsam Funeral Home, after I joined a county association of funeral home operators. We became fast friends. Such good friends that we established a practice of meeting once a month for lunch.

And today, straight out of the gate, Sal was quick with all the numbers. Every month, at lunch, a new set of statistics. Death stats, in all their glorious variety.

Last month, it was average life expectancy. Seventy-eight years. Good, I thought, several decades to go. The previous month it was the percentage of the population that dies every year.

"These numbers are bad, very bad," Sal said over a spinach and sausage quiche. "Tragedies for untold numbers of our fellow citizens." But then, lowering his voice, he added, "But good for business."

For the life of me, I could never tell if Sal's flippant attitude toward death was real or just a way of perhaps hiding deeper feelings. Did he feel what I felt? What I did know was that Sal genuinely loved our business, very much his chosen profession.

Unlike me, for Sal, the funeral business had always been the fulfilment of a lifelong dream. His father had been a mechanic in a local auto body shop. His mother had worked part-time as a nurse's aide in a nursing home. When he was in junior high, one of the teachers in his school had passed away, and the school took a field trip to the teacher's funeral.

The teacher wasn't Sal's, and Sal hadn't really known him, so the whole death thing was more theoretical than real. Sal had gotten to talking to one of the funeral directors and the director told him a few stories about the trade. What you do with dead people became, in that moment, his lifelong passion.

"Chemicals, combs and caskets," Sal told his parents afterward. The combs, Sal enthused to Mom and Dad, were used to set the deceased's hair just right. "His hair was perfect," Sal quipped to his parents, who missed the reference to Warren Zevon's "Werewolves of London."

Sal's parents, he told me long ago, were forever baffled by Sal's strange choice of profession.

It was perhaps no surprise then that Sal and his future bride, Esther, had met at mortuary school. "Most married couples vow that they will stay together until death do us part," Sal had told me. "But in our case, that would have been a very short relationship."

As the owner of a funeral home, Sal was technically my competitor and rival. But as Sal somewhat morbidly reminded me, there is always enough death to go around. "You can put off buying that new car," Sal said. "But when death comes knocking at your door, you're going to come knocking at our door."

This is not to say that our friendly rivalry did not become competitive at times.

And so, today's most important numbers. Whose funeral home had performed the most funeral services in the month just gone by?

As the waitress brought our salads, we each pulled out a manila folder filled with a stack of newspaper clippings. Baseball stats, fans know, are recorded on the sports pages. Funeral service stats, in a similar way, can be calculated by means of the obituary pages.

And so, like baseball fanatics zeroing in on hits, runs and games won, we zeroed in on our relevant statistics. How many funeral services had the O'Toole and Balsam funeral homes each performed in July?

"O'Toole Funeral Home, funerals performed on July second, fifth, tenth, thirteenth and twenty-second and twenty-fifth, for a grand total of six," I said.

"Got you beat, my friend, got you beat," Sal replied, his eyes lighting up and his voice rising. "Eight, count 'em. Behind you when the month started, nothing before the twelfth, but then July twelve, thirteen, seventeen, nineteen, twenty-two, twenty four, twenty-six, thirty."

Sal had obviously done his homework before our lunch date.

Holding his fist before his face to resemble a microphone, Sal continued. "And the home team ekes out a come-from-behind victory, beating out the favored visitors in an end-of-game clutch play," Sal said.

"Quiet," I shushed Sal. "What will the other patrons think?"

"They'll think death likes me more than it likes you," Sal said. "Anyway, today's box score breaks the three-three tie from January to June. The Balsam Funeral Home is now officially ahead four to three. We await your attempt at a comeback performance in innings eight through twelve."

Sal ratcheted up the competition with a hammer of hard numbers. With a score of four to three, with five months remaining, I would have to win four of the remaining five months to win for the year. That would make the score seven to five in my favor. A World Series win.

If I only won three of the remaining months, we would be tied at six months apiece. Two or fewer winning months on my part would hand Sal the full-year win.

"The ball is on your twenty-five yard line, and the fourth-quarter clock is running down," he said. I hated it when Sal upped the competition by throwing in a different sport.

"The New England Patriots," I responded, "rallied for a fourth quarter comeback victory against, what, the Falcons, not so long ago."

It was just after our waitress took our order for dessert, apple pie for me and chocolate cake for Sal, that my friend mounted his favorite high horse. His beloved soap box.

"Your obits are boring, boring, boring!"

Sal had a point. Like many funeral directors, I had families fill out a standard who, what, where and when form, listing such essential items as date of death, education, occupation, survivors, those sorts of thing. All very safe and standard. Boring, but not something that could ever get me into trouble.

"Why don't we tell everyone what the deceased person's life was really like?" Sal said, warming up.

"Like what?" I said. I really didn't need to ask the question, because I had heard his answers many times before. Asking the question was like a straight man asking the right question for his partner's humorous rejoinder.

"Like what his political opinions were, for starters," Sal said, warming to his topic.

"That might offend some people," I replied.

"Nonsense," Sal said. "The people who knew him, already know. And the people who didn't know him, what are they going to do?"

"True enough," I said.

All this was mere pleasant rhetoric of course. Like me, Sal played it safe, and his obits were as innocuous as mine. But we both enjoyed our back and forth.

"What else?" I said.

"How did they meet their spouse?"

Great question, not offensive in the least, and probably quite interesting, I thought. Maybe we should start throwing that in.

"How about what they did they do in college?" Sal said. "Did they do any of those hijinks college kids are always famous for? That would make for interesting reading."

Let's just hope that Sal, good friend that he is, never does my obit, I thought to myself.

Then Sal upped the ante. "Why not include the deceased's history of criminal activity?" he quipped. "Why not ask," Sal added, his voice rising in passion, "What about your uncle's cocaine importation bust?"

It was at this "what about your uncle's cocaine importation bust" that we noticed our waitress standing at our table, holding out our apple pie and chocolate cake.

"Yes, what about your uncle's cocaine importation bust?" she dead-panned. "Our customers and their friends," she said, carefully placing our desserts together with our checks on the table, "are known for their various entrepreneurial enterprises."

And then, "Gentlemen, I'll take your checks whenever you're ready. No hurry, take your time."

TWENTY-ONE: CALL ME

I was working the body for the Patrick Donahue viewing, scheduled for later that afternoon, when the first call came in at precisely ten seventeen.

"I'm calling from the national organ donor registry," the caller said. "Am I speaking with the family of Patrick Donahue?"

"Well, sort of."

"We understand that Mr. Donahue desires to become an organ donor."

"I'm not sure about that."

"That's okay. We appreciate that there is often some hesitation in becoming an organ donor."

"Yes, some hesitation."

"But as you know, becoming an organ donor can save lives."

"I'm sure it can. But…"

"Those who donate their organs give a gift of life."

"But I'm not sure Mr. Donahue has any organs that he …"

"Perhaps Mr. Donahue is hesitant about which organs he can donate."

"Yes, I'm sure he is, because …"

"No problem. You know, organ donors can designate which organs they choose to donate."

"I'm not sure he can choose, because …"

"We understand his hesitation," she continued, without taking a breath. "Choosing which organs to donate needs to be thought through carefully. His heart …

"I'm not sure you'll want his heart."

"Yes, some donors are hesitant to donate their hearts, feeling that their heart is something they've already given to their spouses. Till death do them part, that sort of thing. Giving a heart to seems somehow being unfaithful to your spouse."

"He can't give his heart."

"We understand. Kidneys are also in great demand."

"He's not going to give his kidneys. Now listen here."

"Please, sir, we appreciate that this can be a heart wrenching subject, and we certainly don't want to offend anybody. Perhaps if I called back at a better time."

"You can't call back at a better time," I said. "Mr. Donahue is not going to donate any organs. No heart. No kidney. No brain. No nothing. Not today. Not tomorrow. Not never."

"And why is that, sir, if you don't mind my asking."

"Because he's dead. D E A D. He died last week."

"Oh. I'm so sorry. My condolences. But why didn't you tell me?"

After wishing my caller a pleasant day, I put my gloves back on and returned to preparing Mr. Donahue's body. I had to chuckle. My caller reminded me of me begging a kiss from Susie in the second grade. Same persistence. Same fruitless effort. And yet, maybe it's for a good cause. Looking out over the corpse sprawled out before me, I mused, maybe it was a shame to waste all those good organs hiding inside.

The next call came about fifteen minutes later. I was irritated by the interruption, I hadn't gotten Donahue's ears quite right yet. Still, like most undertakers, I never hesitate to take a call. Calls are customers, and money in the pocket.

"Hello, Mr. Donahue," the caller began. "This is not a sales call and this will only take a minute." That's what they all say, I thought. Where is my stopwatch when I need it? And why am I getting a call intended for him?

"We are offering valued customers a three-week free trial of Facial Magic, the scientifically developed and proven salve guaranteed to make you look ten years younger."

"I'm not sure that's possible," I said. "No cream can do that."

That's not entirely true, I thought. Some of the stuff I put on my "customers," as I affectionately referred to them in private, did wonders for reversing the damage done by a long illness.

"As a special offer," the caller continued, "we will select six customers for a special promotion that will be featured on a cable channel nationwide. Those customers will each receive a promotional fee in excess of a hundred thousand dollars. Does this offer interest you, Mr. Donahue?"

"Mr. Donahue is resting at the moment, and is not currently available," I said. "But as his friend and colleague, I will certainly pass along your kind offer. What was your contact number again?"

By this time, I was ready for a lunch break. I had just sat down for a bologna and cheese sandwich, with my usual touch of mustard, when my smart phone again demanded my attention.

"Our research indicates that someone in your family recently lost a limb in a firearms accident," the caller began. "We specialize in providing replacement limbs for anyone who needs them."

The caller seemed rather forward. "Who is this again?" I said.

"Limbs-R-Us," the caller shouted. "But our service is going to cost you an arm and a leg." Laughter, and then a hang-up.

Oh, well.

A few minutes later, my smart phone went off again.

""This is your electric utility," the voice began. "We have overcharged you. To receive a fifteen percent rebate on your current bill, please push two."

Frankly, I don't mind too much getting sales calls when the company at least hires a real, living, breathing person to make the call. At least they've invested some human capital in the enterprise, and there's an opportunity for some back and forth. What really irritates me are those robo-calls, in which a pre-recorded message does all the talking.

But, of course, when I picked up the phone, I didn't know what I'd be getting. And there was one nice thing about this call. It was for me, sort of, not for my friend on the table.

 Not so the next call.

"Mr. Donahue," the caller began. "Are you suffering from toenail fungus? Surveys show that more than eighty-one percent of adult Americans report itching and other chronic discomfort from the toes on one or both feet, but are too embarrassed to seek professional help."

"But ..."

"We are here to offer you the help you may need but are reluctant to share with your personal physician."

So how were all these people trying to call Mr. Donahue and using my number? Was it that Mr. Donahue had been a long time resident of a nursing home and his family, anticipating that he would soon be under my care, had given out my number? Was it that even death will not free us from the torment of sales calls?

I decided to play along.

"Don't tell anybody, but I'm glad you called," I said. "My toes have been bothering me for months. Especially my big toe, left foot."

"Fungus, huh?"

"Fungus, yeah. Greener than the moss on the north side of a tree. Uglier than Mick and his Rolling Stones band mates. Smellier than socks after a senior high track meet."

"That bad?"

"That bad."

"Okay, we'll send you our catalogue. Let me just check how to spell your name."

"D O N A H U E."

The catalogue, I thought, would work perfectly to keep my kitchen table from rocking by propping up one of the four legs. Yes! A magazine for helping toes will make legs work better!

A few minutes later, as suppertime approached, I got a call from Reggie, my friend who works at the Daily Herald, the local newspaper.

"Have I got some great gossip," he began.

"Gossip?" I said. "That's all your paper ever prints."

"Maybe so. But this is the real deal. The Lucy with the Juicy, the Cutie with the Booty." Reggie, who had worked at the paper as long as anyone could remember, was a poet at heart.

"So, Reggie, what's up?" I said. "Spill the beans. If not now, let's do lunch tomorrow and you can tell me all your salacious secrets."

"It can't wait," Reggie replied. "Tomorrow, and the hot cross buns are cold. The ice cream sundae is melted. Meet me at the Wayfarer's Diner in an hour. Sit in the back, 'cause this is too good to let anybody overhear."

"Okay."

TWENTY-TWO: SCOOP

Reggie was already sitting in the back of the diner when I got there. There was huge smile on his face, so I knew something was up.

"Hey, bro," I said, in our customary greeting.

"Hey, bro, yourself," he replied, giving me a high five.

"So what's the hot news?" I asked. "A Hollywood glamour girl coming to town? A hot new murder? Yet another politico with his hand caught in the cookie jar?"

"You'll love this one," Reggie said.

"So, what is it? I'm out of guesses."

"You know, the Swiss fondue special is really awesome," Reggie said. "You really ought to give it a try."

"Come on, Reggie, I'm dying of curiosity. I'm out of guesses."

"And have you ever had their cherry cheesecake," Reggie continued, removing his black-framed glasses to better read the menu. "It's to die for."

Reggie knew all about drawing out suspense in the reader. Or, in this case, the listener. A longtime reporter covering the crime beat, Reggie wrote stories on traffic accidents, house fires and fatal and non-fatal shootings.

Such workaday reporting is often assigned to rookies, because such occurrences, tragic as they are, can become routine as the reporter's career goes on for year after year.

But Reggie, an African-American in his late 30s, was a veteran, a pro. And every so often, he turned workaday stories into gripping tales.

Some years back, a city resident had been killed when an air conditioner had fallen out of a fifth-story apartment window. Tragic story, and a little out of the ordinary. The local television news broadcast the incident as their lead story on the afternoon news and promptly forgot about it.

Not Reggie. After several weeks' investigation, Reggie retold the story as two unrelated lives suddenly colliding in one fateful encounter. After the story was published, Reggie told me that he thought somebody may have written a similar story, maybe a prize winner, many years earlier. "But what I discovered for our readers was simply too good to pass up," he added.

From one perspective, as Reggie had laid out the tragedy, it was the story of the air conditioner, the apartment building and the fifth-floor tenant. The man, as it turned out, had sought to save a couple bucks on the installation fee by trying to install the conditioner himself.

The man on whom the conditioner fell was running late, fatefully late, to meet a friend for lunch. Shortly after leaving his house, the man remembered that he had forgotten his smartphone. The phone had photos of a recent vacation, pictures he wanted to share with his lunch date. He had gone back to his house to retrieve the device before setting out again.

The detour to retrieve the phone had taken about five minutes, the victim's wife told police.

All this flashed through my mind as Reggie ordered his meal, reexamined the menu after our waitress left, and finally looked up.

"So how are things at the funeral home?" Reggie asked. The twinkle in his eye was unmistakable.

"The funeral home, nothing," I said. "What's the hot news with you?"

"No big news at the home?" Reggie continued. "Any bodies we should know about?"

"Well, you should know, because your own newspaper reported it. In fact, I think you wrote the story, if I remember correctly. City Councilman Ned Jenkins, killed last week in a tragic car accident."

"Yes, tragic," Reggie said.

"Yeah, we're doing the viewing and funeral service," I said. "We're expecting hundreds of people to turn out. So many that we had to rent a larger hall."

"Should be quite a crowd," Reggie said. "Tragic accident, that."

"I wrote up the obit myself, with the usual help from the family," I said. "How Mr. Jenkins spoke up for traditional values. His tireless work as a deacon at the First Baptist Church. A good man, taken down too early."

"A good man taken down too early," Reggie repeated.

"Do the cops know any more about how the accident happened?" I said. "The paper, your paper, said he had just gotten out of his car to change a tire when he was struck by an oncoming vehicle."

"Yes, that's what the cops told us."

"How horrible," I said "All for a tire."

"Yes, that's what the cops told us."

But there wasn't the expected frown on Reggie's face. No, instead, a sly smile.

"Wait a second, Reggie," I said. "You're saying that's not what happened?"

"Well, that's what the cops told us, at first," Reggie said. "The truth is a little more … interesting."

"We like interesting," I said. "So, what did happen?"

"Well, it's true that the cops told us, at first, that Jenkins died when he was struck by a car," Reggie said. "That part is true. And it's also true that he was struck when he was about to change a flat tire. That part is also true."

"So far, so good," I said. "So what part is not true?"

"All true as far as it goes," Reggie said. "But you see, Councilman Jenkins has always been, or should I say, had always been, a great supporter of the police. He always rooted for them when it came to budget time. He always gave them lots of money for salaries, pensions, that sort of thing."

"So what part wasn't true?"

"Again, all true as far as it goes," Reggie said. "It's just what the cops left out."

"Left out?"

"Yeah, left out," Reggie said. "Left out that Councilman Ned Jenkins, family man and tireless supporter of community values, was struck as he was about to change a tire …"

Here, Reggie paused for effect.

"About to change a tire," Reggie said, "in the parking lot of a strip club!"

"Holy moly!" I said.

"Seems the good councilman, dressed so as to hide his appearance, was partaking of some after-office entertainment," Reggie added, "when an unknown somebody, perhaps a fellow patron, decided he would prompt our secret Santa to stick around the club just a wee bit longer. A few knife jabs in a back tire did the trick."

"Yikes," I said.

We were then both silent for a moment. I needed time for this new information to sink in, and Reggie was clearly enjoying the moment.

"It's a Page One in tomorrow's paper," Reggie said. "I wrote the story myself. That's why our little get-together couldn't wait until tomorrow."

"I bet the Jenkins family is furious, what with all that publicity."

"That they are," Reggie said. "They threatened to take legal action if we printed the story. But our editors are gutsy. Old school, ink-on-the-fingers guys and gals. They told the family to go whatever themselves. In a nice way, of course."

"Of course." Stroking my chin and nodding, I smiled.

"Reggie," I said, "You're the man."

The rest of our conversation was tried and true war stories. Reggie would tell war stories about his reporting gig the way politicians would hand out promises to would-be voters. If five was good, six was better.

"Did I tell you about the time a pit bull nearly bit me as I was walking to a crime scene?"

I had heard that one before. But, like eating apple pie, it lost nothing in the repeat.

"Have I told you how neighbors flock to a crime scene when the television cameras arrive?" Reggie said. "And how they all love to tell you how the victim was their best friend, or how they saw the shooting, or how the shooter made his getaway on a motorbike?"

"It's all lies," Reggie and I said in unison. Then he added, "Yes, they all just want to be on television."

Feeling full of food and friendship, I thanked Reggie for his company. Great evening, as it went. But then.

On my way home, I stopped at a 7-11 to pick up some half-and-half for tomorrow's coffee. For some reason, the convenience store was selling Halloween costumes. My eyes fixed on one item after another, and I frowned.

Not just a few items, a full display. Boxes of black-and-white skeletons costumes. Masks colored a putrid green. Snow White with a horrific grin. A full-sized photo of Freddie whoever holding a bloody knife.

Odd, I thought. Halloween is still months away.

Like many convenience stores around nightfall, the place was nearly deserted. The lone clerk stood behind the counter, sipping a soda and munching a bag of chips.

"Why are you selling all that Halloween stuff now?" I asked the clerk. "Halloween isn't for months."

"The shipment came in today," he said, brightly. "It's one of our most popular items, and everybody likes to get their costumes well in advance."

"Do you think it's a good idea to sell all that death stuff to children?" I said.

"What do you mean, death stuff?" the clerk said. "It's all make believe. The kids love it."

"But you're teaching them to love death," I said. "Loving death. Killing people. Did you ever think about that?" I could hear my voice rising.

"What?" the clerk said, a puzzled look on his face. He fell silent for a moment, and then asked, "Is there anything I can help you with."

"I'm sorry," I said, handing him a ten-dollar bill and grabbing the half-and-half. "I didn't mean anything. Keep the change."

TWENTY-THREE: MULE TEAM

The deceased, professionally prepared and ready. The bulletin boards, thoughtfully displaying photos conveying a lifetime of memories. Flowers, tastefully placed throughout the viewing room and outer reception hall.

And so, with such exquisite preparations, nothing could go wrong, right?

Exactly right. On this particular day, with this particular viewing funeral and burial, nothing did go wrong. The grieving family arrived on time, expressed their well-rehearsed remembrances of their loved one, and left for the cemetery.

An hour later, at the gravesite, again, nothing went wrong. Family members said their final goodbyes, and the deceased was respectfully lowered six feet under.

In fact, it was so ordinary that, after returning from the interment and a quick lunch in my office, I had time to step outside to enjoy the sunshine. And if the simple pleasure of a job well done is sometimes rewarded with a chance meeting of good friends, so it was that day.

"Yo, Kevin, what's doing, my man?"

Kevin was my mailman, a service he had performed for the last decade. He shared his route with a handful of others, and he and his colleagues took turns dropping letters, magazines and The Wall Street Journal into my mail box. When he walked by my mail box, it was always about two o'clock.

"Hey, Harry, quite a collection I've got for you today," he said. "National Geographic, Conde Nast, even something from Liberty Travel. I see the travel bug is biting you again."

"It's a disease I can't seem to get rid of," I said. "When I retire, Antoinette and I want to buy a boat, load it up with beer, corned beef and bagels, and strike out for the Caribbean and beyond."

"Me and the missus want to do the same kind of thing," Kevin said. "Only not by sea. I'm afraid we'd both get seasick. What we're hopin' to do is cough up some heavy cash and get one of those fancy Land Rovers, and head out for parts unknown. Or not so unknown, California, or something like that."

"California dreaming, huh?"

"From the Redwood forests, to the Gulf Stream waters."

"This land," we sang together, "was made for you and me."

"So, Kevin, how long until retirement, if you don't mind me asking."

"Eight years, four months and change," Kevin said. "Sixteen days, I think, or maybe seventeen. But who's counting?"

"Sometimes I wish I was closer to retirement," I said. "But always good to see you, and hang in there. Your road trip will be upon you and the missus before you know it."

I wasn't long back inside before there came a knock at the front door. A half dozen men, Hispanic looking, were holding a large wooden box the size and shape of a coffin. Not far away was a station wagon, its back fold-out door open.

Grunting and groaning, but without saying a word to me, the men carried the box inside and placed it in the middle of my entrance foyer. Following this crew were a few other men and a handful of women.

Ignoring me, they began talking among themselves, entirely in what sounded like Spanish. I just stood there, bewildered. A minute passed before one of the men addressed me.

"Nuestro amigo," he said. "Died on a plane. Bogota. New York. Por favor, body for funeral. We pay cash. We come back tomorrow."

"What's his name?"

"Por favor," the man replied.

"Do you want a service?" I said.

It was clear that they didn't quite understand what I was asking.

"Funeral service," I repeated. "Casket."

I spread my hands in a horizontal motion.

"Flowers."

My hands rose up and outward.

"Music."

Palms up and down and fingers extended, I sang, "Dah-dah-dah-dah."

"No service," the man said. "Just pick-up."

To be sure, the request was a little unusual, but I set to work. But as I began to prepare the body, moving the arms and adjusting the face, I began to have some trouble focusing my eyes. I felt slightly lightheaded. Was I imagining things?

That's when the FBI showed up.

"Your friend," Agent Casey said, "is, or was, a drug mule. He had swallowed a bag containing a kilo or more of cocaine, expecting to avoid detection by TSA officials when the plane landed in Miami."

"I've heard about that."

"Alas for him, his stomach juices had other plans, and the bag leaked en route. A hazard of the trade. He made it through the receiving line but collapsed shortly afterward, in the airport parking lot."

Agent Casey explained that the TSA had gotten suspicious about the disembarking passenger's slightly erratic behavior as he walked through the receiving line. Without notifying the passenger, TSA officials had called in extra help, and the FBI soon afterward traced the man in the box to my funeral home.

"So why do guys do it? Why risk your life for a little cash?"

"Well, the bag coming apart in the stomach is pretty rare," Agent Casey said. "And these mules stand to make so much money that your eyes will bug out."

"I feel like my eyes ARE bugging out."

"We'll get you to the hospital," the agent said. "Not sure how much you might have accidentally ingested by working on the body. But a little detox overnight, and you'll be back to normal, as good as new. But when these jokers show up tomorrow to reclaim their friend, I want your staff to call us right away."

So Agent Casey drove me to the hospital. On the way, I gave him a description of as many of my visitors as I could recall under the circumstances. It wasn't a very complete list. He also called in a special agent to sit with me through the night and into the next afternoon as I recovered from my unwitting cocaine high.

The jokers, as Agent Casey called them, never showed up the next morning. Per the FBI's instruction, I released the body to the county morgue. I never did learn the man's name.

A week later, I went to my doctor to confirm I was fully recovered.

"Cocaine, you're clear," the good doctor said. "I don't expect any immediate or long-term side effects."

"That's good news," I said.

"But about your weight," Dr. Sheila Norwood went on. "You're putting on a few pounds. Best to deal with that right away, before you get older and it's harder to shed that unnecessary poundage."

She actually said "poundage."

"Ten pounds extra here, and your odds for a heart attack increases five percent," my doctor said. "Twenty pounds, and it's a ten percent hike in the odds."

"Not good."

"Not good," the doctor repeated. "Also diabetes. Get old and fat, and your odds of diabetes also skyrockets."

"But at least I don't smoke."

"Yes, you don't smoke. That's to be commended. But pounds, you have to watch those pounds. The best exercise? Pushing yourself away from the table when it's time for seconds."

"Or thirds," I said.

The doctor continued on for about ten minutes, but I didn't hear much of what else she said.

TWENTY-FOUR: AN OLD FRIEND

"Hello, my old friend. We meet again. I'm so sorry to see you."

It was on a Thursday afternoon that the body of my old friend, Kevin the mailman, arrived at my funeral home. His family, knowing that he and I had been longtime friends, felt that my holding his service was the right thing to do.

I had prepared the body of many deceased persons over the years, and nearly all the individuals were unknown to me before they passed. Even when I had never met the person in real life, coming face-to-face with his dead body was unsettling enough.

But coming face to face with someone whom I had known in life was different. If death was disturbing when I didn't know the person, it was an alarm bell now, when I did.

Death went from black-and-white to color, from two dimensional to three.

Kevin had died in a way no one had expected. Unlike many folks plodding through middle age, Kevin was in great shape physically. As a postman, he was paid to get hours of daily exercise.

"Look at these abs," Kevin once told me during a discussion on getting and staying healthy. I told Kevin that I envied his having a job in which exercise was part and parcel of the work assignment.

He counseled me to take positive steps. "A daily forty-five minutes on the treadmill will work wonders," he said. "Great way to live longer."

"Great advice," I said. "But I'm just too lazy."

Alas, death is much like a Grandmaster chess player. Guard your king with a rook and bishop on the left side of the board, and your crafty opponent will checkmate you with a queen, knight and pawn on the side of board you haven't been watching as closely.

Kevin was crossing a street to get a snack at the end of his shift when he was briefly distracted by the sound of kids playing. At that moment, he was struck by a car. An ambulance arrived, but he expired on the way to the hospital. I couldn't help but consider the huge irony. Kevin lived by walking and, alas, died in that same activity he so loved.

Kevin had a wife and three kids, a trio of teenage boys. He loved to show me photos of them all, along with a running commentary. The last "picture show" got screen time about three weeks before he passed.

"Andrew wants to be a doctor," Kevin told me, pointing out his oldest. "Mark is aiming for a gig as an attorney. And little Michael isn't yet sure what he wants to do."

"Are you sure 'Little' Michael wants to be called little?" I said. "Fourteen isn't exactly 'little,' you know."

"I call them my family train, with an engine, passenger cars and a caboose," Kevin said. "Every part of the train is important in its own way, even though every part of the train is different. They like that train analogy."

But now, Kevin's body was before me.

Silent.

Silent, of course. But utterly strange that Kevin was silent.

I looked at Kevin for a long time before I began to "work" on him. In looking at him, I noticed several small things I had not noticed before. He had a purplish pimple just under where the collar would be. The collar used to cover it, but not now.

His eyes, always full of enthusiasm, were now glassy and still. His hair was very slightly thinner at the back of his head. Funny, in life, I had not noticed the nascent baldness.

"Hey, Kevin, my man, what's doing?"

I heard my voice ringing out loud the greeting I had repeated to Kevin dozens of times over the past decade. The sound, in the otherwise utter stillness of the room, surprised me, even shocked me.

"Hey, Kevin, my friend, how are things?"

My second greeting, as involuntary as the first, rocked me back on my heels. I was so surprised to hear it that I, with deliberate caution, took off my gloves, laid them on the table and sat down nearby.

I sat for a full ten minutes.

Summoning my courage, I got up and once again approached Kevin's sprawled out body.

"Kevin, my friend," I said. "I'm so sorry that this happened to you."

All reason tells me that Kevin didn't answer. All reason. But in the stillness of that room, I could have sworn that I heard Kevin answer.

"Hey, Harry, my friend, I'm all right. It's good to see you."

"Your family," I said. "Who's going to take care of your family?"

"They're going to be okay," I heard Kevin say. "They're going to be in good hands. But if you could go in and check on them every once in a while, I'd be very grateful."

"Kevin, my friend, I can do that."

Suddenly, the spell was momentarily broken, and I realized the absurdity of it all. I glanced all around the room, looking to this side and that, thinking how embarrassed I would be if anybody saw me talking to a dead man.

A moment later my mind once again settled down, and I stood silently before Kevin.

"Hey, Kevin," I said, once again out loud.

Again, a moment of silence.

"Hey, Kevin," I repeated out loud. "Remember that time you told me about how some teenage boy handed you a dozen postcards he was sending to his puppy love girlfriend? The guy had dipped the postcards in perfume, and you asked him to get a plastic bag to put them in so that they wouldn't smell up the rest of your deliveries?

"Or the time you told me about your son's first date, a tobogganing party, which ended in disaster when he and the girl fell off a sled and she had to be taken to the emergency room?

"Or how proud you were when all three of your sons placed in a math competition?"

At this, my out loud recollection, I started laughing, uproariously. I must have laughed for a full five minutes.

"Hey Kevin," I said. "You were a great friend."

And then suddenly, I broke down, and sobbed uncontrollably.

"Hey, Kevin," I said, getting control of myself and wiping my nose on my sleeve, "You were going to do some awesome road trip with missus, remember that?"

I looked at Kevin in silence.

"The Redwood forests, and the Gulf Stream waters," I said, in barely a whisper. "This land was made for you and me."

Again silence.

"This land was made for you and me," I repeated.

My eyes still filled with water, I smiled.

"Kevin," I said one last time before preparing Kevin's body for his viewing and funeral. "Kevin, you were a good friend."

TWENTY-FIVE: ROOT CANAL

"Dentists!"

"Undertakers!"

"Dentists, modern purveyors of medieval torture practices."

"Undertakers, celebrants of death's final agonies."

"Dentists, the masters of producing pain, excruciating pain."

"Undertakers, the supervisors of sorrow, heart-wrenching sorrow."

"Visit the dentist, and you will experience pain coursing through your mouth and beyond for ninety minutes or more."

"Visit your undertaker, and you will experience pain cascading though your soul for perhaps a lifetime."

Pete, my dentist, and I were engaging in our favorite sport. I had arrived for the first of several visits to undergo a root canal, but the actual dental work could wait. First on the agenda was our ongoing "competition."

Which of our two professions, admittedly neither one popular with the public at large, was in fact the most hated, the most feared? Did people dread more a visit to the dentist or a visit to the undertaker?

Pete, ever the gentleman, gave me first ups.

"Everybody hates going to the dentist," I began, stating the obvious. "Unlike a visit to a 'normal' doctor, which might involve a poke here and a poke there, even a so-called 'examination' involves letting some so-called 'hygienist' tool around in your mouth while you sit by helplessly."

Then, Pete's turn.

"At least our pain is up front and there for everybody to see from the get-go," Pete said. "You guys begin by talking soft and comforting to your 'patients,' the families of the one who has passed. No deceased body yet visible. The deceptive gentleness of the opening gambit makes the rest of the story, the rest of their visit with you, all the more terrible."

My turn.

"You should talk about the rest of the visit," I said. "Once your assistant has finished her work, they bring in the big guns. That's you, my friend."

I continued.

"With a bare concession to easing pain, with Novocain, I think they call it, you begin your deadly work. Like a 42-pounder doing its work from the Battleship Missouri, hey, I'm not sure I got the naval reference right but you get my drift, you go right to work. You blast away. Ninety minutes of sheer pleasure for you, ninety minute of sheer agony for the rest of us."

Now, Pete's turn.

"If we do the work of the Battleship Missouri," Pete said, "your work resembles the as deadly yet more subtle work of a nuclear-armed Polaris submarine. A family is quiet and watchful, knowing they are helpless against the foe."

Pete continued.

"Moments later, unable to do anything but watch, a submarine-like coffin glides into the room. Families feel the full force of this encounter, and you are the professional who orchestrates this engagement."

Needless to say, we carried out this banter out of earshot of the unsuspecting clientele in the waiting room.

After about ten minutes of back and forth, we called it a draw. Both dentists and undertakers, we agreed, were about as popular as some commentators on MSNBC or FOX News. We laughed a bipartisan laugh.

And then, just to make both of us feel better, we rattled off a list of other rather unpopular professions.

How about when an IRS agent calls you into his office? What can be more painful that his rooting though your financial records?

"How doesn't that qualify as a root canal?" I quipped.

Or how about that police officer who suddenly flashes a rotating red light behind your too fast moving vehicle?

"Too many speeding violation points and you'll find yourself undertaking a visit to traffic court," Pete said. "That can't be fun."

Or how about Mr. Patterson, your high school vice principal in charge of disciplinary procedures? He certainly belongs on the list. Both Pete and I agreed that nearly every Mr. Patterson deserved a place on the list.

But not first or second place.

No, the top spots were already taken. Compared to dentists and undertakers, those professionals were merely runners up. Dentists and undertakers, we agreed, were the true bad boys.

But on that day, because I was the one who needed a root canal and because Pete's family and friends were all still alive and mostly kicking, I was the one who would experience the agonies of, drum roll, please, "The World's Most Hated Professions."

Pete's drill, might I add, did not disappoint that day. The drill sergeant went right to work. Whatever latent masochistic tendencies I might be harboring from childhood were fully satisfied.

A week or so later, my follow-up visit was less entertaining. I was waiting to be seen when I picked up several of those magazines that dentist offices love to keep tucked away in over-stuffed shelves. As in dentist offices throughout the land, the magazines were very out of date. Let's hope Pete's dental procedures, I mused, are somewhat more current.

I rifled through the dog-eared collection. People magazine, plus travel and celebrity mags. Few surprises in the headlines.

"Blond goddess in catfight with other blond goddess in boyfriend rivalry."

"Hollywood scribe dishes dirt on your favorite celebrity."

"Once-famous television star living in homeless shelter in Los Angeles."

Nothing to see here, I thought. Move on.

But then, other headlines caught my eye.

"Rock musician dies in tragic motorcycle accident."

"Beloved television personality undergoes Stage Four cancer treatments."

"Have scientists discovered the Fountain of Youth? Is living to a hundred just a scientific breakthrough away?"

Really? Are they saying that death is about to go the way of the Roman Empire?

Still, I was more than a little spooked by these death stories. Piling on, it seemed to me. When I'm on the job, fine. Death, that's normal, expected. But here, why here, when I'm waiting for the dentist's chair? Death seems to be forever nagging me, like a shrewish wife. Tapping me on the shoulder when I'm not looking.

Another magazine. This one an article on yet another anniversary of John Lennon's death. It reminded me of Howard Cosell announcing the fatal shooting outside the Dakota during a broadcast of Monday Night Football. I remembered calling up Cosell on YouTube, and watching Howard's announcement over and over again.

And then, prompted by the magazines, I again remembered the very unpleasant hell fire and brimstone sermon I had been subjected to in college. Since then, I had successfully enforced an arms-length attitude toward my fear of death. I had been able to lock up that fear in a mental box. But coming across these kind of articles threatened to let that demon out of the box.

And so, as I waited for the dentist to call me, I felt almost relieved when it came my turn for a painful bout in the dentist chair.

TWENTY-SIX: BUG OFF

Last night's party had lasted into the witching hour, and Antoinette was, as always, the juice that energized the festivities. Exhausted at the end of the evening, I stacked the plates, saucers, glasses and cups on the counter next to the sink, and mentally assigned myself the task of the next morning's wash-up.

But in the morning, when I reached for a cup for a quick rinse-out before making coffee, I was struck at seeing a vast landscape of black dots scurrying outward from my pile of dirty dishes.

Ants.

Tiny ants. Not the size of those creatures you sometimes see in an ant colony centered on a crack between pieces of sidewalk. No, these ants were pin pricks, the size of the lead tip on a sharpened pencil.

It was almost as though the ants had been partying on my countertop all night, blissfully undisturbed. My turning on the light had been like the curfew police, sending the revelers scampering for cover.

Not standing on ceremony, I poked my finger down on three or four of the slowest fugitives, killing them instantly. With each kill, I wiped the remains of the deceased ant on the front of my pajama.

"Too bad, old buddy," I said, smiling, after each kill.

Antoinette and I had moved from our apartment into one of those classic fixer-uppers, and it seemed that a vast catalogue of the animal kingdom had gotten there first. Not the animal kingdom as in cats, dogs, or parakeets. No, these live-in residents were exponentially smaller. Ants, wasps, flies and other tiny kinfolk.

If ants had taken up homestead on the counter next to the kitchen sink, the wasps were partial to the spaces in some walls. Antoinette and I were sitting out back and enjoying a home-made lemonade, one of her specialties, when we were joined by a pair of wasps.

"Somebody else seems to like your beverage," I said.

"I've never been much fond of wasps," Antoinette said.

"But what about Irish Catholics?" I said.

The good missus assigned me the task of rooting out these unwelcome guests. Can of bug spray in hand, I found a rather small tear in a portion of the outside wall, a tear than was hidden by a growth of ivy. Pulling the ivy aside, I aimed and fired. A cloud of irate insects blew out from the crack, and I stepped back to protect myself.

"Hiroshima!" Antoinette cried out. "Nuke those mothers!"

I can't imagine how those airmen on the Enola Gay felt as they were releasing the first of two bombs that ended the Second World War. Perhaps sadness at the death and destruction they had set in motion, and perhaps relief that their extreme measures were going to finally put an end to the war's seemingly endless destruction.

But for me, in my much more pedestrian "nuking" of those pesky invaders, there was more than a little satisfaction.

When the "victims" are tiny little critters, I rather enjoy death.

If wasps were concentrated in one "home base" and thus easy to wipe out, flies employed a vastly subtler strategy. Their game plan was to attack us, one on one, mostly at night, when we were the most vulnerable.

"What's that brushing against my nose, then my thigh, then my nose again," I said, adjusting my nighttime pillow. "It doesn't feel like you touching me, Antoinette."

"Don't be silly," Antoinette said. "That fly's been buzzing around this room for the last half hour."

Irritated, I swung my feet over the bed, stood, turned on the light, and did a radar-like scan of the room. There was my adversary, alighting first here and then there. As far as I could tell, there was just one of them, doing yeoman duty in fighting The Man.

I couldn't recall us having a fly swatter anyplace handy, so I just bunched up a wad of toilet paper and set out on air patrol. Antoinette loved watching evenly matched opponents engage in combat.

"Missed!" she said.

"Come back here, buddy," I said.

"Missed again," Antoinette said.

"Whose side are you cheering for?" I said.

"I always like to cheer for the winning side," she said.

After about twenty minutes, I decided to call it a draw. I lay back down and placed a towel over my face, covering it up except for the mouth. I tucked the rest of my frame under the sheets. Sure, a little hot, but the best I could do under the circumstances.

In the morning, the fly was still buzzing around. But ...

But, flies are strangely human, at least in one respect. Party all night, and you're exhausted. Like frat boys, like flies. In the morning, this fly was definitely on its second legs. It was flying considerably slower. I, on the other hand, was well rested.

I'll let you guess the outcome of our contest that morning. A delightful outcome.

But the fly was not alone in its assault on our home. So I discovered moments later when I sat down in the smallest room in the house. There, strategically placed between the base of my throne and the arch of my foot, was a spider.

Alas, I was in no position to immediately vacate the premises. There was, to be polite about it, some paperwork that required completion first. I hoped against hope that my adversary would delay its exit for just a moment.

No such luck. I stood up, and the spider was out of sight. But not out of mind. Getting down on my knees, I turned my head to the left and to the right. I spotted the spider. Unfortunately, spiders have their own arsenal when combating their human foe. Poking my head forward, I felt the threads of its web on both sides of my face.

"Oh, gross," said, to no one in particular.

The spider escaped its fate that day. Did it wonder about how close it had come death that day? Did it ponder the brevity of life?

Don't be silly.

Two days later, as I was once again engaging in my regularly scheduled activity on-site, I once again spotted my adversary. Figuring that there was no time for an extended campaign this time, I simply crumpled up some toilet paper and launched my full-fist rocket.

Bullseye!

This was the kind of death I enjoyed.

Three days later, I discovered evidence that the war between me and my animal adversaries was not quite over. I wasn't quite sure what the tiny animal droppings on the floor under the microwave oven pointed to, but Antoinette identified the culprits right away.

"Mice," she said. "Not Mickey Mouse, but Mickey's unsavory cousins."

Setting out the traps was a challenge unto itself. Set the spring too loose and it goes off with a mere bump before the mouse is caught in the trap's clutches. Set the spring too tight and the mouse gets a free meal.

After a few nights of practice, I had honed my hunter skills. In the morning, I turned on the kitchen light, and there it was, on its side, as still as death. Of course it was as still as death.

"He never knew what hit him." Truer words were never spoken.

So how did I feel about this death? Antoinette could not bear to look upon this, my, our, catch. Was it that the mouse, tiny though it was, still resembled, more than ants or wasps, a living creature?

Me, I wasn't quite sure. Mr. Mouse clearly wasn't an insect, creatures I had no pity on. But it was obviously far from anything human, so it really wasn't an object of pity. So, no, my reaction at the demise of the mouse wasn't anything that evoked my genuine wariness at death.

Antoinette let me do the honors. "Into the trash with you, Mister Mouse." Didn't touch it, though. Instead, wrapping everything in a plastic bag, I tossed the mouse-and-trap combo, a single package, into the backyard garbage can.

Later that summer, we discovered an infestation of termites in a hard-to-reach spot just under the floorboards near our spare bedroom. If ants were party animals and flies were flying aces and spiders were espionage agents, these termites were an invading army.

"Think of it as Operation Overlord, except that it's taking place at the edge of your house instead of on Normandy Beach," said Tony, the exterminator. "Not to make light of our boys, those brave soldiers, but this is serious."

Tony took his job seriously, going about it with military precision. "You attack the enemy on this flank, while at the same time ferreting out the enemy on that front."

I was impressed.

"The whole operation should take about three days," he added. "A little mop-up afterward, and the campaign should be a full success."

During coffee afterward, Tony let me in on his professional secret.

"In most professions, you save lives," he said. "Doctors, they go to great lengths to keep their patients alive. Firefighters, they risk life and limb to rescue that person trapped in a burning house. Pharmacists work hard to produce and market medicines that will save lives. Even you, in your job, focus on the lives of the ones you bury to serve their grieving families."

"And you?" I said.

"Me, I kill for a living," Tony said. "The bugs, I wipe 'em out. Totally. Completely. I slaughter every last one of those poor critters. And I love every minute of it."

TWENTY-SEVEN: MUD TO MUD

We were running late for today's graveside service, and the skies were clouding over, threatening a downpour.

Frank, my assistant, was driving the hearse and I was riding shotgun. The funeral procession was crawling along Wilson Avenue, where construction crews had dug up the old asphalt as a first step toward repairing the road.

That initial work had left big ditches on the left and right sides.

"Watch out," I shouted to Frank.

Too late. My side of the hearse plunged down and up as the front passenger tire jerked into and out of the ditch. The casket lurched forward, struck the divider, and bounced backward.

The vehicle's abrupt motion jogged loose the latch holding the back door shut. In an instant, the coffin, like a bullet fired from a gun, burst from the back of the hearse and landed on the pavement.

Frank jammed on the brakes. The back door swung forward and slammed shut.

Looking behind me, I saw that the back of the hearse, home to the box transporting Mr. Jones's mortal remains just a moment ago, was now suddenly vacant. Worse still, the coffin, now on the ground, had sprung open, and the corpse was partially ejected.

"What the?" I shouted.

"Lord have mercy!" Frank cried out.

As soon as I got out of the hearse, the clouds decided that this was also the perfect time to let loose their precious cargo. A few quick drops announced that decision just before the skies opened up completely and the downpour began.

Most of the pedestrians within eyesight merely slowed down as they hurried past. A half dozen or so, however, found shelter under the protruding roof of a nearby clothing store.

"I guess he didn't really didn't want to show up at his party," shouted one.

"Maybe he wasn't dressed for the occasion," said another.

"Perhaps he was wondering if his party was going to be smoking or non-smoking," volunteered a third.

After making his quip, this third man, his head down to get less wet, ran over to help us return the coffin to its previous berth. Some members of the funeral procession got out of their vehicles and likewise joined in. As did I, of course.

I pushed the deceased back into the coffin and shut the lid. The latches clicked shut. With three men helping me, we pushed the coffin, which had landed on its side, back upright.

Now, to get the box back into the hearse.

Mr. Jones' brother, Mark, slipped and fell as he tried to help lift the coffin. "My best suit, you've ruined my best suit," he shouted to no one in particular.

The deceased's brother-in-law, Johnny, tried to get a grip under the coffin. Failing time and again, he let out a string of curse words.

Several female family member huddled together, pointed to the struggling men, and mocked their efforts to return the coffin to the hearse. Others just silently stared.

Finally, success.

"In you go, my friend," Sammy, a cousin, said as we huffed and puffed and hoisted the coffin back into the hearse.

"Thank you so much," I told those helping, who mostly frowned in response.

I looked at my watch. My recalibrated ETA would put us more than 45 minutes late. I phoned the priest, who was waiting at graveside.

"It's okay," a family member told me. "We're not going anywhere."

We pulled up to the cemetery and drove past the sign that has forever befuddled me. "Enter Only."

"Why does it say that?" I asked.

"I don't know," Frank replied.

"But there has to be a reason," I said.

"No reason," Frank said. "It just says that."

This was a conversation, verbatim, that Frank and I had engaged in on numerous previous occasions. We each had our practiced lines down pat.

After several hundred feet of paved pathway, Frank turned onto a grass pathway that led to the gravesite. Unfortunately, the rain made it hard to see where he was going. The hearse slid into a foot-deep rut, a ditch that had been made deeper and muddier by the downpour.

"I think our Titanic just hit an iceberg, and we're listing badly," I said.

Frank revved the engine, hoping for a quick escape from our predicament. The vehicle rocked back and forth, but our total forward motion was a big fat zero.

"Oh, Nellie," Frank said. Frank had the admirable habit of keeping his cool in even the most trying circumstances.

I suddenly remembered that Shakespeare's Richard III had also gotten stuck in mud at a most inconvenient moment, in the midst of a battle. Richard had cried out for a horse to free him. And so I cried out, paraphrasing the long ago monarch. "A hearse, a hearse," I mumbled under my breath, "My kingdom for a hearse."

The man's family began complaining at this last mess-up

"You're late and now this," one man cried.

"This isn't really honoring to anybody," a woman added. "I knew we should have selected somebody else to do the service."

"I'm so sorry," I said.

With help from several male family members, we pushed the hearse out of the mud and back onto the path. The spinning wheels scattered mud. Handkerchiefs were passed around to brush mud off clothing.

The reverend, a Catholic priest hired for the occasion, looked at his watch just as we arrived. He had forgotten to bring an umbrella, but a teenager held an opened umbrella over the man's head. The other opened umbrellas resembled a forest of leafy trees.

The priest was speaking in a soft-spoken voice when a thirtyish woman suddenly cried out.

"Johnny, get back, get back, or you'll fall in."

Truly spoken, but too late. Little Johnny's feet swept upward, his backside hit the ground, and he slid forward and down into the hole. The whole motion resembled what kids do countless times in playgrounds around the country.

The boy's sudden acrobatics broke whatever solemnity surrounded the open gravesite. Father O'Connor stopped talking in mid-sentence. The boy's father jumped into the hole, pushed the boy up to waiting relatives, and hoisted himself up and out of the hole with the help of several outstretched arms.

The young boy was in tears.

The graveside service then went as well as could be expected, given the untoward start.

As we walked back to the hearse, Frank pulled me aside. Imitating the one-two-three finger motions of a major league baseball umpire, he counted off the day's disasters.

"Ejected coffin," Frank said.

"A first," I said.

"Stuck in the mud," Frank said.

"Happens to the best of us," I replied.

"Yeah, but it doesn't look good," Frank said. "And, last but not least, that kid in the hole."

"At least that wasn't my fault," I said.

"True, but they'll probably find a way to blame you," Frank said. "Funeral service gets worse and worse, descends slippery slope."

"Yeah, probably," I said.

"It's like baseball," Frank said. "One, two, three strikes and you're out at the old ball game."

"Some days," I said, "Our batting average just isn't that good."

"Let's hope these guys don't tell their friends about what happened today," Frank said. "If they do, we're not likely to get any repeat clients anytime soon."

As we drove out the cemetery, Frank pointed to a second sign.

"Exit Only."

I felt a twinge of discomfort, but then remarked in a casual voice, "Only for us."

TWENTY-EIGHT: ELEVATOR

"Death and taxes, you can't avoid either one," Jeff told me over the phone. "But I can help you get a break on your taxes."

Jeff was my tax accountant. I had gotten a notice from the IRS, something about possible improperly claimed deductions. I wasn't about to do battle on my own with the taxman, so we agreed on a Friday afternoon in Jeff's office to work out a plan of action.

I walked into the main lobby and read the board listing Jeff's office as on the third floor. Figuring that a two-minute climb up the stairs might satisfy the day's exercise quota, I headed for the stairwell. I took a step or two in that direction when the elevator door suddenly opened. In a moment, I opted for the easier ascent.

I stepped into the empty elevator, and the doors were closing when a man spread the doors open and rushed in. As the doors closed, I pushed the button for the third floor. He followed with a jab at the button for the fourth floor.

Following established social etiquette, neither one of us spoke. The elevator began to rise, and a bell sounded as the elevator moved past the second floor. An instant later, the elevator jerked to a sudden stop. The elevator's standard lights dimmed, the car went dark for a split second, and an emergency light went on, lighting the car at half strength.

"Bummer," the man said. "I think the power just went out."

Cell phone in hand, I called Jeff's office, and his secretary confirmed that the entire building had just lost electricity. "I think it has something to do with the road work they're doing outside," she said. "Let's hope it won't last too long."

After hanging up, I got a chance to eyeball the man stuck with me in the elevator. He looked to be about mid 20s or so, with blue jeans, a dress shirt and longish hair.

"Gary," he said, spontaneously introducing himself. "Sorry about this."

"Don't worry," I said. "I think they'll have to power up and running in no time."

"Let's hope so," Gary said.

A minute passed.

"Excuse me," Gary said. With that, he pulled out a smartphone and began to push some buttons.

I looked around, not saying anything.

"Excuse me," Gary repeated. "Can I ask you a question?"

"Uh, yeah."

"Do you ever think about death?"

"No, why?" I lied.

"I mean, everybody is going to die," Gary said. "Everybody has that appointment ahead of them and yet nobody ever thinks about it. Doesn't that seem a little strange to you?"

"Maybe, whatever," I said.

"Can I read something to you," Gary continued, brushing his finger over his phone.

"I'd rather you wouldn't."

"Here it is," he said. "Anyone not found in the Book of Life was cast into the lake of fire."

"Excuse me," I said. "I thought I said I'd rather you not read anything to me."

"But hey, man, it's important," Gary said. "Cast into the lake of fire, who would want that?"

"Nobody, I guess. But please shut up."

"Into the lake of fire."

"Enough already."

"Trapped forever."

"Shut up already," I said. Then, turning to the door, I pleaded, "Come on, Jeff, let me out of here."

"Trapped forever," Gary continued.

"Jeff, help, I'm trapped in here with a certified nutcase."

"Trapped forever, not just trapped for a few minutes in an elevator, but trapped forever, with no way out."

"At least I wouldn't have to listen to you," I shouted at Gary. Then, softer, "Now would you please mind your own business and leave me alone."

Gary lowered his smartphone and looked me square in the eye. In a clear whisper, enunciating every word and spacing out the syllables, he said, "There is a way out."

With that, Gary stepped back and looked away. Then, in a low voice, he began to sing. "Amazing grace, how sweet the sound, that saved a wretch like me." Looking up again, he said, "Ever hear that song?"

"I thought I asked you not to bother me."

"I don't mean to bother you," Gary said. "I was just wondering if you had ever heard that that song."

I had heard the song, of course. Lots of people sang it at funeral services. But I wasn't about to let on.

"It's some religious song."

"No, it's not just some religious song," Gary said. "It was written by a guy who used to be a slave trader, and then his life got turned around."

"Good for him."

"Doesn't that interest you?" Gary said.

"No, not in the slightest."

"It should," Gary said. "It's good news for everybody who's a wretch."

"That's nice. Maybe you're the wretch it's talking about."

"I am, I am," Gary said. "We're all wretches, you, me, everybody. That's why it's good news for everybody."

"Why am I even talking to you?" I said. Then, turning once again to the elevator's still-shut doors, I yelled, "Jeff, help, get me outta here. There's a crazy man in here, and he's wacko, bonkers, utterly off his rocker."

I took a needed breath.

"But Jesus loves you," Gary said. "Really, man, he really loves you."

"I don't care. Now will you please shut up?"

"Here, take this," Gary said. Reaching into his pocket, Gary pulled out a small folded booklet. He reached over and stuffed it into my shirt pocket.

I pulled the booklet from my pocket, crumpled it up, and threw it on the floor. "I don't want it," I said.

Gary bent down and picked up the paper.

"Here," he said. He un-crumpled the paper, and once again handed to me. "Here, save it for later, put it in your pocket. Read it when you get a chance."

I gave up. I put the paper in my back pocket.

Just then, the lights flickered on and off, and then stayed on. The elevator began moving and completed its long-delayed half-story ascent to the third floor. It arrived at the third floor and stopped.

The twin doors opened, releasing me from my too-long confinement in my involuntary cage. I rushed through the open door, leaving my tormenter behind. Walking briskly, I reached into my back pocket, fished out whatever that Gary guy had handed me, and tossed the unread material into a trash can.

"So how was your drive over?" Jeff said. "Sorry about you getting stuck in the elevator. Hope it wasn't too inconvenient."

"Nah, no problem, nothing to be concerned about," I said. "Now let's try and tackle those taxes."

TWENTY-NINE: MONEY TALKS

"We have some very interesting things to go over," Jeff said, a sly smile flitting across his face.

"Is this room bugged?" I said, returning his smile.

"No, no," he reassured me.

"Good."

"Video recorded," he added. A pause. "Just joking."

Jeff Cotton was dressed the very picture of a tax accountant. His button-down white shirt was expertly ironed. His bright red tie was exactly the right width, neither too wide nor too narrow. His tan khaki slacks were perfectly pressed. His glasses, neither too modest nor too glamorous, made just the right fashion statement. He sported a diamond ring on his left pinkie.

Taking a chair, I mentioned that I had just been to the doctor. Jeff, a perceptive guy, instantly picked up my cue.

"Not your favorite people, we are," Jeff said. "Still, back to back appearances, Harry. I'm impressed."

I had made my appointment with Jeff after the IRS had notified me that they had some questions about the structure of tax liabilities connected with my funeral home. Although taxes and other financial dealings often confused me, I trusted Jeff to do a good job at protecting my financial interests.

Calling up my file on his computer, Jeff printed out the relevant documents. Seeing the dismayed look on my face, he sought to put my mind at ease.

"Your doctor and I," he said, "we have similar callings. You know the old saying, 'death and taxes, you can't avoid either one.' Well, your doctor, he cheats death, or at least he tries to hold off death from coming too soon."

"And you?"

"And I, your tax accountant, I do my best to cheat the tax man," Jeff said. "In a legal way, you understand. But, using every legal option open to us, I work hard to hold off the tax man from taking you captive."

"Sort of like how the doctor uses every available means to keep death from taking me captive, right?"

"Exactly," Jeff said.

I admired Jeff's mix of philosophic flight of fancy with a very nuts and bolts approach to tax issues. Step by step, he began to look through some papers that he would file to reduce my business's tax liability.

Occasionally looking up, Jeff suggested several concerns that needed his attention.

"I've been thinking, you can take better advantage of passive loss rules by diversifying income streams and diluting gains subject to higher marginal rates," Jeff began.

"Oh."

"But we need to be careful, since the AMT has been designed to deter excess contributions stemming from a larger than expected liability for those with prodigious shelters," Jeff continued.

"What's that about my ATM?"

"No, not your ATM," Jeff said. "Your AMT. Alternative Minimum Tax."

"Oh."

"And we need to take a closer look at your phase-out strategy," Jeff added.

"I'm feeling rather phased out by all this tax talk," I said.

"It's okay," Jeff said. "Give me a few minutes and I'll get you all straightened out."

Looking up from time to time, Jeff rattled off a bucket of numbers. Each time, I merely nodded, and he returned to his paperwork.

In the breaks between the numbers, my mind wandered back to my ninth grade algebra class. Speaking in a clipped voice, Mr. Foster would draw two horizontal lines, one above the other, on the blackboard. Then he would write numbers and letters on both sides.

"The lines represent a river," Mr. Foster would begin. "If a three or a five, or any other number wants to cross to the other side, a bandit lurking in the middle of the river issues an ultimatum. 'Your sign or your life.'"

"In any equation," he would then explain, "numbers must surrender their sign in the middle of the river, and go from positive to negative or negative to positive."

I always liked crime stories, but my head ached just thinking about those equations. And taxes, pardon the pun, were numbers raised to a higher power. And so, I found myself mostly nodding as Jeff rattled off his numbers.

Twenty minutes later, the paperwork completed, Jeff handed me a stack of papers. "Place your John Hancock next to each checkmark," he said.

As I handed back the documents, Jeff sorted them into separate envelopes. His work completed, he pushed himself away from his desk, leaned back, and placed his intertwined fingers behind his head.

"The government so wants your money," Jeff said. "But it's our job to give the government as little of your money as possible."

"Will our filling out that paperwork help?" I said.

"It will help," Jeff said. "And let's keep in mind, when it comes to taxes, there's nothing true about the old saying, 'it is better to give than to receive.' As far as the government is concerned, they always operate on, 'it is better that we give and they receive.'"

"Money," I said. "It's always about the money."

"Money has gotten a bad rap," Jeff said. "Contrary to preaching in some circles, there's nothing evil about money. It's not money that's the root of all evil. It's the lack of money that's the root of evil."

I sort of liked Jeff's way of looking at things.

"One more thing," Jeff said. "Remember where those preacher guys say that you can't serve God and money?"

"Yeah," I said. "Everybody's heard that."

"They've got it all wrong," Jeff said.

"How-so, wrong?" I said.

"The preacher guys say that 'can't serve' saying because they want their people to just serve God," Jeff said. "But common sense will tell you to look at it just the opposite. I agree, you can't be religious and serve money at the same time. So drop the religion, which is fake, anyway. Just serve money."

"Just serve money?"

"Of course, just serve money," Jeff said. "If you're honest, that's what people do, anyway. So why not drop the pretense? Go for the gold."

"Interesting."

We parted on pleasant terms, and I was appreciative of his work on my behalf. His saving me money put a little extra in the kitty, and Antoinette and I were able to afford going out to eat at our favorite fish and chips place a bit more frequently.

A few months after our meeting, Jeff landed on the front page of our local newspaper. Landed more than once. Jeff and an alleged co-conspirator were charged with defrauding the government of a substantial sum of money. Thousands of dollars, as I recall.

"Tax fraud on massive scale alleged," declared one headline.

"Millions disappear in tax scheme," shouted another.

The trial went on for several weeks, and the articles spelled out the lurid details of his alleged financial shenanigans. My sympathies were with Jeff and his partner. I appreciated that reporters were always careful to include the word "alleged" alongside any descriptions of supposed wrongdoing. In keeping with my aversion to math, I skipped over the parts of newspaper accounts where specific numbers were referenced.

The jury deliberated just short of a week before rendering its verdict.

Not guilty on all charges.

The following day, I called Jeff to congratulate him.

"You can't serve two masters," Jeff said. "I think money won this one."

THIRTY: COFFIN

I had just returned to my funeral home from picking up some coffee and breakfast sandwiches when I got down to the morning's task. Mopping the floor. Yes, even the owners of funeral homes have to perform such mundane tasks.

I was at the far end of the room when I looked up and noticed that one of the coffins, a display model with its lid open so that families could examine the silky interior, was rocking slightly. I walked over to investigate.

Just when I had almost reached the coffin, a man, lying in the casket, sat straight upright.

I almost had a heart attack. Stuff like this is funny when it plays in the movies, but much less so in real life.

"Who are you?"

Just as I asked my question, Antoinette burst into the room. I wasn't expecting her, but she always made a grand entrance. It was one of the things I really liked about her.

"Jack," she said. "What are you doing here?"

"Who's Jack?" I said. "And what ARE you doing here."

"I'm Jack," the man in the coffin answered. "And I'm the ghoul from the great beyond."

"Get out of my coffin, you idiot," I said. Not wanting this Jack to knock over the coffin as he climbed out, I gave him my hand and helped him out.

"So who is Jack?" I said, looking first at Antoinette and then at this my unwanted guest. "And what's he doing here?"

"Oh, he's just a former friend of mine, somebody I used to know a long time ago," Antoinette said. "And Jack, what ARE you doing here?"

"Oh, I just wanted to see what you're up to these days," Jack said. "You know, long time no see."

"Not long enough," Antoinette said.

"So, what's going on around here?" I said. "Who is this Jack, and why has he made this sudden appearance?"

"Oh, he just came around here to piss me off," Antoinette said. "Come on, Jack, get out of here. Scram."

"Hey, babe, don't be cruel," Jack said. "Don't be cruel, to a heart that's true."

"Oh, a heart that's true, my rear end," Antoinette said.

"Yes, your rear end," Jack said. "And a fine rear end it is."

At this, Antoinette slapped Jack, full palm and clearly unexpected. Jack's glasses went flying. "Leave," she said. "Now."

Walking calmly across the room, Jack picked up his glasses, wiped the lenses with his shirt, and addressed me.

"Any idea who this lady is?" he said.

"She's my wife," I said. "Now do as she said, and beat it."

"But do you have any idea who she used to be?" Jack said.

My jaw clenched slightly.

"Any idea?"

"No, and I don't really want to know," I said. "Now be a gentleman, and leave. Leave, or I'll call the police."

"She used to be my girlfriend," Jack said.

"I gathered that."

"We used to have great sex," Jack said.

At this, I lunged toward Jack, and I would have pushed him over had not Antoinette restrained me.

"Please. Jack, leave, now," Antoinette said.

"Did she tell you about our great sex?" Jack said. "Morning, noon and night."

"Jack, please."

"No, it was great sex," Jack said. "Hey, babe, do you miss it at all?"

"No, Antoinette said, "Not at all. My hubby," she added, pointing to me, "Does it better. Way better. Nobody does it better."

I wasn't sure whether I was relieved or offended.

"Okay, enough, you're out of here," I said, grabbing Jack by the shoulder and leading him out. Two minutes later, he was out the door. I slammed the door shut and made sure it was locked.

"I'm so sorry," Antoinette said. "I had no idea he would show up."

I was still trying to process everything.

"He and I were long ago, a very long ago," she added.

"How long ago?"

"We dated for almost a year, but then broke up a half year before I met you," Antoinette said. "I haven't seen him since."

"So what happened?" I said. "If the sex was so great, how come you didn't marry him?"

"Well, he says the sex was so great, but it really wasn't so great," Antoinette said.

Another thing I really liked about Antoinette. She was the most terrific liar, especially when it mattered most.

"But how come you didn't marry him, even if the sex was only so-so?"

"Well, he didn't really want to marry me," Antoinette said.

"He didn't want to marry you? The sex was great and he didn't really want to marry you?"

"Yeah, that was the weird thing," Antoinette said. "The sex was great, but he was getting it for free. He didn't want to pay the "surcharge" of marriage, as he put it."

"What a skuzzball," I said.

"Yeah, what a skuzzball," Antoinette said. "He said he would never marry me. We had a huge fight, and that was that. Whatever we had was over."

"Oh, sorry," I said. "Well, no, I'm not sorry that it didn't work out."

"During our last fight," Antoinette added, "he gave me lots of excuses why he wouldn't marry me. He said I was too wacko, too out there. He said he wanted a quote unquote normal wife."

I just stood there, silent. When I reached for Antoinette's hand, she responded by tightening her grip on my hand.

"I knew you were different from the moment I laid eyes on you," Antoinette said. Her eyes brightened. "You like a wacked out wife, don't you."

"I do indeed."

"You won't ever let me go, will you?" Antoinette said.

"No indeed."

"Hey, babe," Antoinette said. She planted a big fat one right on my lips.

"But can I ask you a question?" I said.

"You don't even have to ask," Antoinette said. "I can't even remember what whatever was like with that loser. Me and you, now that's the real deal, the real cookie jar. You, Harry, are the love of my life. You are awesome. I'm so glad we're together."

"I'll be right back," I said. Walking to the front lobby, I placed our "Back in One Hour" sign on the announcements board next to the front door. Then I shut off the outside light.

I invited Antoinette into the spare room where we kept a couch for short naps. I locked the door. Then we put practice to our profession of mutual love.

THIRTY-ONE: TINY CAR

Mrs. O'Brian had the most unusual burial request.

"My husband would like to be buried in a Cooper, one of those miniature cars," she said as we sat down in my office. "I'm just letting you know in advance."

"We are happy to accommodate most requests, and we have a fine selection of burial encasements, caskets to match nearly all preferences," I said. "But burial in an automobile, however small, well, I'm not sure we can do that."

"But he's said that he really would like to go into eternity seated behind the wheel of his 2015 pale blue Cooper," Mrs. O'Brian said. "It's the love of his life. After me and the kids, of course."

"Of course," I said. "Would you be so kind as to invite him to come in so that we can come to some sort of satisfactory arrangement?"

"I'm sorry, he can't do that," she said.

"We can arrange a convenient time to make whatever plans need to be made," I said.

"I'm sorry, he told me to make the arrangements," she said. "He won't be making the arrangements."

"Because …"

"Because he's dead."

"Oh. Oh, I'm sorry. I'm so sorry for your loss."

"So, Mr. O'Toole, now that we've cleared that up," Mrs. O'Brian said. "Do you think you could accommodate us?"

"Let me think about it," I said.

"Good," she said. "I've parked said Cooper outside, just to help persuade you." Reaching into her purse, she pulled out a jangle of keys. "Enjoy," she said, turning around and striding out the door.

Like most people, I had heard of hot-shot Cadillac owners who announce to one and all that at their demise they want to go six feet under seated in their Caddies. Good publicity, and Facebook-worthy publicity stunts. But for most funeral homes, it's almost always a no can do. For starters, you'd have to dig a huge hole, a hole the size of a small swimming pool, to accommodate such a gargantuan vehicle.

The little people enshrined around the big guy would not be too happy.

For me, though, there is a more personal reason why Mrs. O'Brian's request made me very uncomfortable.

It was, of course, not I who would be buried in this tiny automobile. And I had buried many people in the even smaller space which coffins are. All rational thinking.

But when it came to tiny, enclosed spaces, which, in a weird way, this Cooper represented, I could not think rationally. I could not think rationally because, and here I must 'fess up, I have long had extreme claustrophobia.

I have always known this about myself. But twenty minutes after Mrs. O'Brian left my office, I went to investigate my longstanding phobia.

As I was walking to the Cooper, I suddenly recalled somebody who didn't seem to mind hiding in a confined space: Antoinette's former boyfriend. That thought made the challenge facing me even more ominous. And then, suddenly, the Cooper stood right in front of me.

Opening the door, I squeezed into the driver's seat. The windshield seemed to dare me to come any closer. The various dashboard dials stared at me like so many alien eyes. The steering wheel pushed against my stomach like a rough truant officer.

After what seemed like an eternity, but probably only five minutes or so, I wrestled my way out of the car. I slammed the door shut, and shuttered with relief.

There, standing just outside the car, was my Antoinette.

'So what's going on, Harry?" she said. "My knight in shining armor is a soldier to battle all giants, except if they're hiding in tiny cramped spaces."

In that moment, I thought back to how my perhaps irrational fear had been one of the things that had helped bring Antoinette and me into our close emotional bond.

During our courtship, Antoinette and I had discussed my utter claustrophobia during one of our early dating "tell me your deepest fears" conversations. I had described to Antoinette how I, as a young boy, had once accidentally locked myself in the family bathroom. Unlocking the door would have been simple enough for any rational adult. But as a panicked child, the door seemed irrevocably locked.

"Wow," was Antoinette's reaction as I related the incident. Then she added, with all the empathy that won my heart, "Harry, you're a wonderful man for sharing that with me."

With that encouragement, I shared a second trauma that had sealed claustrophobia as a permanent part of my make-up.

"When I was a teenager, oh, about thirteen or fourteen, my father took us all on a spelunking trip," I told Antoinette. "I was a little hesitant at first, what with the certainty of being confined in a small space underground, and remembering the time locked in the bathroom."

"Did you remind them about what happened when you were locked in the bathroom?" Antoinette said.

"No, I didn't," I said. "I was too embarrassed to tell them about something like that. It would just make me look like a fraidy-cat."

"Then what happened?" Antoinette sad.

"Well, everything was okay until just before we were going to climb the final incline to get out of the cave," I said. "That's when my father asked to 'borrow' my headlight. After I had handed it over, he 'accidentally' dropped it, and we were in darkness for about 45 minutes."

"The bathroom all over again," Antoinette said.

"The bathroom all over again," I said. "Only that time, ten times as terrifying. But unlike when I was a kid, I didn't scream. I didn't say anything. I didn't want them to know what was going on inside of me.'

"So they never knew?"

"They never knew," I said. "I never told them, even long afterward."

Because I had revealed that perhaps irrational fear to Antoinette, she indulged me in ways large and small. After we had gotten married, and were looking to purchase a house, we always rejected out of hand any house with an abnormally small bathroom.

But now, my thoughts returned to the present and I answered Antoinette.

"Mrs. O'Brian wants to bury her husband in one of these tiny mini Coopers," I said. "I know it's awful big for a coffin, but I just wanted to check how it would feel to sit inside one of these things forever."

"And ..."

"And," I said. "It didn't feel good."

Another thought. Funny how you remember these things, but I had thought a long time ago that hell might be marked by a very unpleasant feeling of falling down, down, down, forever. I remembered thinking that the falling would probably take place while you were locked up in a tiny, tiny space.

Then Antoinette spoke up again. "Harry, your claustrophobia has had one very excellent result."

"And what might that be?" I said.

"Guess," she said.

"I can't," I said.

"Here's a hint," she said. At that, she unbuttoned her shirt and pulled it open wide.

"Still not sure I get it," I said.

"Harry, since you are afraid of enclosed spaces, remember our wedding?" she said. "We pledged our forever love in the most open of spaces."

"I remember."

"In the most open of spaces, with nothing to create a closed space," she said. "No pants, no shirts, no socks or shoes between us and nature's wide open spaces."

"I remember," I said. "And when you look at it that way, you took my claustrophobia and transformed it into the most exciting moment of my life. Even if my freaky friends thought it was somewhat out of the ordinary."

"Out of the ordinary is good," she said.

When Mrs. O'Brian returned the following day, I did not have the heart to deny her request outright. Instead, I explained that the cemetery fees for such an extravagant burial were enormous. I quoted her a price. Including such fees would literally triple the price of her husband's funeral.

"Thank you very much for your time," Mrs. O'Brian said. "I think I'll try someplace else."

THIRTY-TWO: ALEX

Alex McConnell had dropped dead quite unexpectedly.

Alex, 55, had gone to a neighborhood rec center with some friends for a basketball pickup game. About forty-five minutes in, Alex suddenly collapsed at center court. His friends called an ambulance, but Alex was dead on arrival.

Alex died on a Monday and the viewing and funeral were held before the week was out.

His widow, Cathy, and their two sons, both in their late twenties, stood next to the coffin along with Alex's three brothers. Their faces reflected both grief and shock at the sheer suddenness of it all.

After I offered my condolences, they introduced everyone in the family. Cathy, like Alex, was a nurse, she in a nursing home and he in a cardiac step-down unit. Their two boys were starting out in marketing and business ventures.

Alex's three brothers introduced in quick succession. They lived in nearby states, and they had a variety of life paths. Greg, the oldest, was employed by the post office. Alex was next in line. Dan, the fourth sibling, was a tech wizard, working at a number of small start-ups. Paul, last but certainly not least, was a travel writer whose articles appeared in various nationally circulated magazines.

"Wait a second," I said. "You mentioned five siblings, but I count only four. Who's the fifth?"

"Unfortunately, that's our sister, Alice," Dan said. "She and Alex had a falling out more than a dozen years ago, and she has refused to have anything to do with Alex ever since."

"We urged her to reconcile with Alex or else their next encounter might be at a time like this, with one of them stretched out in a casket," Greg said. "But she wouldn't listen. She was quite animated about her refusal."

"And now this," Dan said. "Both Greg and I called her, left messages, emailed and texted her, but we didn't get any response."

"She's not a bad person," Greg said. "She helps out at her church and even helps them with charity food drives. But she's got this problem with Alex."

I had heard about such situations in which a family tie or friendship turned sour, leaving two people at odds for years or even decades. There was a talk show host who sponsored an up-and-coming comedian, only to have the comedian betray him, or so he thought. They both died without ever speaking to the other one ever again.

"So what happened with Alex and Alice?" I said.

"We're not exactly sure," Dan said. "When our father died, he hadn't left a will, so we held a meeting to divide up all the stuff that was in his house. The house itself wasn't up for grabs, because its ownership had been handed over to a nursing home in exchange for them taking care of our mother. But there was lots and lots of stuff in the house, everything from riding lawn mowers to boxes and boxes of tools to everything else."

"So when our father died, it was like a candy store," Paul said. "And when we set up a meeting to work out who got what, Alice came loaded for bear."

"Loaded for bear?" I said.

"Yes, loaded for bear," Paul said. "Alice had a detailed list of everything in the house. Our sister, usually the most charming of individuals, pulled out her notebook and put on her business face."

"I thought we were suddenly meeting with the mafia," Greg said.

"Tell him about the paintings," Paul said.

"Yeah, the paintings," Dan said. "It was the strangest thing. What really seemed to bother Alice was that her brother, Alex, had taken a dozen or so paintings from our father's house while our father was still alive."

"We couldn't understand it at all," Greg said. "The paintings weren't worth much, from either a commercial or even a sentimental point of view. They were just some old paintings that some uncle or other of our mother had painted as a hobby a long time ago."

"Strange, indeed," I said.

"I think what really bothered our sister was that our father had let her brother have paintings that she really wanted," Paul said. "Alice is very competitive, and she loved our father very much. But then the paintings unveiled a very unpleasant truth, at least from her perspective."

"What was that?" I said.

"As in most families, parents have favorites among their children," Paul said. They're not supposed to, of course, but of course they usually do. And Alice was our father's ... second favorite. Alex was his first."

"That didn't bother some of the runners-up in the 'favorites' competition," Paul continued. "But it really did bother, and still bothers, our sister. And what happened with the paintings perfectly illustrated that Alex won the competition for our father's affection. Our sister figured she lost."

"So why didn't Alex just give those paintings to his sister?" I said.

"Well, Alex was no angel either," Greg said. "He figured that his sister should just suck it up and get over it. Not much grace there."

"Oh."

"And then there was the dinner party," Greg said. "Christmastime, I had planned a party and invited all my siblings, including Alex and Alice. My wife cooked up a wonderful feast, complete with shepherd's pie ..."

"And lasagna," Dan said.

"And seven-layer salad, everyone's favorite," Paul said.

"As a courtesy, knowing our sister's attitude toward Alex, I gave her a friendly heads-up," Greg said. "I told her that everybody, including Alex, had said they would come. To my mind, I was just being thoughtful by letting Alice know that Alex would be there."

"And then?" I said.

"And then," Greg said, "she called back a few minutes later to tell me that she wasn't going to come after all. 'But we're all expecting you, and you said you were coming,' I told her. 'I'm not coming,' she said, and abruptly hung up."

"One more thing," Greg said. "Nobody talked about her during the party."

Thanking the family for sharing with me, I left them near the open casket and went to check on the hearse that would transport Alex's body to the cemetery. Each of the three remaining brothers got up in turn to recount some of their memories.

The first one talked about their brother's passion for skydiving in years past. "He had more physical courage than I could ever muster," Greg said.

Another spoke of Alex's work as a nurse. "There are more people healthy and alive today because of what Alex did for years and years, people too numerous to count," Paul said.

"He loved his family," Dan said. "His kids loved it when he would show them how to solve complicated math puzzles."

Alex's grieving widow walked slowly up to the front, helped by both her sons. She tried to speak but was simply not able to utter a word. After what seemed an eternity of silence, she whispered to one son, and they both escorted her back to her seat.

No mention was made of Alex's sister.

Toward the end of service, a thin woman dressed in a plain coat entered the back of the hall where the funeral was being held. She sat down, far away from any of the other guests, and stared forward, motionless. After about fifteen minutes, the woman left without speaking to anyone.

A few minutes later, after a full hour of eulogies, the guests got out of their seats to drive to the cemetery.

THIRTY-THREE:
STREET THEATER

"Ladies and gentlemen, welcome to our afternoon performance," the man on the open air stage began.

"My name is John Tunny, and our theatrical company is called New Look Theater. Today's show should take about 30 minutes. All we ask is that you shut off your cellphones for the duration so as to not disturb others in the audience. We'll get started in just a minute."

Antoinette and I wanted to take a break from the business, so we got one of our assistants to field any incoming calls while we went on a little road trip. I had seen an ad for an antique car show at a nearby county park. But when we arrived, an outdoor play was about to start, and that seemed much more interesting. So we planted ourselves on folding chairs set up for the show.

To the far left of the stage was a large armchair on a platform about two feet off the ground. As the play started, a man in a dress shirt, khaki pants and nice shoes walked over to the chair and sat down. From the opposite side of the stage, a line of actors and actresses walked onto the stage, forming a single file and facing the seated man.

"But I don't believe in hell," the man first in line said to the seated man.

"You're entitled to your opinion," the seated man said.

"Like I said, I don't believe in hell."

"But we're not subject to your opinion. Believe what you like. But now, on to business."

Someone escorted the standing man to the back of the stage and the man disappeared behind a curtain.

"Antoinette," I said, just loud enough that she could hear without disturbing those seated nearby. "I'm not really sure I like this play."

"Harry," she replied, "we just got here. Let's give it a few minutes. Let's see what happens next."

What happened next on stage was that a man about half way back in the line introduced himself to his neighbor, and to us, the audience.

"Harry," he said, offering his hand.

"Jesse."

"Hey, Jesse, what's going on?"

"I'm not sure, but I think we might be dead."

"Dead?"

"Yeah, maybe dead. Bummer if it's true."

"That really pisses me off," Harry said.

At this, Antoinette gave me an elbow shot to the ribs. "You, Harry, it's you," she said. "You're the star of the show!"

"I'm not sure I want to be the star of this show," I whispered back.

Meanwhile, the Harry on stage was going off on a rant.

"This is not how I wanted to die," Harry told his neighbor. "Protecting my family from some guy breaking into our house, that would have been okay. Dying as

Special Forces overseas, that would work. Even breathing my last after a months-long battle with cancer. Everybody's got to go sometime, so give me a good way to kick the bucket."

"So how did you die?" his neighbor said.

"In my sleep."

"In your sleep?"

"Yeah, in my sleep," the Harry on stage said. "I hit the pillow at about ten-thirty, a little later than usual. There was that Netflix feature I wanted to watch. I went to the doctor a week ago and he said everything was mostly fine. Sure, my doctor detected a tiny heart murmur, and he said I could stand to drop a few pounds. But for somebody in their mid-sixties, I was in pretty good shape."

"But now, here we are," Jesse said.

"Here we are."

Harry looked around.

As the Harry standing on the stage was looking around, I, the Harry in the audience, was squirming from side to side in my chair.

"Antoinette, this play is about death," I said. "Those guys standing in line are dead and waiting to go to hell. The guy in line is the chairman of the welcoming committee."

"Let's see what he says," Antoinette replied. "Maybe it's a fun party."

I felt my fear of death rising up, but decided to just play it cool, hoping that Antoinette would get tired of the play and we could get out of there.

No such luck.

"Hey, I think I know that guy," the Harry on stage said, walking back in line to someone about a dozen people farther back.

"Hey, Mike, what are you doing here?"

"Hello, Harry, beats me. What are YOU doing here?"

"I think we're dead."

"You may be right. Strange, isn't it?"

"Is your wife here?" Harry said.

"Not as far as I can tell," Mike said. "Till death do us part, that sort of thing. But she was a good woman, more than I deserved."

"Was she still going to church, and making you go?" Harry said. "I know you guys didn't always see eye to eye about that."

"Yeah, she always loved going to church, and I started going to church with her."

"You started going?" Harry said. "I thought you didn't believe in that stuff."

"I don't," Mike said. "But my wife does. She used to nag me about going with her to that church she goes to. I resisted at first. But then I figured, why not? A few hours being bored once a week is worth peace and quiet the rest of the week."

"Smart man," Harry said. "You always were the practical one."

"Even bought a Bible, a big one, from the church bookstore, just to make her happy."

"And a happy wife," Harry said.

"Is a happy husband," Mike said.

"Well, good to see you, Mike. I better get back in line."

The actors on stage were starting to really irritate me. "Antoinette," I said, rubbing her forearm.

"Shush, Harry, let's see what happens next."

Just then, the action on stage shifted to the front of the line, where a man was having a conversation with the man seated on the elevated arm chair.

"I don't deserve this," the standing man said. "Truth be told, I'm really a good person."

"Remember that girl in high school?" the seated man said. "You were a senior and she was a sophomore. What happened there?"

"We were in love. It was a special time."

"You stole something from her."

"Stole what?"

"Her virginity. Her innocence. It didn't belong to you, and you took it."

"But she agreed. We were in love. So in love that she wanted to try sex."

"What happened then?"

"We broke up a couple of months later. After high school, I'm not sure what happened to her."

"Your theft, your so-called love, so damaged her that she later on became a little hardened when it came to love," the seated man said. "So hardened that I had a difficult time persuading her that my love, a pure love, a costly sacrificial love, was for real."

"Huh?" the standing man said. "That was a long time ago. Let's look at what I've done recently. I supported my family, working my tail off so that they could have food on the table. I did great work at my job. I helped my kids with their homework. Well, some of the time. And our library had a charity food drive. I must have spent five weekends helping out with that. So, Mr. Seated Judge, I don't deserve any of this stuff that you are planning to give me."

"Are you trying to bribe me?" the seated man said.

"Huh?"

"Are you trying to bribe me?" he repeated. "You admitted all the bad things you did, but now you're trying to grease your way to an acquittal by handing me all the supposed good deeds you've done."

"What's so wrong about that?"

"Well," the seated man began. "Remember back on Earth, what if a man accused of rape and murder stood before a judge and made this appeal. 'Yes, judge, I did all these bad things, but it was long ago. Since then, I've led an upstanding life. I've fed my family, and have even helped out with charity food drives, that sort of thing. You've got to let me go.' What would the judge, a just judge, do?"

"I suppose he'd laugh at the man's feeble attempt at getting out of trouble," the standing man said. "Right before ordering him to the slammer."

At a word from the seated man, the standing man was escorted away.

"Antoinette, that's it," I said, loud enough that several people nearby turned toward me. "Let's get out of here."

"Yeah," Antoinette said. "Fun while it lasted, but too weird."

THIRTY-FOUR:
QUESTION AND ANSWER

Halfway into my monthly sandwich and coffee lunch with
Sal, my fellow undertaker, I took an emotional leap of
faith. I trusted a brother in the profession. I asked his take
on something that had long bothered me.

As usual, our meeting started out with a recap of the
monthly "scorecard." Whose establishment had racked up
the most funerals during the month just gone by?

"Seven," Sal said, placing a stack of newspaper obit
pages on the table. We kept score by drawing red magic
marker lines around each funeral our respective houses
had performed.

"Five," I said.

"That means you're treating today," Sal said. It also
meant that I had fallen even farther behind in our month-
by-month funerals tally.

Our waitress came by to take our orders. "Aren't you
the guys whose friend had the cocaine importation bust?"
she said. "As I mentioned, we do admire folks with such
attention grabbing entrepreneurial skills."

"As we do admire your remarkable memory," I said.

We ordered lunch. Reuben for me, Philly cheese steak for Sal. Waiting for our food, we chatted about sports. Sal was a Red Sox fan, and I was partial to the Phillies.

As I gathered up the newspapers used to keep score, I pointed out one obituary of special note.

"Did you see the obit about Derek Friedman?" I said. "He and I went to high school together. I didn't know him that well, but our high school reunion is coming up next year, and I was sort of looking forward to seeing him, along with a lot of other people from back then."

"He didn't quite make it," Sal said.

My throat tightened just a little when Sal said that, but I assumed Sal didn't notice.

As we began to chow down, we began to commiserate about the trials and tribulations of the funeral business.

"It's the odd hours that kills me," Sal said. "Esther and I can never take in a movie, because my phone will go off at the oddest hours. Sometimes I get my assistant to take the calls, but he always feels he has to contact me, even when I ask him not to."

"I don't mind the odd hours," I said. "It beats the boredom of a regular nine to five gig."

"And the people," Sal said. "You know I love people, always have. Helping people when they need it the most is one of the big reasons I went into this profession. But sometimes, sometimes, too much emotion. I know they can't help it, and I don't blame them. But sometimes I feel like I'm just about to burn out."

"Amen," I said. Not in any religious way, but just amen, you're right.

"Yo, brother, amen," Sal said.

At that, I felt so comfortable with Sal that I ventured to ask Sal about what was really on my mind.

"Sal, can I ask you a question?"

"Sure, Harry, what's on your mind?"

"I'm almost afraid to ask you, seeing that we're both funeral directors and all. But here's my question. Are you afraid of death?"

Sal put his hand to his chin and thought a moment.

"No, why?"

"I mean, we're surrounded by death all the time, much more than ordinary people. Our profession reminds us of that appointment each one of us has, whether we like it or not. So, no fear of death?''

"Hey, my friend, what brings this on?" Sal said. "Do you suddenly have a fatal illness you haven't told me about? Is Antoinette threatening to shoot you? Is the mafia coming after you?"

"No, nothing like that," I said.

"Then what's the matter?" Sal said. "To quote the Bard, we've all got to shuffle off this mortal coil. Death is not new information."

"It's just that Antoinette and I heard some proselytizing guys in the park the other day," I said. "It was quite by accident. They billed it as an outdoor theater production. You know how Antoinette and I like that sort of thing. But then they started preaching about religion. They said we're all going to hell."

"Hey, man, I'm sorry," Sal said. "But we're not all going to hell."

"How can you be so sure?" I said. "I've done some pretty rotten things, some rotten things those preacher guys reminded me of. I mean, they didn't point me out or anything like that. It just reminded me of some stuff."

"What did Antoinette think about those preacher guys?"

"She thought it was all nonsense," I said. "Entertaining for a while, but then, just weird."

"So don't worry about it, my friend," Sal said. "Those preacher guys can get carried away."

"They certainly can get carried away," I said.

"So what did the audience think?" Sal said.

"Not much," I said. "They didn't boo, but they didn't clap, either. We left before it ended."

"But to the point, Harry, you're not going to hell, whatever those whack-jobs say," Sal said. "You're a good guy, honest, upstanding. You've got a great wife. You love her. She loves you. You care about people. Nobody's going to waste any space in hell putting you up forever."

"Yeah, probably not," I said. "But that's not what really bothers me. What really gives me the heebie-jeebies is that death sometimes sneaks up on us, unannounced."

"Yes, it does," Sal said.

"Can I tell you a secret?"

"Sure."

Step by step, I described what had happened to me as a young boy when my grandfather died when he was about to take me fishing. Even now, in the busy lunchroom and with my friend listening attentively, the shock of discovering my grandfather suddenly dead welled up in me. I hoped Sal didn't notice my throat slightly tighten as I recounted the painful memory.

"My condolences on the loss of your grandfather," Sal said.

"That's what we're trained to say," I said. "Oh, I'm sorry I said that. I know you're my friend, and not just saying that."

"I really am sorry to hear about your grandfather," Sal said. "And I can see how that memory spooks you."

"It's just that, in our business, death is constantly pulling that sort of surprise on people," I said. "It's always just around the corner."

I decided to not mention the bus accident from high school. On top of my grandfather, that would have been way too much personal.

"Look at it this way," Sal said. "If death comes around unannounced, why worry about it? It's like somebody showing up at your house unannounced. You don't have to make dinner in advance. He just shows up, and that's it."

"And now, yet another visit," I said, "The reaper has knocked on Derek's door."

"Yes, even Derek. And, someday, even you and me."

"Hopefully, far off in the future."

"Let's hope so," Sal said. "Meanwhile, you wouldn't want to quit the business, would you?"

"No," I said. "We do a valuable service for people. Like you said, we meet people's greatest need at the time of that greatest need. It's what we were born to do."

"Yes we do."

At that, the conversation turned back to sports. And the strawberry shortcake was fabulous.

THIRTY-FIVE:
RIGHTING UP OBITS

"You totally screwed up my father's obituary."

I was catching up on some paperwork when a man stormed into my office, waving a newspaper in my face. His father's funeral was scheduled for the day after tomorrow and there were apparently some mistakes in the obituary marking the elderly gentleman's passing.

"Let me see," I said.

"Your obit writer included my father's ex-wife," Fred Jackson screamed in my face. "That woman is a family disgrace, and now you've embarrassed my mother in front of the whole world."

This is one of the things I really like about the funeral business. Somehow, funerals always bring out a family's dirty laundry. But of course I did not speak that heretical thought out loud.

"I'm sorry, sir," I said. "But we got that information from your brother, Andrew, who gave it to the guy whose job it is to write up obituaries."

"Maybe Andrew mentioned the evil woman in passing," the distraught man said. "But I'm sure Andrew told him not to include her."

"I'll check," I said.

"That wasn't the only problem," Mr. Jackson continued. "My father graduated from the University of Michigan, and the obituary says Michigan State University. How could your guy mess up something as simple as that?"

How indeed, I thought. I had hired Nick, a local high school sophomore, as a summer job to write obits. Nick told me that he aspired to be a newspaper reporter, and that writing up obits would be a great way to get a start in his chosen profession.

During the job interview, Nick had handed me a half-dozen articles he had written for his school newspaper. All were well written. But, as I discovered to my dismay, all of those stellar pieces had been heavily edited by the newspaper club's faculty advisor.

I made a mental note to have a serious talk with Nick. Two mistakes in one obit was not necessarily disqualifying, but certainly serious.

Suddenly, a second man burst into my office, also waving a newspaper.

"You, too?" Mr. Jackson said to the newest intruder.

"What is this?" said Mark Johnson, a younger man whose brother's service was planned for several days' hence.

"You idiots stated alcoholism as the cause of death," he shouted. "Why in the world would you do that?"

"We usually don't include the cause of death unless the family offers it," I said. "I believe your sister gave our obituary writer the information. What did she tell him?"

"My sister, that moron," Mr. Johnson said. "My sister hated her brother, so of course she mentioned it. But your obituary writer should have had the common sense not to put it in."

"I'll check," I said.

"And not only that," Mr. Johnson said. "The obituary says my brother got a job in Odessa, Ukraine, when it was really in Odessa, Texas, for heaven's sake. How could your guy make a stupid mistake like that?"

"I'll check," I said.

"And then, he misspelled the name of our other brother," Mr. Johnson continued. "It's Jon, J O N, not John, J O H N."

"Sorry about that," I said.

"And can your obituary writer count?" Mr. Johnson said. "It's nine grandchildren, not eight. Should I list them for you? Get out your fingers."

"I'll check on that, too," I said.

Suddenly, a third angry family member flew into the room. This was Sandra O'Rourke, whose grandfather was to be eulogized the following week.

"This is really beyond the pale," Ms. O'Rourke said. "How could your obituary writer turn my grandfather's best moment into something so shameful?"

"What do you mean?" I said.

"My grandfather's obituary says my father was a draft dodger during the Vietnam War," Ms. O'Rourke said.

This could be a problem, I thought.

"Does it say that he did that out of idealistic motives?" I suggested.

"You're all idiots round here," Ms. O'Rourke said. "My father WAS DRAFTED BY THE DODGERS, the baseball team. How is that so difficult to understand?"

"I'll check," I said.

"That's not all," Ms. O'Rourke continued. "Your guy even got the date of death wrong. He died on the eighth, not on the seventh."

"I'm not sure how our guy could make such a basic mistake," I said. "Exactly when a person dies is usually pretty clear."

"Well, maybe," Ms. O'Rourke said, her tone softening somewhat. "My grandfather died right around midnight, so there was in fact some disagreement about the actual date, Wednesday or Thursday. Different family members said different things. So I'll give you that."

"I appreciate it," I said.

"One other point, maybe a minor point," Ms. O'Rourke said. "My grandfather was always so proud about how he had met the family of Irving Berlin. You know, the famous composer. He met them during a Golden Oldies festival, and they told him a lot of great stories about the great musical genius himself. My grandfather was a huge fan of Mr. Berlin, and remembering that weekend was one of the best stories my grandfather would always tell."

"That's a wonderful memory," I said. "So what's wrong with that? I've got to think that our obituary writer included that."

"He did, but he messed it up," Ms. O'Rourke said. "He told the story in a few well-written paragraphs, but with one crucial mistake."

"A mistake?" I said.

"Yes, a mistake," Ms. O'Rourke said. "He called the composer Isaiah Berlin, not Irving Berlin."

"Isaiah Berlin?"

"Yes, Isaiah Berlin," Ms. O'Rourke said. "You know, the writer and cultural critic."

"Sorry about that." I searched my brain to figure out who this Isaiah Berlin was. I had heard about Irving

Berlin, of course, but I had no idea who this Isaiah guy could have been. I found out later that a lot of people apparently don't either.

"I'll check," I said.

"So what are you going to do about this?" Mr. Jackson said. "This is incompetence on a grand scale."

"Would you like me to redo the obituaries?" I said. "I'll have each of you check them before we send the email with the corrected obituary to the newspaper. No charge, of course. It's the least I can do."

"That would be satisfactory," Mr. Jackson said. "Everyone agreed?"

Everyone nodded.

Later that afternoon, I had the talk with Nick. At first, I wanted to just fire him, given all the embarrassment he had caused and the damage he had done to my funeral home's professional reputation.

What moved the marker for me was my memory of how I had screwed up so many times when I was his age. About the time I accidentally mowed the wrong neighbor's lawn. About the time I accidentally gave a customer change with a hundred dollar bill instead of a one dollar bill. That customer, I remembered, returned minutes later to hand back the larger bill.

Life is forgiving mistakes.

To ensure that the obit disaster would not repeat itself, I put in a new policy. Merely taking the information and writing it up would not be good enough. Instead, all written-up obits had to be emailed to a family member before a copy, corrected if need be, would be emailed to the newspaper for publication.

Nick was extremely grateful that I had not quashed his budding newspaper career before it even got started.

"Thank you so much, Mr. O'Toole," he said. "You've given me a new leash on life."

THIRTY-SIX: DOCTOR HEART

A few weeks after my "fear of death" chat with Sal, part of my private parts started bothering me again. It hadn't bothered me for a while, but here it was once more.

"On and off, on and off," I thought. Just to be on the safe side, I made an appointment with my family doctor. It had been a while.

"Always good to see you," Doctor Vincent said. Then he got philosophical on me.

"You know, the state requires everybody who drives a car to give that car a yearly check-up," the doctor said. "It's a good idea. Good maintenance, and cars last longer."

I could tell where this was going.

"But people," the doctor continued, "People aren't required to have that annual check-up. And so, a lot of folks don't bother to do a regularly scheduled check-up. They don't change the oil or replace the worn-out spark plugs. They ignore the body's 'check engine' light until sometimes it's too late."

"That's true."

"And so you've got to wonder if some people care a lot more about their cars than they do about their own bodies. I can't understand it."

"Maybe it's just that cars are less trouble than bodies," I suggested. "Your car's a wreck, you trade it in for a new one. Not so easy with your body."

"Ah, yes," the doctor said. "No junk yards for worn out bodies."

"So how's my 'Junker Jalopy' doing?" I said.

"Your scrotum seems okay," the doctor said. "No sign of abnormal swelling. Maybe you just strained something. But just to be sure, let's have you checked out by a specialist."

And so, a few days later, I found myself on the second floor nursing station at Baptist Community Medical Center.

I took the elevator to the second floor and stopped at the nurses' station to ask directions to the Oncology section. To my left was a corridor with doors open to patient rooms. To my right would be the room I was looking for. Just behind me was a woman who looked in her early fifties.

I was about to thank the nurse and move on when a "Doctor Heart, Two A" announcement sounded over the hospital loudspeaker. An instant later, a nurse waving her arms appeared outside the door of a room at the far end of the hall. Just as suddenly, three nurses filling out medical charts at the elongated counter inside the nurses' station slammed their metal folders shut and raced toward the end of the hall.

At that, the woman behind me began to run toward the end of the hall. Curious, I walked in that direction.

"Jerry, Jerry," the woman wailed.

One of the nurses caught up with the woman and physically restrained her. "I'm sorry, ma'am," the nurse said. "But you can't go in there."

"But my husband is in there," the woman said. "I've got to see him."

"I'm sorry ma'am, now is not the right time. I'm going to have to ask you to stay here."

At just this moment, a burly security guard reached the distraught woman and gently but firmly kept her from moving any closer to the room at the end of the hall. Also at that moment, four people dressed in green or white hospital gear and pushing an upright metal cart flew past the woman.

It took that crew mere seconds to reach the end of the hall. Suddenly slowing the cart, they turned into the patient's room.

Still restrained by the security guard, the woman was now in hysterics. "Jerry, Jerry, I'm coming, I'm coming," she said. "I'm trying to come, but they won't let me."

The next few minutes seemed to last an eternity. The clerks sitting inside the nurses' station put down their paperwork and waited patiently. "Visiting hours will continue until eight o'clock this evening," the loudspeaker announced in the same matter-of-fact tone with which it had announced the "Doctor Heart."

I checked my watch. I was now ten minutes late for my appointment, but I was not about to budge.

The restrained woman was no longer in hysterics, but rather just weeping profusely. "If only I had come earlier," she kept repeating.

Suddenly, a shout could be heard from the room at the end of the hall.

"Clear!"

And then silence.

And again. "Clear!"

After the second such shout, I tried to keep count of how many times that desperate cry came from the room.

Again, "Clear!"

I lost count, but noticed that the shouts were growing farther apart.

And then, a very long silence. The woman was also very silent, tears cascading down her cheeks.

As I and everyone else waited, my conversation with Sal came knocking on the door of my memory like an unwanted guest "If death comes around unannounced," Sal had said, "why worry about it? It's like somebody showing up at your house unannounced. You don't have to make dinner in advance. He just shows up, and that's it."

Yeah, I thought, try telling that to this poor woman.

A few minutes later, the four members of the emergency crew pushing the "crash cart," as I later learned the name, came out of the room. They were walking very slowly, their heads down. They did not speak a word.

The nurses from this floor remained inside the room.

As the crash cart crew reached the nurses' station, the security guard gently but firmly escorted the woman to the room at the end of the hall. I think he wanted to offer her some physical support, to keep her from stumbling if she were to run on the sometimes slippery floor.

Caught in a morbid curiosity and throwing good sense to the wind, I followed, quietly so as to not be noticed. As the woman entered, the door was left open. I peeked inside.

"Jerry, Jerry, I thought I lost you," the woman wailed. "I thought I lost you."

Her husband's eyes glistened.

A sheet had been pulled over the elongated body of Jerry's roommate. Part of the man's right foot protruded from under the sheet.

When I finally walked to my appointment, I was so late that they told me that they assumed I was a no-show.

"Just like an appointment with death," I thought. "Let's hope It's a no-show."

Ponying up the cancel fee, I simply made another appointment for the following week.

THIRTY-SEVEN:
ASHES TO ASHES

Harriet Smith died at a ripe old age, surrounded by friends and family. Her pastor, at bedside at her passing, closed her eyelids and pronounced a blessing.

"May Harriet Smith's soul rest in peace," he said. I expect that wish was granted.

Not so her body. Two days later, Mrs. Smith's two daughters, Evelyn Rodgers and Madelyn Turner, were in my office to finalize funeral arrangements. All was going smoothly until it came time to decide what to do with their mother's body.

Should a viewing be held, or should her body be cremated?

"How can you even think to have Mom burned up and reduced to ashes?" Mrs. Rodgers said. "That's the most disrespectful thing I've ever heard of."

"Do you really want everybody to stare at Mom's dead body?" Mrs. Turner replied. "Mom would be horrified."

"Did your mother express any preference before she passed away?" I said.

"Nothing set in concrete," Mrs. Turner said. "She made all sorts of funeral plans, what hymns to sing, who to invite, what the pastor should say. But on the matter of viewing versus cremation, she always went back and forth."

"But I think she always leaned toward having a viewing," Mrs. Rodgers said. "Come on, Maddie, Mom was even afraid of campfires whenever the family went camping."

"I don't think Mom is going to notice anything now," Mrs. Turner said. "She's occupied with bigger and better things."

"That's just the point," Mrs. Rodgers said. "Mom is going to a place where she won't get burned up."

"Ladies, ladies," I said, hoping to calm them down. But they paid me exactly zero attention.

"Look, Maddie," Mrs. Rodgers continued. "If we burn up Mom with your cremation, how is God supposed to find her?"

"You've got to be joking, Evie," Mrs. Turner said. "God doesn't need a viewing to figure out where Mom is hiding. God can do anything, even gather up scattered ashes to resurrect a dead body."

"It seems so disrespectful," Mrs. Rodgers said.

"No, it's not," Mrs. Turner said. "Ashes to ashes, dust to dust, even the Bible says that."

"Yes, but let God turn her into ashes," Mrs. Rodgers said. "It's not our place to do that."

I could see that the sisters were going to have a difficult time resolving their disagreement. Perhaps I could help.

"Ladies," I said. They ignored me.

"Mom was always very self-conscious about her looks," Mrs. Turner said. "She was especially concerned about how she looked these last couple years. Do you really want everybody to see her with all those wrinkles and old age spots?"

"What are you saying, Maddie?" Mrs. Rodgers said. "You know our Mom has always been beautiful, old age spots or no old age spots. Why shouldn't she show off that beauty one last time?"

They paused, ever so briefly, allowing me to get a word in.

"We can ensure you that your mother's beauty will be fully visible during the viewing," I said.

"Hear what the man said?" Mrs. Rodgers said. "Mom's full beauty, there for everyone to see and remember her by."

"Yes, maybe you're right," Mrs. Turner said. "But do we really want everyone's last memory of Mom to be seeing her dead?"

"Much better than constantly seeing Mom in some jar stored on somebody's fireplace mantle," Mrs. Rodgers said.

"But at least we'll have her ashes, somewhat close at hand and not hidden away six feet under in some cemetery far away," Mrs. Turner said.

"But even with cremation, the ashes are usually buried in a cemetery," Mrs. Rodgers said.

Turning to me, Mrs. Rodgers posed a question. "Aren't the ashes not exactly those of the person who passed way?"

Clearly she had been reading up on the issue in advance of this encounter with her sister.

"We try to be as careful as possible," I said. "But because the remains are incinerated in a common oven before being gathered up and put in an urn, there are always some ashes left over from the previous person and we also miss some of the current ashes."

"As I thought, terrible," Mrs. Rodgers said.

"I'm sorry for being so graphic," I said.

There was a pause in the conversation.

"Here's another problem with your viewing," Mrs. Turner said. "It might be fine for the first few minutes, but then the body starts to sag, parts of the face moving this way and that. After an hour, you can't even recognize the person. Isn't that right, Harry?"

"Well, not exactly," I said.

"Isn't that why viewings are so short?" Mrs. Turner said.

"We try to make them long enough to be convenient, but short enough not to strain the family," I said.

"And what about family that can't come to the viewing?" Mrs. Turner continued. "Uncle Milton, for example. He can't get off work on such short notice. How is that fair to him?"

"He can come if he wants to," Mrs. Rodgers said. "But just because he can't come, doesn't mean we shouldn't have a viewing for everybody who can come."

"Let me mention something that maybe you haven't thought about," I said. "Some people like a viewing because it gives them a last look at their loved one before the burial," I said. "In that way, the viewing is something like a transition, sometimes making things perhaps slightly easier."

Both sisters were silent.

"Cremation is also less expensive," I added.

"How can you even think about money at a time like this?" Mrs. Rodgers said, turning her head and aiming her impassioned words not at me, but at her sister.

"I didn't say that," Mrs. Turner said.

"But you thought it," her sister replied.

Again, silence.

Mrs. Turner broke the silence. "A viewing is, heaven help us, so public," she said. "Cremation at least respects Mom's privacy."

"But Mom would want to be with us at a time like this," Mrs. Rodgers said.

My mind wandered into irreverent thoughts. There was that Irish patriot, a heavy drinker, who died. Per tradition, the family held a wake. The funeral director, in that wonderful skill that we all possess, had transformed the body into that of a man twenty years younger.

"Sean looks much better," the apocryphal story goes, "since he stopped drinking."

And then there's the story of a city boss who died and was laid out in a viewing. His many friends and more numerous enemies came by to view the body. Said one longtime rival for power, "I just wanted to be sure."

Neither of those resolutions, I reflected, would have been possible with cremation.

But sometimes I recommend cremation, for this reason. Some illnesses or even dying in a brawl can so mar a face that it is almost impossible for us to make the deceased presentable for a viewing. Neither was the case with Mrs. Harriet Smith, however.

The sisters were whispering among themselves. I sat silent, awaiting their verdict.

"We've decided on a viewing," said Mrs. Rodgers.

"Followed by cremation," Mrs. Turner added.

THIRTY-EIGHT: ALICE

I was waiting in my office to meet a Mrs. Anderson for a one o'clock appointment.

In making the appointment, the woman had declined to give the reason for the meeting, but that reluctance was not unusual in itself. Because death regularly shocks everyone, it is not uncommon for some family representatives to simply ask for a meeting without stating its purpose, that of making funeral arrangements.

But now, one o'clock had come and gone, and the time was approaching thirty minutes past the hour.

"I'm so sorry I'm late," Mrs. Anderson said as I escorted her in and invited her to sit down. "Traffic was terrible."

After a pause, she added, "And I'm not really sure this meeting is a good idea."

"How can I help you?" I said.

"You buried my brother three weeks ago."

"Your brother?"

"My brother. Alex McConnell. I'm Alice Anderson."

My confusion was suddenly cleared up. This was THE sister.

"My condolences on his passing," I said.

"Thank you," she said. "Whatever."

"And how can I help you?" I said.

"I just wanted to clear up some of the lies my brothers must have told you about me," she said. "What did they tell you?"

"They said that you and he did not always get along," I said. "They also said that they felt bad that you were not able to attend the service we had for him."

"Did they tell you what a nasty person I am?"

"No, not really," I said. "They said you and your brother had some disagreements, but that you always intended to resolve them."

Oh, well, I thought. Sometimes, in the funeral business, you have to lie.

"I was planning to resolve our disagreements," Mrs. Anderson said. "But then, he died."

A pause.

"The jerk."

Another pause.

"What a jerk, to die without giving notice."

I thought she was joking. The look on her face said that she wasn't.

"So what did they tell you?" she said. "Some details, if you don't mind."

"That you didn't always agree with each other," I suggested.

"Cut the crap," she said, her diplomatic tone tossed aside. "What did they say? Don't BS me."

I figured, why not? She's asking, so let me be frank with her.

"They said you were pissed off because the distribution of things from your father's house showed that Alex, not you, was your father's favorite."

"BS, but okay, that's their line."

"They also said that your story that your brother was the only bad person in your falling out isn't exactly true," I said.

"Whatever. They're peddling the same old pile of BS."

"They also said that you pretend to be religious, but that you don't do basic religious things like forgiving people who have offended you."

"Oh, nonsense," she said. "More BS."

"And that the story that it is only you who has been horribly offended is just so much …"

Here, I paused.

"Is just so much nonsense."

"The whole father's favorite story is a complete hoax," Alice Anderson said. "Our father loved each of his children equally. How can these brothers besmirch our father's good name by telling such an obvious falsehood?"

"Favoritism is often a family problem, but if you say so," I said.

Mrs. Anderson's attack opened up on another front.

"Did they tell you what a nasty person Alex could be?" she said.

"They did say that Alex was no angel," I said.

"Whenever I came to visit," she said, "he would always ask, with a mocking sincerity, how my job was going," she said. "But he would only ask that when he knew that I didn't have a job. Never when I actually had a job."

"Okay."

"Our mother passed away a long time ago, but something she told me when I was just a teenager stuck with me," Mrs. Anderson continued. "She said, 'Avoid nasty people.' Alex was nasty people."

"Why are you telling me this?" I said.

"I want to set the record straight," she said.

"I'm not a counselor."

"You seem fair-minded."

"Your brothers also mentioned that you go to church," I said. "Doesn't your church teach you to forgive people, to make amends?"

"He never did that," Mrs. Anderson said. "Did they tell you that he went to church like clockwork?"

"They did not mention that," I said. "But they did say that he had made steps to be family. They said he invited you to come to his house for several family get-togethers, but that you always refused."

"Refused, because he just wanted to gloat," she said. "To show off all the things our father had given him."

"How do you know that's why he did that inviting?"

"I just know him," she said.

"How do you just know him?" I said. "I mean, maybe those were real steps."

"I just do," she said. "Those steps were just pretend steps."

At this point, I was just weary of the conversation. But I thought I would try one last tack.

"Mrs. Anderson, can I ask you a question?"

"Go ahead."

"Do you pay your taxes on time?" I said. "Do you make sure that everything is filed by April 15?"

"Of course."

"Do you pay your electric bills on time?"

"It's automatically deducted, but I get your drift," she said. "I pay my bills on time."

"So obviously," I said. "It would have been smart to reconcile with Alex on time. Why in the world didn't you do that?"

"As I tried to explain to you, I was going to," she said. "But, as you well know, he didn't cooperate."

Yes, I thought, he died when you thought he wasn't supposed to.

With that, Mrs. Alice Anderson stood up and pulled a bouquet of flowers and a box of expensive-looking chocolates out of her purse.

"For you and your family," she said. "For the funeral home. Not for Alex or his family."

A sadness gripped me as she walked out the door.

THIRTY-NINE: BORED

Antoinette burst into my office and showed me a new dress. Always drop dead gorgeous, she looked even more stunning, if that were possible, in her new apparel.

"How do you like it?"

"Sweetheart, you look terrific," I said. "So where did you get it?"

"Lord & Taylor."

"Lord & Taylor, excellent," I said. "Very nice. So how much was it?"

"Nothing."

"Nothing?"

"Nothing. I got a five-finger discount."

"A five-finger discount?"

"A five-finger discount, but maybe it only took four fingers plus a little creative thinking to outsmart store security," she said. "I shoplifted it."

"You stole it?" I said. "What did you do that for? We're not exactly strapped for cash."

"Excitement," Antoinette said. At this, she did a two-step dance and took a bow. "I wanted to drive away the boredom blues."

"What about your bounty hunting?" I said. "That's always exciting."

"Haven't had much business lately," Antoinette said.

"Yeah, I know," I said. "Work on my end has been a little hectic recently, and maybe we haven't had some good quality time together."

"It's not that, Harry," Antoinette said. "It's not your fault. It's just that burying bodies was pretty exciting at first. But now, it's become rather routine, if you can call death every other day routine."

I hoped a little humor might cheer up Antoinette.

"We're like farmers," I said. "We've got to keep planting if we want to eat."

Alas, it did not.

"I'm bored," Antoinette said. 'Not with you. With life."

"Would a road trip help?" I said. "Maybe we could drive someplace we haven't been before. See some new sights."

"Okay."

No viewings or funerals were scheduled for the rest of that day or the next, and I called one family to postpone a meeting to work out funeral arrangements. Antoinette and I packed up the SUV and set out for a two-day adventure. We had no specific destination mapped out.

At about two that afternoon, we were barreling along a country road that was unfamiliar to both of us. To the left and the right of the two-lane winding road were empty fields, fields planted with corn and tobacco. Occasional gatherings of cows and horses mostly stood around eating.

Suddenly, Antoinette cried out. "Harry, let's stop."

"Stop? Whatever for? This is the middle of nowhere."

"Harry, it's perfect."

I pulled over, parked mostly on a narrow shoulder, and we both got out. Antoinette took me by the hand and walked me about two hundred feet from the road. Then she faced me and began kissing me, passionately.

"Antoinette."

"Harry, it's perfect." Continuing to kiss me, she began removing her clothing, tee-shirt, jeans, and her undergarments.

"Antoinette, outside? What if somebody comes by?"

"Nobody's going to come by, unless it's some horse or cow," she said. "Harry, time to live a little. Time to throw boredom to the wind."

"There is a peasant wind," I said.

An hour later, we were still lying there, naked as two jaybirds. Antoinette was sleeping, drawing in gentle breaths. That's when the two state police troopers came by.

"Excuse me, sir, madam, we're going to have to ask you to cover up," one trooper said.

I covered up Antoinette and then awakened her. "We have visitors," I told her. Antoinette broke into a wide smile. "Hi there, gentlemen," she said.

The troopers explained that several drivers along this road had called 911 complaining that there was an abandoned vehicle blocking part of the roadway. Other callers said that they thought they had seen at least one naked person a few hundred feet from the parked vehicle.

"We're going to have to issue you a citation for public nudity," one officer said. "Can we see some identification?"

"Make sure you spell our names right," Antoinette said, again smiling. Then, turning to me, she whispered, "Harry, we're going to post this citation in a prominent place in our living room!"

"See, I told you our road trip would cure your boredom," I said.

But two days later, Antoinette had again fallen into a bit of ennui. "Harry, I'm sorry, I'm still bored," she said. "You've got to help me. Think of something."

That's when I suggested a whitewater rafting trip. Oregon. The Columbia River. Not a river for beginners, but for those who are ready for a full-on challenge.

"But I can't swim," Antoinette reminded me.

"All the better," I said. "Sheer terror is a sure cure for boredom." Never one to shy away from a challenge, Antoinette agreed.

Working out the details of the trip took a little doing, and it was just over a month before we boarded our flight to Portland, Oregon, followed by a bus trip to the whitewater launch site some distance upriver. As we got into the raft, Antoinette held my hand and stepped carefully.

"Tighten your lifejackets and make sure that they are secure," the instructor told the dozen or so people in the 20-foot raft.

"Harry, I'm nervous," Antoinette said.

"But not bored, I trust," I said.

"Not bored."

Dashing downstream over a disorganized assortment of riverbed rocks, the raft moved up and down, to the left and to the right, like trees in a windstorm. Everyone's screams were drowned out by the sound of the rushing waters.

Then came a moment's pause as the raft glided onto a pool of still water between two stairwells of gurgling water. Everyone took a deep breath and relaxed. The next set of rapids was a minute or two away.

Suddenly, the left side of the raft, the side Antoinette was sitting on, was thrust upward as it struck a rock underneath the calm surface of the water. The raft's sudden upward motion tossed Antoinette overboard.

I immediately stood up and followed her into the water. Her head was bobbing up and down, making her alternately visible and invisible. She screamed something, but I couldn't understand anything she was saying. I didn't need to. She couldn't swim.

It is folk wisdom that "it seemed an eternity" before someone is rescued out of such a perilous situation, but I didn't find my experience anything like that. No, as I grabbed Antoinette and held her head above water and paddled furiously toward the ever moving shoreline, it was more like a scene from Raiders of the Lost Ark playing out at hyper-speed.

How long did the rescue take? Twenty minutes? Ten minutes?

"Are you all right, babe?" I said. "We almost lost you there."

Antoinette coughed several times and spat out some leafy material. Then she broke out into a terrific smile.

"All right?" Antoinette said. "I'm awesome! And you, Harry, the love of my life, are super-awesome." Then she planted a kiss, smack-dab on my lips. When she was finished, I wiped away some of the vegetation that her kiss had left on my cheeks.

Looking downriver, we saw the raft pulled up against some rocks along the shore.

"Are you ready to try again?" I said.

"Let's go," she said.

On the flight home, we got philosophical. "We almost lost you back there," I said.

"Oh not really," Antoinette said. "You don't go until it's time to go. And as long as I'm with you, Harry, it's clearly not my time to go."

"Did we solve our boredom problem?" I said.

"Yes, we solved our boredom problem."

But two weeks later, as we finished up a discussion of the day's events, Antoinette sighed.

"Harry," she said. "I'm bored. The river trip was great, and you did a wonderful rescue, and who can forget our afternoon escapade on the side of the road. But something's missing. I'm still feeling kind of bored."

FORTY: ENNUI

Maybe it was contagious.

A few weeks after we went to great lengths to solve Antoinette's boredom affliction, I caught the same disease.

Our trip to the Pacific Northwest was certainly exciting. Antoinette's narrow escape when our whitewater raft tossed her into the raging rapids momentarily piqued her adrenalin and ramped up her passion for life. But as Antoinette expressed it some weeks later, the boredom she had felt before the trip -- indeed, one of the reasons we had taken the trip – had returned.

And now, a month later, on a Monday morning on a very ordinary summer day, I, too, was feeling very bored.

"What's the point of it all?" I muttered to nobody in particular as I drove to our funeral home.

As soon as I heard myself utter those words out loud, I instantly felt rather foolish. After all, how could I complain? I had a wonderful wife. We loved each other passionately. I had friends, Sal and Reggie among them. I had a job, a respectable job, and finances were not particularly tight.

Still, as I sunk into thought during the drive to my business, I felt a little discombobulated.

Yes, the funeral business was doing well. We had a steady supply of families. People died with amazing regularity, and we were the beneficiaries. Money was flowing in.

But the problem, on that start of yet another work week, was exactly that. The funeral business, and my life in general, were very steady. Too steady. Sure, there were occasional adventures. Families fighting. Oddball viewing requests. But overall, nothing much out of the ordinary. And, in that moment, as I pondered my future, a horrifying thought occurred to me. This is how every morning was going to play out over the next several decades.

"Just a tad depressing," I muttered.

Also seemingly pointless was a recent letter I had received from yet another government office. As you might imagine, the funeral business is very much regulated, with regular reports going first to this and then to that bureaucracy. I usually keep those matters under careful watch, responding promptly to each and every directive.

But will the requests, the demands for compliance verification, ever end? No, they will never cease. But surely, life is more than completing the government's endless requests for more documents.

My mind wandered to the personal. I wondered if Antoinette and I would ever have any kids. If we ever had a son, would he be the ungrateful jerk that I was toward my father. Fair is fair, he probably would be.

Now there's a happy thought.

Why is my mind even going there? Perhaps it was my earlier glance at the morning's newspaper. There, on the front page of the local section, was the outcome of a long-running story.

More than a year ago, a guy had carjacked a woman, and then murdered her and her two pre-school children, who were seated in the back. And now, yesterday, the guy had gotten off scot-free.

It seems that the cops, incompetent as usual, had fabricated some evidence to help the case along. It turned out to be not too difficult for the defense team to point out the police wrongdoing. The result? The judge tossed what seemed an open-and-shut case.

"My client has been vindicated," the man's brazen defense attorney had announced to the assembled reporters.

"Outrageous," I said upon reading the story. "Simply outrageous."

Yes, reading that story did not help my mood.

Perhaps surprisingly, the day at the funeral home went well. I presided over the viewing of a gentleman who had died at the ripe old age of 83. Mr. McCormack was eulogized by all five of his children, who came from the four corners of the nation to pay him tribute.

"We're so grateful to you for all you've done for our family," the oldest son told me as we prepared to head off to the cemetery.

After the gravesite ceremony, I drove back to my office and finished up some paperwork before heading home. In the car, the morning's blues again tapped on my shoulder.

Something that was said during the eulogy sparked a memory. Or, more accurately, something that was said caused me to strain to remember something I had learned in a college American history class.

It seemed that the deceased had taken his family to visit a museum commemorating someone once famous and hailing from the Chicago area. Driving home, I couldn't remember the name. But I did remember that I had heard the name when my long-ago professor had mentioned it during one of his lectures. The man, I remembered my professor telling us, was involved in a controversy that had dominated the newspapers for weeks on end.

I scratched my head, trying to remember what the controversy was all about. I rubbed my thumb and forefinger together, trying to summon the memory. But no such luck.

Oh well. Life goes on, and we do our best. After I got home, Antoinette and I went out to eat with Antoinette's friend, Andrea, and her husband, Joe. The restaurant was the Mandarin House, an all-you-can-eat Chinese buffet.

In between mountains of fried shrimp and sushi, Joe recounted how he met his wife. Students at neighboring colleges in the Pittsburgh area, they met while standing in line to pay a traffic ticket. They struck up a conversation, and went for lunch afterward.

"Shakespeare doesn't know what he's talking about," Joe said. "The course of love can run true."

"Always," his wife said. "Well, mostly always."

"With us," Antoinette said, squeezing my hand underneath the table, "Like you two, with us, always. Yes, mostly always."

With that, the four of us again pushed our chairs back and headed over to the dessert bar.

Pittsburgh, I thought, in what years did they win the Super Bowl? I could not remember. Fame, I thought, how fleeting.

But what a dessert bar. Wonder of wonders. Cookies, from chocolate chip to raisin. Cheesecake. Strawberry shortcake. Chocolate cake. Cut up melons. Strawberries. Apple pie.

Back to the table, again great conversation. College era war stories. Local politics. Career plans. Hopes for children.

At around eleven o'clock, the waitress gently informed us that the place was closing for the evening. In the parking lot, we said our goodbyes.

On the ride home, I thanked Antoinette for a wonderful evening. And truly, it was a wonderful evening. I slept soundly.

But Tuesday morning, I drove once again to the O'Toole Funeral Home, in business since time immemorial. In my car, I did some rough math. At 365 days per year, and roughly forty years to go, I would be doing this drive some fourteen thousand and six hundred times.

Not counting leap years.

A slight sadness settled over me as I pulled into the funeral home parking lot.

FORTY-ONE: AUTOPSY

"How'd you like to look at a dead body?"

"That's my business, looking at dead bodies."

Reggie, my newspaper reporter friend, was on the phone. He was even more excited than usual.

"I mean," he continued, "seeing somebody cut up a dead body. An autopsy, man, watching somebody do an autopsy?"

For all my time in the funeral business, I had never seen an autopsy performed. Death was unpleasant enough taken whole. But watching a dead body being cut up would be like going from just looking at an unsavory meal to actually eating it.

Reggie had arranged to observe an autopsy and write up the experience as a feature story to appear in his newspaper. An ace at the crime beat, Reggie had experienced death in all its forms: murder, car accidents, house fires, you name it. But an autopsy? This was a new one, and Reggie was stoked.

Me, not so much. But Reggie was a good friend, and he had gone to great lengths to secure a ringside seat for both himself and for me. So I could hardly refuse.

When I walked into the exam room, Reggie was already there, standing next to the medical examiner, who was about to make the first incision. The room was a little chilly, and I rubbed both my arms to fend off the cold.

Reggie handed me a white apron, and I tied it in back. It was like tying your shoelaces, only backwards.

The medical examiner pulled back the white sheet covering up the corpse, revealing the naked body of a middle aged woman.

I had seen naked corpses before, of course. What always surprised me was how asexual dead bodies are. Same features, slightly protruding breasts, exposed pubic hair and puffy lips that a naked living woman might display. But about as arousing as meat in a supermarket cooler.

"We suspect she died of extensive Stage Four cancer," Doctor Palumbo began. "A CAT scan revealed much of the damage, but the family asked for an autopsy to fully ascertain the extent of the disease."

Reggie shuffled his gaze back and forth between the body and his notebook as he took extensive notes. In the age of everything smartphone, it warmed my old-fashioned heart to observe a true scribe at work.

When the medical examiner cautiously cut into the deceased's left breast, his scalpel punctured a pool of blood. A rivulet of blood burst forth, landing a splotch of red on the doctor's nearby apron. "One of the hazards of the trade, and why we always wear an apron," he said calmly.

Slicing through the deceased woman's breast was one thing, quiet and mostly orderly as it was. Except for the sudden squirt, of course. Exploring the inner recesses of the woman's brain was quite another matter.

What struck me was just how jarring that step was. There's nothing delicate about it. Lifting the head from the metal table, Doctor Palumbo sawed a full circle around the top of the head, just above the eyes. Then, laying aside his saw, he grabbed the top of the head with two hands and gently separated it from the rest of the head.

The exposed brain looked like a convoluted glob of foam rubber. Reggie whistled when he saw it. I leaned in close to get a better look.

The entire procedure required less than an hour. The physician replaced the severed top of the head, removed his gloves and tossed his blood splattered apron into a nearby dirty linen hamper. Reggie stuffed his pen and dog-eared notebook into his back pocket.

"How about lunch?" Reggie suggested as we walked out of the room.

"Just so long as it's vegetarian," I replied.

I cheated somewhat because my Caesar's salad was chicken side-by-side with tomatoes and lettuce. As for Reggie, he ordered pizza, his perennial favorite. But I did notice that he passed up his usual meat lover's slices and opted for cheese and mushroom.

"So what'd you think?" I said.

"Terrific, simply terrific," Reggie said. "Very informative. And the doc's slice into the left breast causing a stream of blood to gush out and splatter onto his lily-white apron, who could ask for more?"

"Pretty dramatic, I've got to admit," I said. "But sawing open the skull was nothing to sneeze at, either."

"The blood splattering, that's my lede," Reggie said. "It's stuff like that that gets the reader hooked and wanting to read the rest of the article."

"Better than the skull being sawed open?" I said. "For my money, sawed-open head beats blood splattered on white-aproned doctor every time."

"Yeah, you're right, more dramatic," Reggie said. "But we don't want to scare off granny from reading the article before we get started."

"Maybe you're right," I said. "The parting of the skull was kinda creepy. Not so pleasant breakfast reading material."

"And we always want to give our readers some excellent breakfast reading material," Reggie said.

Then conversation was going so well that I ventured to ask Reggie the kind of question had put to Sal. "Reggie, my old friend and buddy, you and I encounter death like other people come up against homeless people. They're everywhere. You meet death in murder and accidents, I make death's acquaintance with every corpse I bury. So, my question, does death ever bother you?"

"No, not really."

"Really? This death thing never bothers you?"

"No, really, this death thing, as you call it, it really never bothers me."

"Can I ask why?"

"Hey, Harry, you're freaking me out. But no, it never really bothers me."

"Because ..."

"Because it's all part of life," Reggie said. "You're born, and you die. You've seen it yourself, so you should know more than anybody. You get a dead body, and after a bit of gussying up and some family tears, where does it go?"

"Into the ground," I said.

"Exactly. So why worry about it?"

"But what if there's something past that?" I said. "What if there's something after we go into the ground?"

"I guess we'll find out when that happens," Reggie said. "It's just not worth worrying about before we get there."

"I guess not." But in my own mind, I wasn't quite sure. It sure seemed like a waste of a still pretty good body to let it just rot in the dirt someplace. Nature seemed pretty efficient most places. The most obvious example. Isn't it worth noticing that we need to sleep eight hours a day, and that it happens to be dark half the day?

"Reggie …"

"Yes, my friend?"

"Reggie, really, nothing after we die?"

"Hey, Harry, not nothing, that is, just not something we can be sure of," Reggie added. "It's just that we don't know, we can't know, so it's not worth worrying about."

"Okay."

Reggie's autopsy story was published ten days later, leading the Sunday paper's feature section. As Reggie had told me, he led with the blood splattered on the apron. The editors had placed a remarkable headline over the story: "With Help from a Skillful Medical Examiner, Dead Men (and Women) Do Tell Tales."

I read though the story, as always impressed by Reggie's uncanny ability to weave a compelling tale. Reggie called me up a few days later and asked me how I liked his story.

"It was excellent, simply excellent," I said.

"Did you notice anything unusual?" he said.

"Nothing unusual except that it was very well written," I said. "But with you, that's never unusual."

"Did you notice the woman's name?"

"Come to think of it, I did not," I said. "What was her name?"

"No name," Reggie said. "She had no name. We just called her, 'the woman.'"

"Interesting," I said. "I know you would want to protect the woman's identity in an article like this. But don't you guys usually give the person a made-up name, followed by 'not her real name'?"

"That's exactly what we did," Reggie said. "But then my editor got nervous. 'Maybe there's somebody out there with that made-up name, and their family would get very upset with us, even though we put in, not her real name.' So he just changed everything to 'the woman.'"

"So what was the problem?" I said.

"Fortunately, my editor always does a final check of the Sunday paper by quickly going through the feature section as it comes off the press on Friday afternoon. That's when he caught the mistake."

"What mistake?"

"As he was editing the story, my editor had changed the made-up name to 'the woman' each time it appeared," Reggie said. "Unfortunately, he missed one 'Mrs. Everett' late in the story. The made-up name was still there, but without the 'not her real name.'"

"Not good," I said. "So what did the editor do when he saw the mistake in the print run?"

"Well, in my many years in the journalism profession, it was a once-in-a-lifetime experience. The editor ran up to the pressmen and he yelled ..."

"Let me guess ..."

"He yelled, 'Stop the Press!' And yes, we threw away about ten thousand copies of the press run. Then he fixed the mistake, reshot the page, and once again cranked up the press run."

FORTY-TWO:
RUSSIANS LONG FOR CHURCH

Mr. Igor Ivanov, 89, seemed the most unlikely candidate for a church service to mark his passing.

Like many of his generation, Mr. Ivanov, born in Moscow, was an atheist by habit if not conviction. Vodka was his close friend, his family told me. He attended Russian Orthodox services roughly twice a year. He came once every Christmas, in January, as was the Orthodox custom. He usually made a second annual appearance on the Easter holiday.

Mr. Ivanov had come to this country in his late-50s. Once here, he made no effort to learn English, and had lived out his life in a Russian colony in New Jersey. His work history was spotty at best, and he often fought with his neighbors.

Which is why I was surprised that the family declined a simple graveside service and insisted on full ceremonies at Saint Vladimir's Church, located in the greater New York area.

"Church is what Russians do at a time like this," his son, Sasha, said.

I had never been inside an Orthodox church, and my only previous exposure to that tradition was a slide show during a European history class at college. But as I stepped inside, it felt like I had suddenly been transported back several centuries in time.

Inside the church, huge portraits, done up in that abstract medieval style, showed saints holding up pinched fingers and staring straight ahead. Scattered around the sanctuary were waist-high stands topped with pictures of additional saints enclosed in glass. Perched on other stands were forests of flickering candles.

Unlike in other churches, the choir was not front and center, but above and behind. The choir members sang in a language that I was told was something akin to old-fashioned Russian.

But all that was not what I found most strange. Rather, it was the constant bowing and crossing themselves that everybody did, everywhere and all the time. Just before walking into the church, people bowed toward the building and crossed themselves. They repeated this gesture in front of the wall portraits and again in front of the stands holding up pictures of various saints. And as they walked out of the church, the churchgoers turned around to face the church and again bowed and crossed themselves.

Also unusual was just how long the service lasted.

An hour into Mr. Ivanov's funeral service, I tapped on his son's shoulder and told him that I needed to step outside for a smoke break. My appeal to smoker's mercy was a lie, a sin no doubt made more egregious for having been committed inside a church. My only exposure to cigarettes was one time in high school, and on a dare, to my great displeasure. But as the service promised (or threatened) to continue for an hour or two more, I was sorely in need of an intermission.

Walking outside, I remembered my high school English teacher. Don't do run-on sentences, Mr. Samuel told us repeatedly. Religious services, I thought, should follow the rules of good English sentence construction. They should not run on and on and on and on and on and on.

I was seated on a concrete bench outside the front of the church when a priest approached me.

"We are grateful to you for doing the funeral for Mr. Ivanov," the priest said.

"I am honored to do so," I replied, moving to the side of the bench and inviting the priest to join me.

Father Sergei was a pudgy man in his thirties, with jet-black hair and a beard that dropped down to nearly his navel. The beard, together with his imposing eyebrows, accented his pale complexion. His outer garment, also jet-black, stretched down to his ankles.

Following the customary Russian greeting, Father Sergei attempted to kiss me on the cheek, but I politely waved off that gesture.

"Igor was a good man," Father Sergei began. "He was a faithful son of the church."

I wasn't quite sure what to make of his statement. I certainly did not want to disrespect the deceased, but his family had told me of their father's secular lifestyle and spotty church attendance. I decided to play it safe.

"So how did Mr. Ivanov like going to church?" I said. "It's a beautiful church."

"He came on the days it was important to come," Father Sergei said. "He celebrated the birth of Christ on Christmas, and the resurrection of Christ on Easter."

"That he did," I said, hoping my skepticism would not show in the tone of my voice.

"Mr. Ivanov always enjoyed breaking the shells and eating those Easter eggs blessed by the patriarch," Father Sergei said. "His family told me how he always took a special pleasure in that."

I noticed a slight emanation of alcohol on the father's breath. "So how long have you known Mr. Ivanov's family? I said.

"They've been part of the parish for decades," Father Sergei said. "I christened every one of their children."

"What's that ceremony like?" I said.

"Their godfather brings the child, and I personally sprinkle them," Father Sergei said. "Then we have a wonderful Russian feast afterward, with piroshky, kvass, a table set with traditional Russian food. We have a similar table set for today."

"It's a shame Mr. Ivanov won't be joining us today," I said.

"He's in a far better place," Father Sergei said. "I don't think he's disappointed that he's not joining us today. He's missing his family, of course, but I think he's in better company."

"But he wasn't too sure about his belief in God, according to his family," I said. "Do you think he's persuaded now?"

"Oh, he knows now," Father Sergei said. "As a Russian, he's always been a faithful son of the church, and God welcomes faithful sons of the church."

"Doesn't it matter that he said he was an atheist?" I said.

"Oh, many Russians say that," Father Sergei said. "Even Stalin said that. But when they die, they always return to the church. Russians are always sons and daughters of the church."

No fear of death here, I thought. Your life doesn't matter.

Some minutes later, a deacon came out of the church and told Father Sergei that it was time to move the coffin from the church and into a hearse I had provided for the drive to the graveside.

I looked at my watch. More than two and a half hours had elapsed since the service began.

Six pall bearers, each man dressed in a formal black suit and white shirt, carried the coffin. I swung open the back door of the hearse and the men slid in the coffin.

The coffin secured, I sat behind the wheel, inserted the key and turned it to start the engine. No response. I removed the key and repeated the steps to start the engine. Again, no response.

It was then that I noticed that the headlights likewise did not work. The switch was on, but no lights.

It dawned on me. After driving to the church at the front of the funeral procession with headlights on, I had failed to turn off the lights after the pallbearers had removed the coffin to carry it into the church.

How could I have made such a stupid mistake? I thought. And at this very long Orthodox service?

Apologizing profusely, I asked Mr. Ivanov's nephew, Boris, if he would be kind enough to jump-start the hearse. He quickly agreed, and maneuvered his car to face the hearse. Opening both hoods, he attached the jumper cables.

My engine jumped into action. Just then, another member of the funeral party, a man in his 20s, signaled for me to roll down my driver's side window. As I did so, he leaned inside, and spoke in a stage whisper that I, but no one else, could hear.

"While we're at it, why don't we also jumpstart Grandfather?"

FORTY-THREE: WIVES

Family members regularly dress up to attend the funeral of a loved one. But the 20-something woman standing next to Mr. Frank Osbourne's casket was noticeably more decked out than most.

Black ruffles circled her exposed shoulders and neck. Black gloves reached to mid-forearm. Black fishnet stockings reaching to mid-thigh showed off her shapely legs. High heels added a half-foot to her height. A black beret was tilted at a fashionable angle.

My assistant had made the arrangements for the funeral for Mr. Osbourne, 49, who had died after being shot in a tragic hunting accident. All funerals are traumatic, but given Mr. Osbourne's sudden and unexpected demise, I was anticipating an especially difficult afternoon.

"I am so sorry for your father's passing," I said, addressing the smartly dressed woman. "I'm told he was a wonderful man."

"Excuse me, Harry," the woman replied, fire in her eyes. "That is, I assume you're Harry O'Toole, the guy in charge. This gentleman, Mr. Frank Osbourne, is my husband, not my father."

"Oh, I'm so sorry, I just assumed ..."

"Don't assume," the young woman said. "I'll have you know that I am Jennifer Osbourne, this poor gentleman's bereaved widow."

Just then, two men and one woman, each looking in their 20s, walked briskly into the room. They were wearing dark clothing, of the sort you would wear to a funeral, but nothing too formal.

"Hello, Jennifer," one of the men said, addressing the woman standing by the casket.

"Jennifer, when did you get here?" the woman in the group said.

Jennifer Osbourne did not respond to their greeting.

Avoiding Mrs. Osbourne, the three 20-somethings walked around to behind the casket and peered at the deceased's body.

"Oh, Dad, I'm so sorry," the young woman said.

"We love you, Dad, and we're so sorry this happened," one of the young men said.

"Mom can't believe this happened," said the third.

Suddenly, an older woman stormed into the room. Ignoring the deceased, she began to rail against the decked-out woman standing by the open casket.

Although obviously older than the first woman, the new arrival still retained the appearance of a naturally attractive woman. Her figure retained its youthful form. Her face displayed soft contours. Her reddish brown hair was perfectly coiffured. She was dressed modestly, her attire moderately formal.

"You did this to him," she said, aiming her face and outburst directly at the high-heeled woman. "If it wasn't for you, you slut, this never would have happened."

"You have no idea what you're talking about," the decked out woman said. "It wasn't me who shot him."

"Mom, calm down," one of the young men said. "We know you don't like Jennifer, we don't like her, either. But she didn't shoot him."

"She might as well have," the older woman said. "She stole him, and then she shot him."

"Mom, it was a hunting accident," one of the three adult children said.

"He never had a hunting accident when he was married to me," the older woman said. "If she hadn't stolen him, this never would have happened. It's her fault, and he had it coming."

"Let's not fight in front of Dad," one of the young men said. "He would not want us to do that."

At this point, the most recent Mrs. Osbourne began shaking noticeably. Ignoring the others, she turned to face the deceased. "Frankie, Frankie," she said before dissolving into tears.

The original Mrs. Osbourne rushed up to her younger rival and pushed her aside, causing the younger woman to nearly lose her balance. The original Mrs. Osbourne then looked straight into the casket, setting her face six inches from the oblivious Mr. Osbourne.

"You S O B, you big fat S O B," the original Mrs. Osbourne shouted. "I loved you so much, I gave you my everything, three kids and twenty-eight years together, and you betrayed me for a common whore."

Having recovered her balance, the most recent Mrs. Osbourne marched up to her displaced rival and attempted to kick her. "You witch," she said. But instead of landing a solid blow, she only managed to send her high heel flying across the room.

In response, the original Mrs. Osbourne removed her own shoe and waved it at her replacement. "I should smack you across your pretty little face," she said. But good sense, it seemed, restrained her.

I stepped forward, put my outstretched hands between them and firmly but gently pushed them apart. The three adult children crowded around their mother and helped her as she sat down far from the open casket. A few minutes later, she got up and walked out of the room.

The original Mrs. Osbourne did not reappear for the rest of the viewing and did not attend the funeral service.

The replacement Mrs. Osbourne stayed for both the remainder of the viewing and the entire funeral service, weeping openly. As the pallbearers were carrying the coffin toward the hearse, I chanced upon seeing her get into her car. She was dry-eyed.

Both the most recent Mrs. Osbourne and the adult children attended the graveside service. The original Mrs. Osbourne did not. All were in tears as we lowered his casket into the ground.

At the end of the graveside service, I asked the adult children how their father had died.

"It was the third day of deer hunting season and he was out with a buddy of his when he tripped and fell," one of the adult sons said. "His friend called 911, and the emergency crew came minutes later. But he was pronounced DOA when he arrived at the hospital."

"It must have been quite a shock, so sudden and all," I said.

"Yeah, it was an awful shock," the adult daughter said. "We were still mad at him for dumping Mom, and then this happened."

"Mom was in a double shock, finding out what he was really like, and then, this," the son said. "But she chalked up his sudden death to karma taking its revenge."

In response to their forthrightness, I felt emboldened to ask the obvious question. "How did your father meet his new wife?" I said.

"In a strip club," the three said in unison.

"I'm so, so, sorry," I said.

"So are we," the adult daughter said.

Later that evening, I was sitting at my desk when Antoinette walked up to my left side and planted a kiss on my cheek.

"Rough day at the O.K. Corral, lover boy," she said. "How are you feeling?"

"Could be better," I said. "Those two ladies really went at it."

"They did indeed," she said. "So let me ask you something."

"Anything."

"When I'm an old jalopy, you would never trade me in for a newer model, would you?"

"Of course not," I said. "But who says you'll ever turn old and gray?"

"But if I do, on the off chance, you'll never pull a Mrs. Harry 2.0 on me, would you?"

"Sweetheart, you know I'd never do something like that."

"If you try, do you give me permission to pluck out your eyes?"

"I give you permission to pluck out my eyes."

"Can I slit your throat?"

"You can slit my throat."

"Can I cut off your do-hickey?"

"You can cut off my do-hickey."

"It's a deal," Antoinette said.

A pause.

"Antoinette, can I ask you a question?"

"Sure, lover boy."

"Antoinette," I said, "What's a do-hickey?"

"Oh, Harry," Antoinette said, "You're such a tease."

FORTY-FOUR:
OVERSEAS MISSION

Sal, my fellow undertaker and good buddy, was a well-respected professional in our local community. But today, as we waited for our spinach soufflé (his choice) and ham-and-cheese quiche (my selection) during our monthly lunch get-together, he had some big news about taking his craft overseas.

"You know how doctors and nurses head overseas on short-term trips to help when there's an outbreak of some strange disease?" he said.

"Sure," I said. "That ends up in the news."

"And you know how people show up in some places beyond our shores to help clean up the mess when a tsunami strikes?"

"Of course," I said. "I've thought about doing that myself."

"But what's missing from these pictures?" Sal said.

"Not sure."

"You and I should know better than most people," Sal said. "What's missing is somebody to take care of all the unfortunates who die during those tragedies, not to mention somebody to help all their families."

"I never thought of that," I said. "But you're right. Nobody talks about what is done with all those deceased individuals. Somebody has got to care for them."

"Esther and I are flying to Haiti next week to do just that," Sal said. "We made the arrangements a couple of weeks ago. We're going to be part of a team of funeral directors in charge of giving a proper burial to those who died in the recent mega-storm. We're also going to organize proper funeral services for family members so that they can say goodbye to their loved ones."

"How many dead do they estimate?" I said.

"In the thousands," Sal said. "The local officials are completely overwhelmed."

"Will you be having an individual service for each person who died?" I said.

"No, most of the time, we will have services for multiple dead," Sal said. "But we'll do our best to honor each of the dead and give each family an opportunity to show their love to their loved ones."

I sat back, impressed. I had heard of the disaster that had struck the island nation, of course. The news also mentioned that several well-known relief agencies had sprung into action. But among all the attention to the disaster, news reports had said nothing about that additional funeral directors would be needed to bury the dead. That need seemed obvious, especially to us undertakers. But no, there was no mention of anything like what Sal was telling me in the news.

"So, how long will you be overseas?" I said.

"About four weeks."

"And how much will you be paid for this overseas gig?" I said.

"Nothing."

"Nothing?"

"Nothing. Nada. Zilch," Sal said. "It's all volunteer. Each of us, about a half dozen in all, are going as volunteers."

"Nice," I said.

This wasn't the first time that Sal had forgone cash in his funeral business. This lack of an 'it's all about the money' mentality was one of the things I most admired about Sal.

For many people, the funeral business comes across as a cash cow. A huge cash cow. Everything the bereaved family encounters just reeks of money. The hearse is brand new. Everyone is dressed to the nines. The funeral home building resembles an expensive classical Greek or Roman temple.

And then, of course, there's the final bill for services rendered. Typically, it seems, almost enough to pay a semester's tuition at Harvard.

Sal wasn't like that. Of course, most of the time, Sal would collect large fees, just as any self-respecting funeral director would. But, and this is huge, there were those occasions when a truly needy family was unable to pay, and Sal would wave some or all of his fee.

What was most remarkable about that charity was a telling detail, or rather the lack of telling. It wasn't Sal who would tell me about that forgoing of charges. It was invariably a family member. Sometimes, when they came back to me afterward, asking me why I would not perform certain services at Sal's cut-rate price.

Sal also donated money to charities. But almost exclusively to charities that served animals. The SPCA, those sorts of organizations.

One more thing. Funeral directors, for some strange reason, seem to all like to drive brand new, expensive, cars. It seems to go with the territory. Maybe it's an unconscious rebuke of the deterioration that death brings to everything.

Not Sal. Sal always drove a used car, just a few steps above clunker.

Why Sal was this kind of person about money was always a mystery to me. He wasn't religious. His philosophy was, when you're done, you're done. And he certainly wasn't above a little gossip, some of which would either fry your ears or qualify for the front page of the most scurrilous supermarket tabloid.

But when it came to money, Sal was a saint. But non-religious, a secular saint.

And so, I piped up.

"Sal, I'm so proud of you for going," I said. "You are an honor to our profession."

"A profession that often gets bad press," Sal said.

"True, true, and more than true," I said. "We perform a very valuable service, but it's not always much appreciated, at least when you don't need our services."

"Let me give you an example," Sal said. "It's from ancient history, but it speaks to the point."

"Okay."

"Did I ever tell you about my remarkable blind date when I was in high school?"

This was, as Sal acknowledged, ancient history. Sal was married to his lifelong sweetheart, Esther, for many years. They had met in mortuary school and married shortly after graduation. Theirs was a full partnership, personally and professionally.

"My buddy, Tommy, had set it up, and the girl wasn't bad looking," Sal began. "We met for lunch at Denny's.

She was from a school across town and so I had never seen her before. Just a sprinkling of zits, but slim, nicely dressed, and a good talker."

"So, what happened?" I said. "Did you and she hit it off?"

"Well, everything was chugging along famously until she happened to ask what I wanted to do after high school and, presumably, college," Sal said. "I told her, in all innocence, that I wanted to go into the funeral business. That I wanted to be an undertaker."

"Oh-oh."

"It was like she had suddenly seen a ghost," Sal said. "Her face froze. She politely excused herself, saying she was late for an appointment. She walked out of the restaurant without a word. And yes, the cheeseburger she had ordered arrived five minutes later."

"Did you ever hear from her again?"

"Never heard from her ever again," Sal said. "But Tommy told me later that she yelled at him for setting her up with such an 'inappropriate' date."

"Another one bites the dust," I said.

"And that, my good man," Sal said, "is why I so appreciate my Esther. Dead bodies are her passion. The family that lays out corpses together, stays together."

Sal was wrapping up his recounting of high school misery when the waitress brought our lunchtime selections. Because Sal would be leaving for overseas in several weeks, today's scorecard for who had performed the most funerals in the previous month held especial interest.

"Five, my friend," I said.

"Five, good buddy," Sal said. "Tie."

After we were finished eating, the waitress engaged us in a brief conversation. She seemed even more outgoing than most servers, and Sal, ever the extrovert, asked her why she seemed so happy.

"I was at the animal shelter yesterday, and I got a border collie as a rescue dog," the waitress said. "His name is Sparky, and he's the cutest thing ever. Would you like to see his picture?"

The waitress pulled out a smartphone, and showed us a photo of the lucky dog. The puppy was indeed a looker. Sal nodded and smiled.

The waitress handed us our tab, and we spilt the check. Sal left the tip. On a twenty-nine dollar and change check, a brand-new Hamilton.

FORTY-FIVE: LOCKED UP

"Harry, you're a sight for sore eyes."

Seated in front of me was my good friend Reggie. Unfortunately, where he was seated was in the county lockup. What he was wearing was prison blues.

A few days earlier, Reggie was enjoying some late-night socializing with some fellow scribes at a local bar. As the hours went by, Reggie had lost count of how many beers he had consumed. Not a first-time drinker, Reggie appeared perfectly sober when he left the bar.

The accident happened less than thirty minutes later as Reggie was nearly home. When the police arrived, they determined that Reggie's Chevy Malibu had crossed the center line, colliding with the oncoming Honda Civic.

A passenger in the Civic, not wearing a seat belt, was thrown from the vehicle. The 32-year-old suffered a paralyzing injury. The police administered breathalyzer tests to both drivers and the one passenger. Reggie registered just over the legal limit. The second driver and his passenger were both stone cold sober.

And now, Reggie was incarcerated and facing a host of charges, including drunk driving and causing bodily injury.

"I'm scared," Reggie said.

A half hour earlier, I was a little nervous myself, just walking into the jail, and I was not the one locked up. A concrete structure set down in the middle of its own campus at the edge of town, the jail consisted of a large building and three smaller adjacent wings. The large building and two wings housed exclusively male prisoners. The third wing housed female prisoners.

The outside of the entire building was painted various shades of worn-out blue, brown and gray. The building's massive size and dull colors seemed to shout depression.

The guards patted me down. After emptying my pockets into a tray the size of a shoe box, items held for safekeeping at the front desk, I walked through a metal detector.

I wondered if death is like this. You empty your pockets, you pass through a special detector, and that detector checks that you're not carrying anything of value as you pass through and into a strange world beyond.

And now, Reggie and I sat across from each other, separated by a glass window reaching from the table to the ceiling. We spoke by means of a telephone connected by a metal-encased cord connected to the table.

I had come to the county prison after reading the newspaper article detailing Reggie's accident and subsequent arrest. A follow-up article listed the charges and possible jail time if convicted.

"It's not the jail time that bothers me the most," Reggie said. "It's what my beers did to that poor guy."

My heart went out to Reggie.

"Don't tell anybody what I just said," Reggie added, "because of course I'm going to plead not guilty. But I can't get over what I did to that poor guy."

I didn't say a thing. I just listened.

"Another thing," Reggie said. "I'm so embarrassed. For years and years, I've written about things like this. But I never imagined that I would be the lede in some police story."

"Do you know the guy who wrote up the story?" I said.

"Yeah, I know the guy really well," Reggie said. "He's the back-up police reporter, the guy I work with on the cops beat. He was as surprised as anyone when the cops told him the name of the quote unquote suspect in the police story."

"Did your editors try to play down the story when they found out that you were the guy?"

"Just the opposite," Reggie said. "Ordinarily, a drunk driving story without a fatality would go inside. But when they found out it was about one of their own reporters, they moved it to Page One. Bottom of the page, but still Page One. Journalistic integrity and not playing favorites. I can't say I blame them."

"Have you met any of the guys you've written about?" I said.

"They're keeping me in some sort of protective custody," Reggie said. "They told me it was standard procedure for 'celebrity' prisoners. Imagine, me a celebrity prisoner."

"You probably do have a bit of notoriety among these guys, even if you're not famous nationwide."

"So how are you doing, Harry?" Reggie said. "It's always good to see you. You and the missis doing okay?"

Clearly, Reggie appreciated the opportunity to focus on something other than his difficult plight. Antoinette and I had talked about making another road trip, but I decided to not mention that, given Reggie's confined circumstances.

"So why does stuff like this happen?" Reggie said, becoming suddenly philosophical. "You know, when I first got here, I thought about hanging myself. But I talked myself out of it pretty quickly."

I was taken aback by that revelation. "I'm so glad you didn't, Reggie."

"I did notice that, when I first got here, the guards watched me pretty closely," Reggie said. "They took away anything I could have used to hang myself, like my belt and shoelaces. I asked them about that, and they told me that a lot of new prisoners think about hanging themselves when they first get locked up, and so they do a very strict suicide watch for the first 48 hours."

"I'm glad you didn't try," I repeated.

"So what's it all about, Harry?" Reggie said. "Why did this happen, to me and to that guy in the other car? It's not like I'm a big drinking guy, I just wasn't paying attention. Is God trying to get me or something?"

"I don't know, Reggie."

"I'm not religious, Harry, but maybe God is trying to tell me something. What do you think?"

Suddenly, Reggie's question didn't seem like just rhetoric or the jail talk of somebody facing some prison time. There was a hint, just a hint, of something more in the question.

And so, I did something completely out of character. I recounted to Reggie what happened when Antoinette and I came upon that theater performance in the park several weeks earlier. I did not leave out any of the religious parts, including the part about the guy in line who thinks he's a good guy until the seated guy started asking him some questions.

I spoke for maybe ten minutes. Reggie did not say a word. When I was finished, Reggie asked simply: "Is any of what those guys said, true?"

"I don't know," I said.

"You know, I've always thought of myself as a good person," Reggie said.

"Me, too," I said. "But that seemed to be their point. Maybe we're not the angels we think we are."

"Yeah, maybe I've always thought of myself as a good guy because of all the bad guys I've written about," Reggie said "But now, here I am, locked up like the rest of them."

"Sort of puts a different spin on things, maybe," I said.

"Yeah, maybe," Reggie said.

Not wanting to end on a downer note, I asked Reggie about what legal steps were next. It turned out that he was scheduled for several hearings in the next few days, from a so-called preliminary hearing to a second hearing to set bail.

"Got a good lawyer?"

"The best," Reggie said. "The paper's paying for top tier talent."

A guard tapped on my shoulder, indicating that visitor time was up. I promised Reggie that I would come back to see him tomorrow or the next day.

"By the way," I said, "what are you going to do in here while you're waiting for your bail hearing?"

"I'm just going to try and keep my sanity."

FORTY-SIX: FATHER

Three years after my parents died, I did something I had resisted doing with all my being. I went to visit their gravesite.

It was my first visit since the September and November when I looked on as we laid first my father and then, two months later, my mother in their final resting place.

And now, I stood before their side-by-side portraits, pictures engraved on one vertical stone. My father's picture displayed movie star good looks that scarcely resembled how I remembered him. My mother's picture was likewise glamorous, in a Greatest Generation sort of way.

Weeds creeping up the side of the gravestone gave evidence of my lack of visiting.

I stared at the portraits for about five minutes, unsure as to what to do. Then, I spoke, out loud.

"Hello, Dad." After a pause, "Hi, Mom, you too."

A flood of memories came rushing into my mind, in no particular order, and in no order of importance. First. I was in high school, and my father had just picked me up from a dance at the local YMCA. We were in the car, and a stream of teenage boys and girls were leaving the dance and walking past our car.

Suddenly, one of the boys, fully engrossed in a conversation with the girl at his arm, unconsciously taps on my father's car. My father instantly stops the car, gets out, and collars the boy. He yells at the teenager, who, no doubt, is totally humiliated in front of the young lady.

But no one, repeat no one, taps on my father's car. I wonder if those teenagers ever remember that incident from so long ago.

Coming out of my memory, I looked around before speaking. Satisfied that no one was within earshot, I spoke aloud.

"I'm sorry, Dad, that we never communicated very much."

Being at my parents' gravesite was the most eerie experience. As an undertaker, seeing the dead was an everyday occurrence. But when it's your parents, it is just not the same thing.

Again, my mind wandered.

I remembered another occasion, but this one more positive. When I entered high school, I was terrible at math. No pun intended, but when it came to manipulating numbers, I couldn't put two and two together.

My father always prided himself on being an Enlightenment kind of guy. He had read Voltaire, on his own, as a teenager. In his later years, he had wrestled with the proof of Fermat's Last Theorem, claiming that he had solved the puzzle that had eluded generations of mathematicians.

I think my father must have felt rather embarrassed that his son was nearly beyond the pale when it came to things mathematical. And so, he patiently taught me some math fundamentals. The lessons went so far that I even came to feel, in my senior year, a passion for calculus. A brief passion, however, as it turned out.

It was this very precise and mathematical nature that made my father so good at his chosen profession. In laying out a corpse, he always made sure that every eyebrow and every lock of hair was precisely in place. For my father, preparing a body was like working out a math proof.

His 'cross your t's' nature also made my father appreciate the place that tradition has always had in the funeral business. Like me, he inherited the family business from his father. But unlike me, he never doubted that he would continue in the family business. As far as I could tell, he never displayed any of the doubts I experienced.

That, I realized later, was why he was so surprised when I expressed my hesitation about continuing in the family business.

Looking at my parents' graves, my mind continued to wander.

I recalled the time my father taught me how to drive a stick shift. "It must have been utterly frustrating for you," I said, out loud. What was it like, I thought, to be patient with a son who, even if his life depended on it, could not figure out how to let up on the clutch with one foot while pressing on the gas pedal with the other? Maybe fathers are unsung heroes, I thought.

My mind returned to the present, and I noticed that I had been ignoring my mother. My father was in many ways larger than life, what with his razor sharp mind. And so now I wondered, as I often did when my parents were still alive, just how much my mother felt slighted when standing in Dad's shadow.

"Mom," I said, again out loud, "You were a wonderful mother."

My mother, I mused, was the very opposite of Antoinette. If Antoinette was flamboyant, my mother was steady and down to earth. There was a reason my parents "sat out" being present at our clothing optional beach wedding. I remembered that Dad tried to talk Mom into showing up for the ceremony, even with clothes on, but she adamantly refused.

"You would have enjoyed it," I said, out loud, and with a smile. But I knew that wasn't true.

It dawned on me, and not for the first time, that this was one reason why I was so taken with Antoinette. It was exactly because Antoinette was the yang to Mom's yin. Mom was solid rock, Antoinette was rushing water. Mom was steady, Antoinette was flighty. Mom was conventional, Antoinette was nowhere near conventional.

I appreciated Mom. But I was passionate about Antoinette.

Perhaps surprisingly, the thing I remembered most about my mother was an argument. An argument I had with my father.

As I stood there looking at my parents' graves, I could not recall what the argument was about. I think it was an opinion I had expressed, not something I had done wrong. Given my father's forceful personality, I was shrinking back as the discussion progressed.

Then my mother told me to be a man and stand up for myself. This was remarkable, mostly because my mother usually deferred to her husband.

And I did. I did stand up for myself.

"Mom, I appreciate what you did," I said, out loud. Then I unconsciously glanced over to my father's portrait. It was, of course, silent.

And then, as I continued to look at my parents' gravestones, Shakespeare's words blew over me with fresh power. All the world IS a stage, and we ARE merely players. My parents appeared in Act One, but that part of the drama was now concluded. I was speaking my lines in Acts Two or Three.

And, not many years hence, my children, if I ever acquire any, would take to the stage in Act Five.

What a stage director death is!

My reverie once again left me, and I felt that I needed to make a report to my father on my progress in the undertaking business. It was the most curious thing. Here I was, an adult, supporting myself and my family by the sweat of my brow, and I still felt that I needed to make a report to this man, my father, my father deceased and long ago gone.

"It's not a bad business," I said, again out loud. "I'm slowly getting the hang of it. It's just that the dead bodies still freak me out."

Hearing my words, and seeing the gravestone in front of me, I felt suddenly sheepish.

"I'm sorry," I said. "Nothing wrong with dead people."

Then I stood silent. I thought about whether I should confess my still lingering doubts about being in the funeral business. That is, the fact that dealing with dead bodies on a daily basis reinforced by still unresolved fear of death.

"Dad," I began. Carefully considering my words, I thought how I might articulate my feelings on that delicate subject. After all, it was very possible that my father, like me, had wrestled with this very same fear of death. And that he, like me, had kept those feelings very much under wraps during his long lifetime in the business.

"Dad," I repeated. But then I decided that no, this fear was too personal. My father and I had not communicated, and now was not going to be a time to start. Besides, I would not have wanted my mother to hear such a personal confession. It would have been entirely too personal. Such words would have offended her very practical nature.

And so, I punted, or half-way punted. "Dad, and Mom, I miss both of you very much."

I turned to leave.

FORTY-SEVEN: HEARTBREAK

Mr. and Mrs. Robinson, weeping and nodding, sat up front as their pastor spoke words of encouragement during the funeral service for their loved one. I was seated in the rear of the room, holding my tongue and just barely able to conceal my anger.

The Robinsons' child, three-month-old Benjamin, had died of crib death three weeks earlier. The young African American couple, both in their mid-20s, had miscarried twice before giving birth to Benjamin. Their joy at his birth was everything you might imagine.

"But when Benjie died," Larry Robinson told me before the service began, "we thought God hated us."

And now, with Mr. and Mrs. Robinson a captive audience, Pastor Ezekiel Jarred was giving them a song and dance, and I was beginning to boil inside.

"We don't know why the Lord took Benjamin," the pastor intoned. "His thoughts are not our thoughts, and his ways are not our ways."

"Yes, Lord, your ways, your ways," the couple, holding hands, were saying in unison.

At this, it took all my willpower to keep from running to the front and strangling this guy, pastor or no pastor.

Clenching my teeth in a firm grip and grabbing my seat with both hands, I remained seated.

Not that an imaginary conversation did not run through my mind. Picturing myself face-to-face with the pastor, I fired off questions obvious to anyone with a brain or half a heart.

"How can you say that it is somehow God's will, even if there is a God, to take away their child from this beautiful couple? Why would God be so cruel as to do that? What did they ever do to deserve this?"

Throwing off my silent questions with a shake of my head, I once again focused on listening to what the pastor was saying. And that, rather than calming me down, further inflamed me.

"We don't know why the death of Benjamin is part of God's plan," the pastor was saying.

"We don't know?" I thought. "You're up there, trying to give answers to this grieving couple and you're telling them that you don't know? What kind of answer is that?"

At this, I got up. Drawing on common sense and a small remaining measure of self-control, I simply strode to the men's room. I spent some time in a stall, got out and washed my hands, walked over to use a urinal, walked back to a stall, sat down, got back up and out, walked over to the sink, and washed my hands slowly and carefully, exercising good hygiene. All this to kill some time until the good pastor would likely be finished with his absurd sermonizing.

As luck would have it, the funeral service was nearly over when I returned to the hall. The tiny casket was still up front, but the line of friends and family was nearly fully past the child whose loss they were grieving.

I walked up to Mr. and Mrs. Robinson and spoke my final condolences. "Again, I'm so sorry for your loss," I said.

"God is good, and his ways and wisdom are beyond ours," Mr. Robinson said. "Mr. O'Toole, we so much appreciate your kindness for the wonderful service."

I nodded my head and shook his hand.

Just as the last of the family members walked out, the pastor came up to me and asked for directions to the men's room. "Right over there," I said.

I decided then and there that I would "ambush" this dubious purveyor of truth. When the men's room door closed behind the pastor, I walked over to the hallway outside that room and rehearsed the questions I had put to him in my earlier mental combat.

The pastor emerged from the men's room.

"Pastor Jarred," I said, thinking to ease into the ambush, "can I ask you a question?"

"Sure."

"Aren't you even a little upset that the Robinsons' baby boy died, died when he was not even old enough to walk?" I said. "Doesn't that just seem a little bit unfair to you?"

"Of course I'm upset," the pastor said. "I'm grieving with them in the loss of their child."

"So why did God, if there is a God, why did that God let this happen?"

"As I tried to explain, we don't know," the pastor said. "There are a lot of things, some things that hurt very much, that we don't know."

"What do you mean, we don't know?" I said. "Isn't it pretty obvious that either God doesn't care about these people, or that the whole story about God is just a made-up fairy tale?" I paused to let that sink in.

"Okay, now it's my turn," the pastor said. "Let me ask you a question."

"Okay."

At just that moment, our conversation was interrupted by Joe Scranton, who had scheduled an appointment to prepare for his father's funeral. Jack Scranton, 91, had died in his sleep at home.

The elder Mr. Scranton was known to his neighbors as a retired bank executive, but the authorities saw him otherwise. So did I, thanks to some earlier inside gossip by way of Reggie, my cop reporter friend. "The FBI tried to pin money laundering on him, but they could never prove anything," Reggie had told me. "Mostly because he had an army of good lawyers."

The elder Mr. Scranton's funeral was tentatively scheduled for the day after tomorrow. Bouquets by the dozens had already arrived, as had a wide assortment of cheeses, canned meats and fruit baskets.

I asked the younger Mr. Scranton to take a seat in my office and told him that I would be with him shortly.

And then, ignoring that it was the pastor's turn to make his rebuttal, I fired a question at my captive.

"So, if your God is so fair, what about this elderly gentleman we're going to bury in a couple of days?" I said. "He's had a pretty long and happy life, and who knows what he got himself into?" With my client just out of earshot, I did not want to be too specific concerning what Reggie had disclosed.

"Tell me why this gentleman got a good deal and young Benjamin and his parents got a rotten deal," I continued. "It just doesn't seem fair, whatever your happy talk religious sermonizing."

The pastor was silent for a moment. Maybe he was thinking, maybe he was just giving me a chance to calm down.

"You may not like what I'm going to tell you, or maybe you will," the pastor began. "But since you were straightforward enough with me to ask me an honest question, I'm going to be frank with you and I'm going to give you a straightforward answer."

"Fair enough."

"Two answers, actually."

"Okay. I'm listening."

"First, let me answer you by asking you a question," the pastor said. "Can you explain to me how the brain, which is material and made of things we can see, can process thought, which is invisible, private, and somehow interactive with the made-of-matter brain?"

"No, I can't."

"And can you explain to me how we have both sexual desire and the physical ability to engage in sex?"

"Again, no, I can't."

"And can you explain to me how we have, as you so eloquently asked about, a sense of right and wrong? A universal sense, shared by all humans?"

He continued.

"One last question," the pastor said. "Given that you don't know these things, and that God does know these things, because he created these things, isn't it just possible that God is a little bit smarter than you? That God operates with a wisdom a little higher than yours?"

"I see your point."

"But one more point."

"Fire away."

"The cross."

"The cross?"

"Yes, the cross that Jesus died on."

"What does that have to do with anything?"

"Just this," the pastor said. "Your question was, at its core, the question of whether God is a good God. Whether God cares about people."

"That's right, that's the million dollar question," I said. "Does God care about people? But what does Jesus have to do with that?"

"The point is that God has demonstrated that he cares about you and me," the pastor said.

"How is that?"

"Each of us has violated God's law, the ten commandments," the pastor said. "And since God is a just judge, each of us owes a payment for our breaking that law. Each of us deserves hell."

"Hell?" I said. This is not helping me with my fear of death, I thought.

"That's the bad news, but here's the good news," the pastor continued. "Out of love for us, God allowed his son, Jesus, to take our punishment, in our place. And Jesus willingly took that punishment."

I remained silent.

"And in doing that," the pastor continued, "In doing that, God demonstrated, not just talked, but demonstrated, in a pro-active way, at great cost to himself, that he loves people."

I wrinkled my brow.

"That demonstration of self-sacrificing love puts everything else into perspective," the pastor said. "Even things we can't understand, like the death of Benjamin. Since God has shown his love for us in the cross, we can trust God, even for things we can't understand."

I was silent.

"Are you going to think about this?" the pastor said.

"I'm not persuaded."

But as I drove home, I began to mull over the pastor's way of thinking.

FORTY-EIGHT:
TAP ON SHOULDER

"Harry, it all started when the dental hygienist would not shut up."

Antoinette had just returned from a visit to the dentist to get her teeth cleaned, and she was super excited. I was sure something was up, because she, like most of us, was not a fan of visits to that place where they root around in your mouth.

"I sat down in their fancy armchair," Antoinette began. "And as they always do, they tilted the chair back to a 45-degree angle, and then they placed that heavy x-ray bib over my chest and stomach, to take some pictures. They didn't strap me into that electric chair, but it sure felt like it."

"Antoinette, that sounds like a normal dentist visit," I said. "They always do that."

"They made me open my mouth."

"Yes?" I said. "That's what they do."

"Then Denise came in," Antoinette said. "You know Denise, right?"

"I know who Denise is, but I've never really spoken with her."

"Well, Denise says hello, pulls up my x-rays on her computer, and then gets out her tiny pickax," Antoinette said. "Then she gets out her rotating drill and starts going over my teeth, starting with my bottom left molars."

"So far," I said, "everything sounds normal."

"Normal, not quite," Antoinette said. "First, she starts asking, 'How's the family?' things like that. I can't answer because I can't move my mouth, so I just groan."

"I can relate to that."

"My mind started to wander off when all of a sudden she starts to talk about religion," Antoinette said. "She said, 'Antoinette, have you ever thought about how much Jesus loves you?' Stuff like that."

"I bet that went over well."

"Yeah, you can imagine how I felt," Antoinette said. "Number one, you know me, your friendly neighborhood atheist. Number two, you've got me captive here, sitting in this chair, with you digging in my mouth."

"Did you protest?" I said. "Did you tell her to take her religion someplace else?"

"I couldn't," Antoinette said. "I tried, but all I could get out under the circumstances was a groan. She ignored my groans."

"Bummer."

"Well, not exactly," Antoinette said. "After a few minutes, I started listening, mostly because I couldn't do anything else."

This reminded me of the time I was stuck in the elevator with that fanatic pushing his Bible. I had sloughed off that incident, and I never told Antoinette about it.

"What happened then?" I said.

"It was the strangest thing," Antoinette said. "It started to make sense. I can't explain it, but it started to make sense."

"What made sense?"

"She started off very simple," Antoinette said. "She said God cared about me. She said God loved me. That God had created me, and that, whether I realized it or not, God was passionately concerned about me. She quoted some Bible verse, 'For God loved me,' I can't remember the rest, something about Jesus dying on the cross."

"What did your atheistic soul think about that?" I said.

"I think it must have been hiding in a corner or something, because I started really liking what she was saying," Antoinette said. "That is, until she got to the next part."

"The next part?"

"She said that it was wrong to disrespect your parents," Antoinette said.

"I know you haven't always gotten along with your father," I said. "He wasn't much of a happy camper when you had that argument with him after you dropped the wafer."

"I didn't really tell you all of that story," Antoinette said. "I made myself seem nicer than I really was. I didn't just get angry with him. No, I actually cursed him out. I said things I should not have said."

"Did you tell Denise that?" I said. "I mean, when she was finished cleaning your teeth?"

"I couldn't, I was too embarrassed," Antoinette said. "She finished up, rinsed out my mouth, and handed me a piece of paper that she said outlined what she had told me."

"What did you do then?" I said. "Did you read the piece of paper?"

"No," Antoinette said. "But I did do something. I drove to my father's house. My father was home. He was lukewarm toward me, as always. You know he's always been that way toward me since I told him I was an atheist."

"What happened then?"

"I told him that somebody told me that God loved me, and that I wanted to apologize for cursing him out."

"You apologized to him?"

"Well, I tried," Antoinette said. "I tried to apologize. In fact, I tried to apologize several times, using different words, but …"

"But?"

"But, he wouldn't accept my apology."

"I'm sorry."

"Yeah, I'm sorry, too. He told me that if I wanted to apologize, I should go to the priest and confess to him. I told him I couldn't do that. And so he told me he couldn't accept my apology."

"I'm sorry," I said. "That must have hurt."

"Yeah," Antoinette said. "Then he outright yelled at me. He told me, 'Go talk to your atheist Baptists.'"

"So what did you do?"

"I took his advice," Antoinette said. "I was so pissed that I decided to do that, just to spite him."

"And?"

"And so I drove down to the Baptist church just down the street, knocked on the side door, and asked to see the pastor."

"Did you talk to the pastor?"

"No, the pastor was out somewhere," Antoinette said. "But I did talk to his secretary. She was a nice lady. She listened to my story, I even told her about what had just happened with my father. And then she asked if she could talk to me about what she believed."

"And then?"

"I figured, why not?" Antoinette said. "And guess what, it was just about the same thing that Denise had tried to tell me. Except, this time, I was listening. She told me that God loves me, that I have broken God's law, and that Jesus took the punishment for what I did wrong by dying on the cross."

"I think that's what Baptists believe."

"But here's the frosting on the cake," Antoinette said. "The lady told me that if I believed that and if I trusted Jesus for what he did, I would go to heaven when I die."

"That seems a little strange to me," I said. "What did you think about it?"

"I told the lady that it seemed to make sense, and that my dental hygienist had told me something similar just a couple hours earlier. She smiled and said, 'Maybe God is trying to tell you something.'"

"I told her, 'Maybe.' But then, something else strange happened. After I left the Baptist lady, I went to the supermarket to buy some half-and-half for tomorrow's coffee."

"What's so strange about that?"

"Harry, it's the oddest thing," Antoinette said. "Guess who I ran into at the supermarket?"

"Not sure."

"Remember those weird people we saw in the park a few weeks ago? The people playing that guy standing in line after he dies? The guy named Harry? The guy who thinks he's a good guy until the man sitting in the front of the line starts asking him some questions?"

"I remember."

"Those are the guys I ran into in the supermarket," Antoinette said. "The dairy aisle. We started talking. They asked me what I thought about their play. I told them that I didn't like it at the time, that we had left early, but that I was now having second thoughts."

"Second thoughts? Since when?"

"Since today," Antoinette said. "The guys in the supermarket asked if they could talk to me about Christianity. I wasn't sure what they wanted, but I said, whatever."

"And then?"

"And then, they told me more or less the same thing that Denise and the pastor's secretary told me," Antoinette said. "That God loves me. That I've messed up, like everybody else, and that Jesus died on the cross to pay the penalty for the bad stuff I've done."

Antoinette started to tear up.

"And then," Antoinette continued, "that if I turned away from the bad things I'm doing, and trust Jesus for what he did on the cross, that I would become a new person on the inside. Forgiven. A new life starting today."

A broad smile came over Antoinette's face.

"And then," Antoinette said. "Heaven when I die."

"And?" I said, dumbfounded.

"Harry," Antoinette said. "Right there in the dairy aisle, I bowed my head and prayed. I asked God to forgive me for all the stupid stuff I've done. I gave my life to Jesus. Harry, I became a Christian."

I just stood there, stunned. And not too happy, I might add.

FORTY-NINE: FREAKED OUT

"You've got to be kidding, Antoinette. You've gone JESUS FREAK on me?"

We were standing in our kitchen when Antoinette, the love of my life, announced that she had suddenly gotten religion. I was dumbfounded. Her declaration blindsided me. It was if Ronald Reagan had proclaimed that he had suddenly become a disciple of Karl Marx.

And I was not a happy camper.

My first reaction was simple disbelief.

"Antoinette, this is completely ridiculous," I said. "Religion is what wacko Bible thumpers do."

"Not religion, Harry," Antoinette said. "Christianity."

"What's the difference?" I said. "Christianity. Whatever. I don't like it."

"What's not to like?" Antoinette said. "Christianity says you have to love people."

"We do love people, Antoinette. We love them as part and parcel of our job. It's just that I don't like religious fanatics. And I don't like it that you've become one."

"But you do like me, don't you, Harry?"

"Of course I like you, Antoinette, You know I love you. I just don't want you to be one of those Jesus freaks."

"But I'm not a freak, Jesus or any other kind." Just then, Antoinette hunched over my neck and playfully feigned a Dracula-style vampire bite, but I shrugged it off. I wasn't in the mood for games.

"Okay, fine, Harry. But you know that I love you. And my becoming a Christian will help me love you even more."

"But we made a deal, Antoinette."

"What deal?"

"When we got married, I married a wild and crazy girl, the wild and crazy girl I fell passionately in love with."

"Yes, you did," Antoinette said.

"The wild and crazy girl who perfectly balanced the dull and boring guy that I was and still am," I said. "And now, this so appealing wild and crazy girl has just decided that she wants to be a dull as dishwater Baptist."

"Wait a second, Harry. Make up your mind."

"Make up my mind?"

"Yes, make up your mind," Antoinette said. "First, I'm a Jesus freak, wild and crazy. Then, I'm a dull as dishwater Baptist. Bonkers or boring, make up your mind."

"You know what I mean," I said. "Those Baptists don't have a brain in their head. They hate science. They're anti-evolution. You don't think Darwin was wrong, do you?"

"Actually Harry, I hadn't really thought about Darwin."

"And gays," I said. "Baptists hate gays, don't they?"

"I hadn't really thought about that, either," Antoinette said. "But that isn't the issue."

"What is the issue?" I said.

"The issue is that Christianity is true, and I've become a Christian," Antoinette said. "And I would very much like it if you also became a Christian."

"Fat chance," I said.

At this, Antoinette reached over and kissed me on the cheek. I could hardly refuse her gesture.

"You never play fair," I said in response. Antoinette merely smiled.

We stood and looked at each other, neither one of us saying anything for about ten minutes.

"Besides," I added, "I thought I was the love of your life. And now you say that this Jesus, whoever he is, is the top dog, the big man in your life."

"Did I say that?"

"No, but you certainly implied that."

Again, a few minutes of silence.

In the silence, I felt more than a little foolish implying that this Jesus was somehow a rival for Antoinette's love. Still, that's what it felt like. Antoinette was choosing this Jesus over me. I did not like the competition. It felt like Antoinette was being disloyal.

Finally, Antoinette spoke.

"Harry, Jesus makes me love you more, not less."

I wasn't persuaded.

Again, silence.

I had other ideas for taking her out of this new-found religion. And, if Antoinette was going to use emotion, as she did with her kiss on my cheek, I was going to rely on logic and reasoning.

First up, hypocrisy among those who claim religion. This was something I was quite familiar with, in ways both well known to everybody and in ways unique to my profession.

Way back in college, some of my supposedly Christian dorm mates didn't exactly live up to what they said they stood for. They typically got plastered on Saturday nights before going to church on Sunday mornings.

This hypocrisy in religion got even worse after I became an undertaker. As anybody who had ever been to a funeral knows, only the good die, be they young or old. If eulogies are to be believed, everybody's going to heaven. Doesn't matter what kind of rotten person you were before you kicked the bucket. Hypocrisy, thy name is religious profession in the funeral business.

I broke the silence.

"Antoinette, you know as well as I do that everybody who claims to be religious is really a hypocrite," I said. "They're all faking it, sounding religious just to impress other people."

"Harry, be fair," Antoinette said. "Are you saying that I'm faking it?"

"No, of course, not," I said. "It's just that you don't want to associate with those people."

"But, Harry, let's be honest," Antoinette said. "We're all hypocrites. We all pretend a little bit, every now and then. Don't we, now?"

"Well, maybe."

"So what's the problem?" Antoinette said. "I don't have to be, we don't have to be, hypocrites, or at least not as much as everybody else."

"What's with the we?"

"We, us," Antoinette said.

"No," I said. "Not we. Not us."

"Harry."

"Antoinette, let me be real honest with you," I said. "Here's what really bothers me. It's not the hypocrites. That can't be helped. What really bothers me is that if this religion thing is something you've really bought into, it means that the wonderful woman I married has turned into an altogether different creature. Something I did not expect, and someone I do not know at all."

Antoinette was silent.

"I do not like the turn our lives have taken," I said. "The turn your life has taken, and so, our lives."

Baptists hate sex, everybody knows that, I thought. There goes our sex life. I knew enough not to mention that out loud.

Antoinette was silent, but I could see that she was beginning to tear up.

I decided to dial down my speech. I was angry, but her silent response and watery eyes were starting to make me feel like a heel. But after a few minutes of silence, I considered whether a different approach might lead to a better result. Better than the confrontation we had just gone through.

Antoinette, as I learned both during our courtship as well as into our marriage, was prone to suddenly latch onto strange fancies. Some months earlier, Antoinette had suddenly expressed a desire to learn parachuting, and passionately begged me to join her. I have always had a fear of heights, and thus had no desire to take part in any such airborne folly.

What worked in that case was simple enough. I simply delayed a trip to the airport. I found various excuses (mostly work related) to delay making an exploratory trip to the "sky adventure" club she had found advertised in the newspaper.

Three weeks later, Antoinette had forgotten all about parachuting. I didn't need to say a word.

So there was hope. I could simply wait her out. But this strategy depended, of course, on my playing it cool, being non-confrontational, and assuming that Antoinette's sudden religious insanity would go away of itself.

And so, I apologized.

"I'm sorry, Antoinette," I said. "I didn't mean to be so harsh. I love you, and would never do anything to hurt you. I respect your decision. Let me think about what you've said."

"Okay, Harry," Antoinette said. Again, a kiss on my cheek, before quietly walking away. And yes, the part about my loving Antoinette was true. The part about giving serious thought to whether her new-found religion was a good idea?

Not so much.

FIFTY: IN BLUES

"Hey, Reggie, good buddy. How you doing? How you holding up?"

"It's the pits, Harry," Reggie said. Then in a mocking voice, he added, "I'm stuck in Folsom Prison, I hang my head and cry."

Today was my second visit to Reggie, awaiting trial for a drunk driving accident. The charges had been upgraded as the condition of the person paralyzed in the accident worsened and authorities discovered that Reggie had several previous drunk driving arrests.

I sat down in a booth in which visitors could talk by telephone to incarcerated friends or family members. Reggie was wearing "blues," the prison garb mandated for all inmates, and a wristband with his name and newly issued ID number.

"Harry, don't tell anybody, but I'm terrified," Reggie began.

"I'm sorry."

"The days are bad enough, because the walls are everywhere, staring you in the face," Reggie continued. "But it's the nights that are really depressing, because I can hardly sleep, and the dead quiet kills me."

"I'm so sorry, my friend."

"And then, in the morning, when you wake up groggy, the walls again remind you that it's another day, exactly like the last one. You're reminded, you're going to be here for a very long time. You're going to be locked up forever."

"I'm sorry," I said. "I wish I could help."

"But you know what's really bad for me personally?" Reggie said.

"No, what?"

"For years, I wrote about guys doing crimes, and going to prison, and never once thinking about what it was like for them after they got locked up," Reggie said. "'Lock 'em up and throw away the key.' It was a big joke. Some joke."

"Yes, some joke," I said.

"And the food here," Reggie said. "Three squares. Three squares, but just awful."

"Yeah."

"And here's something else that's just embarrassing, humiliating," Reggie said.

"What's that?"

"The female guards," Reggie said. "I tell you, they're all on a power trip."

"Oh."

"Here, man-hating women in uniforms can boss you around, absolutely boss you around," Reggie said. "I think maybe they're just trying to get revenge on some past boyfriends."

"Could be," I said.

"And now, they're on a power trip," Reggie repeated. "And if you don't do exactly what they say, it's in the hole for you, pal, one day, two days, even a week or more at a time."

The hole was a special isolation area which serves to punish rebellious inmates.

"You haven't gone there, right?" I said.

"Not yet," Reggie said.

"How about the other guards?" I said. "Are any of them at all pleasant, given the circumstances?"

"It depends," Reggie said. "As long as you do what they tell you, some of them are not too bad. It just that most of them have a thing about bossing you around. They're the ones who are hard to get along with."

"I Imagine so," I said.

"And don't ever call them guards," Reggie said. "We do, but not to their faces. They always want to be addressed as CO's, corrections officers."

"CO's it is."

"The CO's who are sometimes really nice, you know, they're the ones who have been locked up before," Reggie said. "As they say, in a former life. And then they remind me that this, too, will pass. Maybe they're right."

"That must have been encouraging," I said.

"Yeah, in a way, it was."

Hoping to continue with something positive, I asked if Reggie if there were any other bright spots, even minor, over the past few days. To my surprise, Reggie smiled.

"I've learned some new words," Reggie said. "As a wordsmith of long standing, I am always open to imbibing new slang."

"For example?"

"Well, my cellie says he's facing a body," Reggie said. "He said there was a gat involved."

"Translation?"

"He said he was facing a murder charge, and that there was a gun involved," Reggie said. Reggie explained that "gat" was slang derived from, of all places, "The Great Gatsby."

"Do you get along with your cellie?" I said.

"Passably well," Reggie said. "A surprising thing, that. A lot of these guys make a lot of good friends here on the inside. As you might imagine, sometimes they know guys from the outside, and they get to know them even better being locked up together for months and years. And of course, you can't trust everybody and things can get pretty tense sometimes. But some of the friendships are tight."

"Not bad."

"Except if you get a tune-up," Reggie said.

"What's that?" I said. I had a feeling Reggie was trying to show off yet another new word he had learned.

"That's when they beat you up because you've ratted out your cellie," Reggie said.

"Yes, you don't want to do that," I said. "Other newsworthy tidbits about life on the inside?"

"Prisoners are rabid movie buffs," Reggie said. "But not all kinds of movies."

"You guys on the inside get to watch movies?"

"Sure, but don't tell anybody," Reggie said. "Sometimes on TV, sometimes on old television sets with places for push-in cassettes."

"Life of Riley."

"No, not life of Riley, but some creature comforts," Reggie said. "But guess what kind of movies the guys in blues like to watch."

"No idea."

"Crime movies," Reggie said. "Mafia movies. 'Scarface.' 'Chinatown' The absolute favorite? The three 'Godfather' movies."

"They let you watch that stuff?"

"Sure," Reggie said. "It keeps the brothers happy."

I wasn't sure that keeping inmates happy was a top priority, but it is what it is. "Reggie," I said, "You are an education in itself. So what else have you learned?"

"Not something I learned, because I pretty much expected it," Reggie said. "But being locked up can be, and most of the time is, extremely boring. Depressing, and boring."

"Yes," I said. "I imagine it is." I frowned.

"Anything else a surprise?" I said.

"Yes, a surprise, or maybe not so much a surprise," Reggie said. "The guys in blues are absolute news junkies. We're fanatics about watching the news."

Now, that was a surprise to me. I figured that prisoners might watch sports to pass the long days, but news? Why news? Why on Earth would inmates care about news?

Reggie clarified things. The news that inmates cared about was not news about politicians promising new programs to fix this or that problem. It was not news about celebrities talking their new picture.

No. Think O.J. Simpson.

"The courts ain't fair," Reggie said. "Somebody gets off, and the next jury wants to convict, whatever the evidence." Inmates are very aware of the way the public thinks about this, Reggie explained. So inmates watch the outcomes of those trials, like gamblers sizing up odds before placing a bet.

"I hope you get a fair trial," I said.

"Let's hope not," Reggie said. "If I get a fair trial, my goose is cooked."

The guard, excuse me, the corrections officer, tapped on my shoulder. My visitation time was expired.

FIFTY-ONE: IN CLASS

"I only went there because I was utterly bored."

Several weeks into being locked up awaiting trial, Reggie, who had never before given a thought to religion, showed up at a Bible class held inside the prison.

During my weekly visits over the last several months, Reggie had mostly talked about how difficult it was to get adjusted to prison life. But now, this was something new.

Most of the time, Reggie told me, inmates are confined to their cells or a common recreation area. After a while, you get to know your cellie and those locked up next door pretty well.

"After a while, even television in the common room gets pretty boring," Reggie said. "At least with a Bible study, you get to get off your floor and go somewhere else."

Reggie had fallen into one piece of good luck when he first arrived at the prison. As he was being processed, the intake officers asked him what "religion" he was. Reggie had never much thought about religion, but he remembered going once or twice as a child to a local Baptist church. And so, he replied, "Christian."

As a result, "Christian" was entered onto his wrist band. Without that designation, he would not have been allowed to attend the "Christian" services, and he would have been stuck upstairs.

I wondered why the intake workers did that. I found out later that classifying inmates by religion helped keep the peace by making sure that inmates would not be able to disrupt religious services they were hostile to.

"So what was the service like?" I said.

"It wasn't too awful, and I certainly liked getting out of my cell," Reggie said. "They made an announcement over the loudspeaker. I was lounging in my cell, and so I asked the guard if I could go. He checked my wrist band, and then said okay."

As Reggie related the procedure, he and his fellow inmates headed over to a large classroom. "We had to go through a metal detector to make sure we weren't carrying any shanks," Reggie said.

"Was anybody?"

"There sure was," Reggie said. "At least, one guy was. I couldn't believe he tried to get away with it. He tried to go around the detector, but the guards waved him back, and told him to go through. When he did, the buzzer went off. Then they searched him, and found a three-inch blade tucked away inside his shoe."

"What happened to the guy?"

"Into the hole, of course," Reggie said. "A full week, I think."

"How about the rest of the guys?"

"Of course, everybody had to take off their shoes," Reggie said. "But everybody else was clean."

Any inmate whose shirt was not tucked in was also reminded to tuck in his shirt right away. "I think they want to make sure nobody is hiding something in their waistband," Reggie said.

"And then, into the study?"

"No, not right away," Reggie said. "They checked everybody's wristband, to make sure they were registered as Christians."

"Big crowd?"

"Seemed big to me, about forty guys or so," Reggie said. "But they told me later that attendance goes way down during Ramadan, because a lot of guys get their wristbands changed to switch to Muslim."

"They switch to Muslim?"

"Yeah, a lot of guys don't want to offend the Muslim brothers during the holiday," Reggie said. "It's a watch your back kind of thing. Don't stick out if you don't want to get into trouble."

The room for the study was the size of a high school lunch room, Reggie said. Several dozen folding chairs had been set up, all facing in the same direction. One of the guards opened a locked closet, walked inside, and then handed out Bibles to everyone who asked for one. Some of the inmates brought their own Bibles.

"Sounds like church."

"I haven't gotten to the strange parts yet," Reggie assured me.

"Like what?"

"Well, first of all, what was on the walls," Reggie said. "There were some charts I couldn't understand, and some pictures of a temple. I think it had something to do with the Old Testament."

"Could be," I said.

"That wasn't the strangest thing on the walls," Reggie continued. "There were some cloth tapestries, with scenes from what I think must have been the Bible."

"That sounds like what you would have at a Bible study," I said.

"Yeah, except Jesus in every picture was black," Reggie said. "I didn't know Jesus was black."

"I didn't know that, either," I said. "Maybe he was. Maybe Jesus looked just like you, my friend."

"Yeah, maybe," Reggie said, smiling.

Reggie paused for a minute before continuing.

"Then it got really strange," Reggie said. "Everybody got up and started singing."

"What's so strange about that?" I said. "They do do that, you know, at Baptist churches."

"I know that," Reggie said. "It's just what they started singing. Nothing sounding like an old-fashioned hymn or anything. No, they just started singing, and I quote."

At this point, Reggie began in a sing-song voice.

"The blood the blood the blood, the blood the blood the blood, the blood the blood the blood for me. One day I was lost, Jesus died on the cross, I know it was the blood for me."

"That sounds morbid," I said.

"It was morbid," Reggie replied. "I think it had something to do with Jesus dying on the cross."

So what was the teacher like?"

"Actually, there were two teachers," Reggie said. "The guys kept referring to those guys as the outside ministry."

"Makes sense."

"Interesting story, Harry. The main teacher was a black guy, middle-aged with gray-white hair, with tattoos on both arms. The other guy, a white guy, didn't say much. The first guy started with a prayer, but it didn't sound like a prayer. It sounded more like just talking."

"And how was the sermon?"

"Actually, it wasn't too bad," Reggie said. "At least they didn't tell us we were all going to hell."

"Surprise, surprise."

"Yeah, what a relief," Reggie said. "We're all going to hell is certainly what I expected to hear."

"A relief, I'm sure."

"Yeah, not too bad," Reggie said. "The guy opened his Bible and read a paragraph. I'm not sure where it was from. Then he told us not to give up hope."

"Sounds encouraging."

"He told us not to give up hope because he had been where we were," Reggie said. "He told us a story about how he had been locked up for selling drugs and stealing a car when he was twenty two, and how he had quote unquote found Jesus while he was locked up."

"What did the guys think about that?"

"I think most of the guys had heard the story before, but you could tell they were still impressed. Some of the guys shouted 'amen, brother.'"

"So what happened then?"

"Well, you could tell that not everybody was interested in what he had to say," Reggie said. "Some guys kept talking, especially some guys in the back of the room."

"Talking."

"Yeah, talking, and passing notes," Reggie said. "Everybody could see them passing notes, but I don't know if the guy talking up front could. They were talking, laughing, and passing notes."

"So what did the guy up front do?"

"The guy kept having to ask two guys in the back of the room to stop talking," Reggie said. "He told them, 'if you want to talk, please leave.'"

"Did they stop talking?"

"No," Reggie said. "So he did ask them to leave. The guys got up and, as they were leaving, they gave yo-bro handshakes to all their buddies."

"Sounds like high school."

"Very high school," Reggie said.

"Then what?"

"Well, after about thirty minutes, the guy asked if anybody wanted to 'get saved,'" Reggie said. "Three guys went up, and the main preacher man and his buddy prayed for them. Then everybody clapped."

"Did you go up?"

"No," Reggie said. "It was too strange for me. And I'm hoping to get out of here soon. My attorney says I've got a chance, maybe even an even-steven chance, of getting out of here with time served."

"Let's hope so."

"But then the strangest thing happened," Reggie added. "Before the study started, the preacher man had prayed for one of the guys. I forget what his name was, but everybody seemed to know him. The man prayed that 'God would turn the heart of the judge' and give the guy a reduced sentence."

"Always something to hope for, I guess," I said.

"And guess what?" Reggie said. "Just before the service ended, a guard came into the room and called out a name, the name of the guy the preacher man had prayed for."

"You're kidding."

"When the guy stood up, the guard told the man to come with him and pack up his things. The guard said, 'You're being released.'"

"I can imagine what happened then."

"Yes," Reggie said. "Complete and utter bedlam. Crying. Hugging. Shouts, 'Thank you, Jesus.'"

"Couldn't ask for a better ending," I said.

"Well, maybe, maybe not," Reggie said. "After the crowd calmed down, the preacher man said that God answered prayers, but did not always answer them in exactly this way. But when I talked with guys afterward, everybody told me that if I prayed hard enough, God would get me out. They told me that God is better than the best lawyer."

"What do you think?" I said. "Do you believe that?"

"No," Reggie said. "The guy who got out was just plain lucky. This Bible stuff, it just seems like so much nonsense to me."

FIFTY-TWO: HANG-UPS

When Antoinette started hanging up her clothes, that's when I started to panic.

As the months and years of our life together rolled out, we had come to a loving standoff in which each person tolerated the other person's eccentricity.

But one Saturday morning, Antoinette, without saying a word, began picking up her clothes. Socks, jeans, blouses and other items that, for as long as we had been married, had always been scattered all over the floor.

I thought her behavior strange, but at first did not give it much additional thought.

Until the next day.

Again, Antoinette hung up her jeans, dresses and blouses. She folded her socks and placed them in a drawer. A few minutes later, I discovered her toothbrush, ordinarily thrown to the side of the sink, placed in the cup next to mine.

By the fourth day of such strange doings, I knew something was up.

"Hey, Antoinette, what's with you turning into Felix Unger?" I said. "You seem to have undergone some sort of transformation."

Antoinette, usually a fountain of words, merely smiled.

A few days later, I discovered Antoinette in the bathroom, reading. She was seated on a folding chair set up next to the bathtub, and her feet were propped up against the side of the tub. Now, Antoinette was a voracious reader. That habit was one of the many things I liked about her. But reading in the bathroom, that was something new and unusual.

"So, what are you reading?" I said.

"The Bible," she said. She put her hand inside the pages to mark her place and held the paperback book aloft. "It's really quite interesting." And then, with that winning smile that always left me smitten, added, "You really ought to try it sometime."

"To each his own," I said. Inwardly, I kicked myself for not being able to come up with a wittier reply.

I went downstairs to make myself a sandwich. I noticed that Antoinette had placed a piece of chocolate cake, my favorite, on a plate next to the microwave. Next to the plate was a note. "To my dear husband, Harry, who always lights my fire. With my love and undying passion, your Antoinette."

Now, Antoinette was never shy about love talk, but this was a little over the top. I became immediately suspicious.

"Antoinette," I shouted, loud enough that my once and always bride could hear me upstairs in the bathroom. "I appreciate you putting out some cake for me."

"Did you like my note?" Antoinette said. Antoinette always had a remarkable way of getting right to the point.

"It lights MY fire," I said. "You light my fire. You've always lit my fire."

At this point, Antoinette came downstairs, making exaggerated steps to pretend I wouldn't notice her arrival.

Then she wrapped her arms around me and planted a big kiss, lips to lips.

I waited, enjoying the moment, until the kiss was finished. Then I asked, the pleasure flown and now annoyed, "What's this all about? Does this have anything to do with you and Jesus?"

"Harry," Antoinette said. "I've become a Christian. I would love it if you would become one, too."

What have I gotten myself into? I thought. Why has the love of my life turned into a religious fanatic, a Jesus freak?

"Is that why you hung up your shirts and folded up your socks?" I said. I felt my tone a little harsher than I intended, so I added, "Antoinette, I really appreciate that you did. But I was just wondering why."

"I thought you would like it if I did," Antoinette said. Then, with that winsome smile, Antoinette added, "Imagine us, Harry, Felix One and Felix Two!"

"But this Jesus stuff, Antoinette, I don't know about this Jesus stuff," I said.

"What's wrong with Jesus?" Antoinette said.

"I don't know," I said. "Being religious just seems kind of boring."

"Harry, let me ask you," Antoinette said. "What do you like most about me?"

"Lots of things. Everything."

"Most?"

"I'm embarrassed to tell you this, although you probably know it already," I said. "What I really like about you is your free spiritedness. Your simple wackiness. That you're off the charts wild and crazy."

"I'm not boring, right?"

"You're not boring."

"So, Harry what makes you think that God, who made this wild and crazy creature" – here, Antoinette made an expansive bow – "What makes you think that that God is boring?"

"You've got a point."

"And what else," Antoinette said, "what else do you like about me?"

"Well, Antoinette, you're a kind person."

"True, with all modesty," Antoinette said. "And what makes you think that God is not a kind person?"

"Well …"

"And let me ask you another question," Antoinette said.

"Wait, not another question, Antoinette," I said. "Too many questions."

"Okay, not a question, just something I want to say from all my heart," Antoinette said. "Harry, I've always loved you, from the first time you came tripping into my life. It's just that Jesus has made me love you now even more, if that's possible."

"How possible?"

Antoinette fell silent, just looking at me, and then began again.

"Harry, remember how you told me about those times you went fishing with your grandfather, and how you so loved your grandfather?"

"I remember."

"And remember how that terrible day arrived, that terrible day when your grandfather died?"

I just nodded.

"And that school bus accident," she added, "when your friends died?"

I remained silent.

"And how you've been terrified of death ever since?"

Why is Antoinette talking about this? I thought. This is completely unfair, her bringing this up.

"I'm so sorry, Harry," Antoinette said. "I know this is very painful, that this still hurts very much."

I kept silent. I wasn't even looking at Antoinette.

"Antoinette, your Jesus has nothing to do with this," I said. "People die. My grandfather died. People all around us die. Heck, we see more people dead in a week than most people do in a year. And I'm going to die, Antoinette, and yes, even you are going to die. Of course I'm afraid to die. With all the death around us, why would I not be? The train is barreling down upon us, and we're tied, bound hand and foot, on the tracks."

"That's just the point, Harry," Antoinette said. "When we die as Christians, we go to heaven."

"For God so loved the world, that he gave his only son," I said.

Antoinette looked surprised.

"I looked it up after we talked the last time," I said.

"That whosoever believes in him would not perish, but have everlasting life," Antoinette said, completing the verse. "That's me, Harry, and I want it to be you, too."

"Antoinette …"

"We could be there, together, you and me," Antoinette said, mischievously.

I couldn't help but smile.

"Plus a lot of other people, of course," Antoinette added. "Let me give you something to read."

I stood there as Antoinette walked into another room and came back with a small booklet with a folded-up piece of paper inside. The booklet had a religious title and the paper listed a series of steps to becoming a religious person.

"Harry, it would be great if you would read through these."

"Okay, maybe."

FIFTY-THREE: DEATH BED

Bob Marsden had undergone a deathbed conversion and therefore, for that reason alone, the notorious gangbanger was safely in the comforting arms of Jesus at this very moment.

That, at least, was the reckoning put forth by the pastor speaking at his funeral.

"Just before Bob passed," Charlie Harrington told the assembled friends and family members, "Bob repented of his sins, and they were many, and cast his soul onto the mercies of Jesus."

Bob's friends, many of them decked out in Hell's Angels motorcycle regalia, and family members, including two women with who he had produced children out of wedlock, were not persuaded.

Pastor Harrington was standing in front of the room and next to Bob's open casket as he delivered his eulogy. "It took a long time and much heartache for Bob to come to Christ," the pastor said. "But in the end, and just in time, he did."

The pastor was about to continue when a motorcycle gang member in the back of the room interrupted him.

"Bob is having a blast today, partying hardy with the devils in hell," the gang member said.

A woman, whom I learned Bob had left pregnant and thereafter without the least token of child support, had a different assessment. "He's rotting in hell, now and forever, and he deserves every minute of it."

I was tasked with overseeing this funeral after the pastor, the leader of a mid-sized evangelical church, had called me up a few days earlier. As I made arrangements, no member of Bob's family had offered to help or suggest anything that needed to be included in the ceremonies.

"Bob pretty much alienated his entire family," Pastor Harrington told me. "And nobody was present when he passed, so they're all getting this news second hand, the news of his deathbed conversion."

I must admit that I was more than a little skeptical myself of this sudden so-called deathbed conversion. You hear about these things, but I didn't believe they were real.

What was real was the venom spit out toward Bob during the services. "Bob could be counted on to start a fight, especially when he got stark raving drunk," said an older guy. "And don't ever lend him any money," a younger man added. "And watch out if he tried to hit on you," added a younger female sporting a dark tattoo across both shoulders.

Many of the people were attending, as the pastor told me before the ceremony, "just to make sure he's really dead."

What made the eulogies still more interesting, though, was that not everyone had a negative take on Bob's unsociable habits. Some of the assembled crowd brought up Bob's nasty habits to praise him for that lifestyle.

"Bob and I were best buddies," said one man clad in motorcycle fashion. "And we had the best times getting plastered together."

A visibly overweight woman added her endorsement to Bob's multi-faceted resume. "Bob was the best you-know-what, I don't want to say the word, because we're in polite company here," she said, "But Bob was the best ever performer under the sheets."

"Tell it, sister," rang out a voice from a far corner of the room.

"Right on," said a voice from another corner.

A few minutes into the service, Pastor Harrington proceeded to tell the story of Bob's final hours. Pastor Harrington, a Baptist, was visiting St. Luke's Hospital at the request of the family of a certain Tom Franklin, who had suffered a heart attack. That man, recuperating, was Bob's roommate in a double room.

When Pastor Harrington arrived at the roommate's bedside, the man's family was already there. The man, his wife and grown children were having a lively discussion about heaven, Pastor Harrington explained. "How the pain and suffering of this life would be no more."

The pastor continued.

"I joined in the discussion and we discussed many hopeful things," Pastor Harrington told the crowd assembled at Bob's funeral. "But just as I and the family were leaving, I happened to glance over at Bob's bed, and I noticed something very unusual. He was listening intently."

And now, as the pastor spoke, the crowd at Bob's funeral had settled down.

"I noticed something else," Pastor Harrington said "Bob's eyes were glistening."

"Crocodile tears, not doubt," someone in today's crowd said.

"No, something else," the pastor said. "So I said goodbye to the family and pulled up a chair next to Bob. I sat down and gave Bob my full attention. He began speaking, slowly at first, but then in a steady pace as he told me his story."

By now, the crowd was silent.

"Bob told me how he had end-stage cancer, and that he was about to be transferred to some sort of hospice program, probably the next day," the pastor began. "Bob told me he had been in the hospital for three days, and that he had had only one visitor over that time, a guy he used to work with a long time ago."

Some in the crowd shifted from side to side in their seats.

"Then," the pastor said, "Bob got very emotional. Bob said he had wasted his life on stupid stuff like drinking and fighting, and that he felt very bad about all the people he had hurt. How he had wrecked his family. How he had messed up almost everybody he had come in contact with. He named a few first names. David, Sandra, Sally, if I remember correctly."

Some people in the assembled group twitched.

"Then," the pastor continued, "Bob was suddenly silent. He didn't say a word. It must have been a full five minutes, though it felt like more. I just sat there, praying silently."

Among the assembled guests, you could hear a pin drop.

"Suddenly," the pastor continued, "all of a sudden, Bob began go speak again, now in a low, guttural, voice. 'I'm about to go to hell, I just know it. I've messed up my life,' he used a different word than messed up, 'and I'm about to end up in hell. I've screwed people over my whole life, and now I'm about to get screwed over.'"

"That's right, buddy boy," someone in the back of the room shouted out.

"Oh, screw you," someone else said.

"I just sat there, and let Bob's words sink in," Pastor Harrington continued. "Then, ever so gently, I asked Bob if I could share something with him. He nodded."

Again, the room was quiet.

"That's when I told him that Jesus died for every one of us, for good people and for bad people alike. That Jesus died on the cross to pay the penalty for the bad things each of us has done. That it was still not too late to ask God to forgive him on the basis of what Jesus had done."

"What did Bob say?" somebody asked.

"He said, 'It's too late. I've screwed up my life, and it's too late.' I reassured him that, as long as he was still breathing, that it was not too late. All he had to do was trust Jesus, to believe what Jesus said, that if we call on Jesus, he will in no way cast us out."

"So, where's the death bed conversion?" somebody in the audience challenged.

"Well, after Bob told me it was too late, I waited a few minutes and then again suggested that Jesus would welcome him if he would only cast aside his disbelief and trust that Jesus would forgive him if he, Bob, would only ask."

"And?" someone said.

"And again, Bob said, 'No, I have messed up too many lives, my own included, to get out of hell just before I die. I'd be a complete hypocrite to ask Jesus to forgive me now."

The audience was riveted. I had presided over many funeral services, but this pastor's tale was certainly one for the ages.

"That's when I told Bob," the pastor began once again, "that Jesus died for hypocrites. That Jesus died for prostitutes, drug dealers, self-righteous church goers and ordinary scoundrels just like himself. He smiled when I used the word scoundrels."

"So, did he fess up and break?" somebody said.

"No, not quite yet," the pastor said. "I gently told him once again that God cared about him, and that Jesus died to rescue sinners. Prostitutes. Drug dealers. Just plain jerks. That we were all equally rebels against God, and that Jesus was holding out his hand, inviting Bob to receive forgiveness."

"Did he respond?" someone said.

"Well, Bob was quiet for a moment," the pastor said. "I could tell that he was wrestling with his conscience, thinking it over. And then, suddenly, a surprise."

"A surprise?" someone said.

"A surprise," the pastor said. "From the neighboring bed, from the gentleman whose family had just left after visiting him, came a low baritone voice."

"Just like this," the pastor said. Pastor Harrington began singing, "Amazing grace, how sweet the sound. That saved a wretch like me. I once was lost, but now I'm found, was blind, but now I see."

The pastor returned to his speaking voice. I looked at the pastor, curious.

"When the neighbor finished his song, Bob's eyes were filled with tears. A minute passed, and Bob spoke. 'If Jesus will have me,' he said, 'I'm asking Jesus to forgive me.'"

The pastor then addressed the assembled crowd, speaking slowly and, looking first at this person and then that one, addressed individuals, one after another. "I led Bob in a prayer to become a Christian," the pastor said. "Bob confessed that he was a sinner, that he had broken God's rules and deserved hell, but that Jesus had died in his place. Bob asked God to forgive him, and to make him a new person in Christ, even at this late hour."

"What the hell?" somebody said.

"No, hell is where Bob is definitely not at this very moment," the pastor said. "He is enjoying the very presence of God at this moment, loved, forgiven. And by the way, Jesus makes that same invitation of forgiveness to each and every one of you."

There was a moment's silence.

"Party time!" someone yelled.

"Let's party!" another person said.

The crowed rushed out, talking loudly. I was stunned by the abruptly empty room.

"And when did Bob die?" I asked the pastor.

"The next day."

FIFTY-FOUR: TALL TALES

The viewing for Brian Mulvane was set to begin in about half an hour, and family members had begun to enter the receiving hall. His widow, his brother and sister, three children and five grandchildren all arrived within minutes of each other.

Per the family's instructions, I had decked him out in an expensive pinstriped suit, complete with a white carnation on his right lapel.

Funerals are often a quiet affair, with a mix of both sadness at the loss mixed with subdued smiles as family members recount this memory and that. But what was odd here was that all five grandchildren, adults in their twenties and thirties, were holding a spirited if friendly discussion among themselves.

"It's all tall tales," the oldest said. "Wonderful, witty, fascinating stories, and we love him for them. But they're all made up."

"No, they're all true," said another grandchild, age-wise somewhere in the middle.

"How could he have done all that stuff he told us about?" said another. "They're great stories, but how could all that stuff happen to any one person?"

"Why would he pretend if they weren't true?" said another, clearly the youngest. "I, for one, believe every word."

"He would have made a great novelist," the oldest replied.

At this point curiosity got the better of me. I know it is undertaker policy to let family discussions stay with families, but I couldn't resist.

"I couldn't help overhearing," I said. "Your grandfather sounds like an interesting guy. What kind of stories are you talking about?"

I didn't have to ask twice.

"Well, he told us about the time that he single handedly captured an enemy machine gun nest," one of the grandchildren said. "We know that he was in the war, and that he did some pretty brave things. But we always thought that the 'single handedly' part was a little over the top."

"Not over the top at all," another said. "People did those kind of things in those days. You should believe him."

"I do believe him," another replied, "I just think he was exaggerating a little. War stories are like that."

"And what about his story of foiling a bank robbery by sticking out his leg and tripping the bank robber as the guy was running out the door?" another said. "Sounds pretty incredible to me."

"Not incredible at all," another pitched. "Unusual, for sure, but not impossible."

"Or what about that trip to the Amazon, where Grandpa was held prisoner for three days before he managed to escape?" another said. "That's quite a story."

"Grandpa was always in pretty good shape," another said. "And he's always been quite resourceful."

"And what about that Egyptian artifact Grandpa donated to the Met?" another said. "You know, we've all seen that item, haven't we?"

"But we don't even know if Grandpa had ever been in Egypt," another said.

"Yes, but we've all seen what he said he donated," another said. "We've all looked at it very closely. And the donor is listed as anonymous."

"But of course it's listed as anonymous," another said. "Grandpa was too modest to put his name there at the Met for everybody to see."

"So why did he tell us?" another said.

"That's different," one said. "We're family. It's not bragging if you're telling family."

"What do you think?" they said, turning to me.

"I don't know," I said. "People do donate things to museums anonymously. Sometimes it's modesty, and sometimes they just don't want other people going after them."

"Maybe," several said.

"But tell Harry here Grandpa's favorite story," one of them said. "The story he was most proud of."

"Yes, this is the story we can all agree on, that this was the wildest of them all, that this was the story that made Grandpa's eyes light up the most," one of them said.

"Let me ask you, Harry, have you ever heard of Foxy Roxy?"

"No, I haven't."

"Well," the speaker continued, "Foxy Roxy was a singer at a nightclub in Paris many decades ago. She was what you call a torch singer, an honest woman, but one with a low gravelly voice that exuded sex appeal.

"According to Grandpa," they continued, "he was in his early twenties when the made a business trip to Paris.

While there, during a break from business, he stopped in at a local café for a bit of lunch. And there, in this café was this torch singer, the so-called Foxy Roxy.

"This was a couple of years before he married Grandma, but as he tells the story, he was utterly smitten with this Foxy Roxy. He told us that was her stage name, and even though he knew her real name, he would never tell us. Grandpa said he went back to the café day after day, just to look at her and hear her sing."

"And then," another broke in, "Grandpa said, he had to go back to the U.S. But he told us that he never forgot about those five days looking at Foxy Roxy."

"A few years later, back in the U.S., he met Grandma and they started dating, and they eventually married. They had children and grandchildren. That would be us."

I asked the obvious question.

"So what did your Grandma think about this Foxy Roxy story?" I said. "Wasn't she a little jealous of this youthful Roxy obsession, and how he seemed to brag about it?"

"Nah. Grandma would always wave it off with a flick of her hand. 'Your Grandpa is just imagining things about how exciting this Roxy lady was,' she would tell us. She would just smile and say, 'Foxy Roxy's are just something men in their twenties are obsessed with.'"

"And Grandpas in their eighties make up and tell their grandchildren about," added the oldest grandchild.

The formal part of the viewing was just about to start when my assistant came in with a special telegram postmarked from the Metropolitan Museum business office. He handed it to me and I, given our discussion, waved it before the grandchildren just before I opened it.

"Evidence!" one grandchild shouted.

I began reading from the top. "This invitation is extended to all members of the Metropolitan Museum family as a token of our appreciation of your previous financial support."

"See, it's not evidence at all," a grandchild said. "Grandpa, bless his soul, was just a regular contributor to their financial supporters' fund."

I flipped through the three-page business letter, obviously a monthly appeal to regular contributors asking for additional support. I was about to hand the envelope and its contents to one of the grandchildren when I noticed another piece of paper in the envelope.

Under an official Metropolitan Museum of Art letterhead was a handwritten note. I read the note aloud to the grandchildren.

"To the family of Brian Mulvane. Our deepest condolences on Mr. Mulvane's passing. On this sad occasion we want to thank him, and you, for his generous financial support of the Museum. We especially want to thank him for his priceless contribution to the Museum's Egyptology exhibit. We appreciate his desire to keep that generous gift anonymous, but felt that a personal thank you was in order at the time of his passing. Sincerely, Alan Todd, director, Metropolitan Museum of New York."

The grandchildren listened in stunned silence.

About this time, an older woman pushing another elderly woman in a wheelchair entered the room. They approached Mrs. Mulvane, who was sitting near the open casket, some thirty feet away.

"We read the obituary in the paper," the woman in the wheelchair said. "Our heart goes out to you."

"We're so sorry," the standing woman said.

"Thank you so much for coming, Sally," Mrs. Mulvane said. "I really appreciate it, Doris."

Mrs. Mulvane hugged them both.

"We had a wonderful life together," Mrs. Mulvane said. "Sixty-one years together. Three wonderful children, five wonderful grandkids."

"And it all began ..." Sally said.

"Shush," Mrs. Mulvane said.

"It all began, when a hungry businessman ..." Doris said.

"Quiet," Mrs. Mulvane said.

"All alone in a city we won't mention ..." Sally said.

"Please," Mrs. Mulvane said.

"Stopped by a small café ..." Doris said.

"Shush," Mrs. Mulvane said. "I don't want the grandkids to hear. They'll tease me all the way to kingdom come."

FIFTY-FIVE: THE WHEELCHAIR

"The man in the wheelchair asked if he could speak to me, privately."

I was once again visiting Reggie, only this time not in the lockup where he had been awaiting trial. No, today's visit was taking place in the state correctional facility to which he had been transferred after the end of his trial.

Weeks earlier, Reggie had been convicted on nearly all charges in connection with his drunk driving accident, a crash that had left a man in the other car paralyzed from the waist down. Following a jury trial, the judge had sentenced Reggie to up to 20 years in state prison.

In a way, all of this was for Reggie nothing new. After all, he had covered similar trials as a crime reporter. Still, this time it was personal. Reggie had just experienced all the trauma of being chewed up by the jaws of justice.

And now, we sat down in the reception area for visitors, he on the inside of the protective glass and I on the outside.

"When the trial started," Reggie said, "my lawyer said there was some hope. He said that we had a fifty-fifty chance of persuading at least some of the jurors that the police investigating the accident had acted improperly."

"I'm sorry that didn't work out," I said.

"My lawyer tried," Reggie said. "He tried really hard. I can't blame him. But the jury just didn't buy it."

The trial had lasted four days. I remembered sitting in on the first and final days. After the lawyers gave their closing summations, the judge had addressed the jury, giving them their instructions before sending them off to deliberate.

I had brought "The Spy Who Came in From the Cold" to read while waiting for the jury to return, but found I could not concentrate. After summations, the judge had charged the jury just before lunch. The jury had deliberated until suppertime, had taken a dinner break and had returned for further deliberations. They had returned with their verdict shortly after darkness fell.

Reggie had sat motionless as the judge asked the foreman if they had reached a verdict. The foreman said they had. Each count was read off and the foreman had responded in a clear voice. I could see Reggie's head jerk back ever so slightly as each pronouncement of "guilty" had rung out.

"I thought I had prepared myself for a guilty verdict, but it still stung," Reggie said as we spoke now, weeks later and a world away from the courtroom. "As it turned out, I wasn't ready for that verdict at all."

All I could do was slowly shake my head and frown.

I had left the public seating area immediately after the verdict was announced, and had not been able to speak to Reggie before he had been escorted from the courtroom. But now, weeks later, Reggie described an unexpected epilogue to the jury trial.

After the jury had filed out, the officers who would escort Reggie back to prison to await a second appearance for sentencing gathered around him. But then, as Reggie explained to me now, another officer approached Reggie and addressed him in a firm, clear, voice.

"Mr. Steele would like to speak with you, privately.'"

Mr. Anthony Steele was the man injured in Reggie's drunk driving accident. "I was so shocked, I had to sit down," Reggie said.

"What did he say?" I said. "I expect he was furious, that he would remind you that you would probably get away with prison for a few decades, while he was stuck in a wheelchair for life."

"No, that's not what he said at all," Reggie said. "I expected something like that, but that's not at all what he said."

"What did he say?"

"He said that he had forgiven me, and that he wanted me to know that he had forgiven me," Reggie said.

"What?"

"Yes."

"Did he sound believable? I said.

"From his tone of voice, and from his facial expression, he did," Reggie said.

"What went through your mind as he said that?"

"You know, I'm a little ashamed of the first thought that went through my mind," Reggie said. "The first thought that went through my mind was this. That if this guy has forgiven me, then the court should also forgive me, and that the judge should sentence me to time served."

"That didn't happen, obviously," I said.

"That didn't happen," Reggie said. "But in the days between the verdict and the sentencing, I fully expected the judge to let me go."

"That must have made the judge's sentence an extra tough blow."

"It did."

"So why did the guy say he was forgiving you?" I said. "What reason did he give?"

"Well, at first I couldn't understand it," Reggie said. "The guy started saying something about the Bible, and how Jesus commanded people to forgive other people."

"What did you think about that?"

"Two thoughts," Reggie said. "First, I thought, who is this religious wacko? Then, I thought, wow, this is my lucky day. This religious wacko, if he talks to the judge, and if he sounds normal, this guy is going to get me out of jail."

"Did he talk to the judge?"

"I don't know," Reggie said. "Maybe. But as you know, it didn't make any difference. Talk or no talk, the judge slammed down the hammer."

"Did you at least ask him to talk to the judge?"

"No," Reggie said. "I was still too stunned by the verdict, and then this surprise."

"So how long did the guy talk to you?"

"Maybe twenty minutes."

"Did he say anything else? I said. "Did you at least thank him for forgiving you?"

"You know, it's the funniest thing," Reggie said. "When he told me that he had forgiven me, all I thought about was how that might get me out of jail. And then, about ten minutes into our meeting, it suddenly dawned on me. This guy says he has forgiven me."

"Suddenly?"

"Suddenly," Reggie said. "Harry, remember how I told you before how what really bothered me about the accident, what really bothered me, was that somebody was going to be crippled for life because of my irresponsibility? That the worst thing wasn't that I was probably going away for a long time, but that somebody was going to be crippled for life because of my stupid drunk driving."

"I remember."

"So it suddenly dawned on me," Reggie said, "that it wasn't just somebody was going to be crippled for life. Not just a nebulous somebody, but this very man who is sitting in front of me."

"That must have been a shock."

"It was a shock," Reggie said. "I was so shocked, I just sat there for a minute, dead silent. The guy, too, was silent. The officer started to pull away the man's wheelchair, but the guy waved him off, asking for just a few more minutes."

"And then?"

"And then, Harry, and I had no idea where this came from, I asked the man, why was he forgiving me," Reggie said. "I know that he had given me some religious mumbo jumbo about being commanded to forgive people a few minutes earlier. But, as I just told you, I wasn't really paying attention then."

"I remember."

"But now, suddenly, I was paying attention. And so I asked him, I asked him in a respectful tone of voice, why he was forgiving me."

"And?"

"The guy, and now, I've got to call him by his name, Mr. Steele, Mr. Steele said he had forgiven me because his savior, Jesus the Messiah, had earlier forgiven him. Mr. Steele said that he had been an alcoholic, that had ruined his family, and that he was at the end of his rope when somebody had told him that Jesus offered forgiveness to the most rotten of sinners. Of whom, Mr. Steele said, he was the chief."

I was stunned. Antoinette had recently told me a similar story. I had not told Reggie about my conversations with Antoinette on the topic, but now this.

"I started to tear up, but tried very hard to hide it," Reggie said. "The man recited a Bible verse from memory. He said that God will forgive people if they forgive others."

I was silent.

"Harry," Reggie said. "After the judge sentenced me and they sent me here, I sat in my cell for a long time, thinking about what Mr. Steele said."

"I can't imagine what went through your mind."

"I began to realize that if Mr. Steele had forgiven me, maybe God could also forgive me."

"I didn't think you believed in God."

"I didn't," Reggie said. "But sitting alone in your cell, realizing you're locked up for the start of twenty years, starts to make things very clear."

"So what did you think?"

"I resisted, resisted, resisted, fought it with every fiber of my being," Reggie said. "I had heard the stories about how bad guys get religion, but I wasn't a bad guy."

"No, Reggie, you've never been a bad guy," I said. "I've never heard anybody say a bad word against you, except maybe those guys you wrote about, but that's to be expected."

"And I'm not a bad guy," Reggie said. "Not sold drugs, not robbed anybody, nothing like that."

"I agree," I said. "Nothing like that."

"Except," Reggie said. "Except that somebody was in a wheelchair. In a wheelchair for life, because of something I did."

"In a moment of weakness," I said. "Nobody could fault you for that."

"Maybe," Reggie said. "But I just couldn't get over the fact, and it is a fact, that something I did meant that somebody was in a wheelchair for life. And not just any old somebody, a very specific somebody. A very specific Mr. Steele."

"So what did you do?"

"Remember the Bible study I went to?"

"Oh no, Reggie," I said. "You got religion?"

"No, Harry, not religion. The verse Mr. Steele told me started penetrating, and I got this very strong sense that if I only asked, God would do Mr. Steele one better, and that he would also forgive me."

The officer, waiting patiently for our conversation to finish, was listening intently.

"Remember the Bible study I told you about when I was first locked up," Reggie said. "How I went because I was bored? Well, when I got here, they also have a Bible study. So, a few weeks ago, after Mr. Steele's talk with me and my reconsidering things while alone in my cell, I went to the Bible study here."

"And?"

"Harry, I became a Christian. God has forgiven me."

FIFTY-SIX: TWO CHAIRS

Reggie's newfound religion cost him his life.

Several weeks after Reggie told me of his religious awakening, I went once again to visit him in the state prison where he was serving a lengthy sentence for seriously injuring someone in a drunk driving accident.

When I arrived for my visit, I was directed to the chaplain's office. It was there that I was informed that Reggie had been killed by two inmates just days earlier.

I broke down at the news.

"I am so sorry about the loss of your friend," Chaplain Josiah Smithson told me, his eyes moist. "He told me what a great friend you were, and how much he appreciated your coming to visit him after he got locked up."

Then the chaplain told me of what transpired during what turned out to be Reggie's final weeks.

After coming forward to become a Christian during a prison Bible study, Reggie found himself a changed man, Chaplain Smithson said. Once completely uninterested in anything religious, the former newspaper reporter then became a passionate reader of the New Testament.

"Reggie began to eat through the Bible like a man working his way through an all-you-can-eat buffet," the chaplain said, laughing.

As a new believer, Reggie began to regularly participate in the prison's twice-weekly Bible studies. Not one to shy away from singing, Reggie exercised his deep baritone in songs led by chaplain's aides, inmates specially selected to encourage fellow inmates in singing worship songs. He listened carefully as the "outside ministry" followed up after the singing with an exposition of some Bible passage.

During most weeks, the volunteer leaders of the study invited inmates to come up front and give a "testimony" of what God had done in their lives. Most of the time, the testimony was an account of how God had prompted a judge to shorten a sentence or otherwise drop charges.

When Reggie went forward to give a testimony, a few weeks after coming forward to receive Christ, he told a different story.

"Reggie told the inmates that God didn't give him a shorter sentence," the chaplain explained. "He told them that God had done him one better. That God had given him a whole new life, now and forever."

"How did that go over?"

Some inmates at the front of the room applauded, Chaplain Smithson said. Some inmates in the back of the room looked bored, and continued talking among themselves.

All was going well until a week later, Smithson continued. The room for the study was filling up when two inmates bumped into Reggie. They did not say anything before they sat down in the back.

Reggie sat in the front row, and thus had no warning before what happened next. About ten minutes into the

Bible exposition, the two men rose from their seats. Without a word, they walked up to the front. Each one picked up an empty chair and began repeatedly striking Reggie over the head and about his body.

Prison guards ran into the room seconds later, but they were too late. Reggie was bleeding from large gashes to his head, torso and arms. An ambulance was called, and Reggie was transported to a local emergency room. He died the following morning without regaining consciousness.

It turns out that the two men who attacked Reggie were the very same men who a volunteer preacher had kicked out of a study for refusing to stop disrupting the service a few weeks earlier.

After the attack, murder charges were filed against the men. Those charges, unfortunately, did not seem to matter because the men were already serving lengthy sentences.

"So why did they kill Reggie?" I said.

"Both of them were vocal in their contempt for the Christian faith," Chaplain Smithson said. It wasn't clear how they managed to obtain 'Christian' armbands when they entered the facility, he added. But in doing so, they were able to attend Christian services.

"Mostly they came so they could talk," the chaplain added.

"So why did they target Reggie?" I said.

"I think Reggie's enthusiastic testimony about how Christ had changed his life really irked them," the chaplain said. "Reggie went on for about twenty minutes, looking at individual inmates and pleading with each one to stop doing drugs and sex outside of marriage and to start reading the Bible."

"Sounds strong," I said.

"It was strong," the chaplain added. "Toward the end of the twenty minutes, Reggie looked intently at the two guys. Inmates often know what charges other inmates are facing, and Reggie told the guys that God would forgive them for anything, even murder, if they would only become Christians."

"I'm sure they didn't like that."

"No, they did not like that," the chaplain said. "I think they decided then and there to show up at a later meeting and kill him."

"Awful."

"Besides," the chaplain added, "They figured it wouldn't cost them any additional time."

"Reggie was my good friend," I said. "I don't believe what he believed, the Bible and all that, but he was a terrific friend, and I'm going to miss him terribly."

Then, suddenly, the chaplain said something that threw me back on my heels.

"Don't waste his life," the chaplain said, "Or his death."

"Say what?"

"Reggie died because he had the guts to tell people what Jesus had done for him," the chaplain said. "Speaking the truth about Christ cost him something very precious."

I wondered whether I should tell the chaplain about what Antoinette was talking to me about.

"A great cost," the chaplain added, "to honor a great Savior."

"You know, Mr. Smithson, my wife has been talking to me about the same thing. Neither of us have been very religious, but she recently told me that she has quote gotten saved, as she calls it. I also recently caught her reading the Bible. In the bathroom, of all places.

"Maybe God is trying to tell you something."

"Maybe."

"Is she acting any different otherwise?"

"Yeah," I said. "It's the weirdest thing. She started hanging up her clothes."

"Hanging up her clothes? That's unusual?"

"For us, very unusual," I said. "I'm the Felix Unger in the family, and she's always been the Oscar Madison. But now, she's hanging up her clothes, and folding up her pairs of socks. I think she's doing it because she wants to be extra nice to me."

"God does change people in extraordinary ways," the chaplain said, laughing.

"And Reggie?"

"Reggie, too," the chaplain said. "When I met him, briefly, when he first got here, he was using the f-word like a sailor. But when I spoke with him a few weeks later, after his going forward, his language was cleaned up."

I asked the chaplain if I could do Reggie's funeral service.

"I think Reggie would be honored to have you do that."

The funeral service, ten days later, was attended by one of the largest crowds at our facility ever. The newspaper's obituary writer insisted on writing up a "feature" obit, a mini-biography that went way beyond the usual "just the facts, ma'am" obituary send-off. Reggie's obituary, blown up into large print, was prominently displayed next to the open casket.

Reggie was an only child and never married, and so the newspaper was his family. Reporters and editors, many of them entirely unaccustomed to wearing coats and ties, got dressed up for the sad occasion. During the time for eulogies, many got up to describe Reggie's compelling reporting on the city's more colorful denizens and their activities.

The last to speak was Chaplain Smithson.

"I didn't know Reggie as long as many of you have," he said. "But in our short time of knowing each other, he became a good friend."

The chaplain described how Reggie had suffered at knowing that he had caused a permanent physical injury to someone. Revealing something that Reggie had told me privately, Chaplain Smithson explained that experiencing that guilt was more painful to Reggie than his conviction on the drunk driving charge.

Reggie's friends and former colleagues were listening intently.

"But Reggie found a freedom in Jesus," the chaplain said. "He found forgiveness."

"Then why did Jesus let him be killed?" Reggie's city editor piped up. "The judge only gave him twenty years. God gave him much worse than twenty years. God gave him the death sentence."

I thought the question was rather impolite, given the occasion. But, okay, why?

"We don't know," the chaplain said. "God's ways are not our ways, his thoughts are not our thoughts. But I suspect that Reggie, at this very moment in heaven with Jesus, is not missing prison, not even one little bit."

The crowd was silent.

"In heaven, in eternity," the chaplain added, "there is complete freedom. No guilt. No sorrow. No fear of death."

No fear of death, I wondered. Driving home after the ceremony, I decided to give this religious question some serious thought.

FIFTY-SEVEN: A STONE'S THROW

Several weeks into our conversations about her recent encounter with religion, Antoinette determined to once again visit her father to try to resolve their estrangement.

"I've got to make things right," she told me before starting out. "Best I do it by myself."

At mid-morning, Antoinette was driving along a country road, about a half hour from her destination. She was singing at the top of her lungs. "Jesus loves me, this I know," she belted out, "for the Bible tells me so."

Because Antoinette was not sure what kind of reception she would receive, she decided to visit without asking her parents in advance. As usual, Antoinette was driving our Honda Accord well over the speed limit.

In the open countryside, Antoinette's open window let in both a cool breeze and that special aroma of barnyard animals. As she approached an overpass, Antoinette tapped on her brakes to slow her vehicle.

The rock burst through the windshield with a thunderous fury. Glass went flying as the windshield shattered into dozens of fragments. The rock struck Antoinette's right arm and careened into her torso, causing her to jerk the wheel sharply clockwise. The abrupt motion sent the car sharply to the right and off the roadway. Continuing to spin clockwise, the car collided with a tree, causing it to suddenly jerk in the opposite direction. Bouncing off another tree and plowing down an incline, the car flipped over and came to rest upside down.

It was only the fastened seatbelt that kept Antoinette from being thrown from her car. Tangled in those straps, Antoinette quickly lost consciousness.

A passing motorist called 911. Antoinette did not regain consciousness until just before she and the rescue crew arrived at the hospital. "What happened?" Antoinette mumbled through the oxygen mask. "You had an accident, but you're going to be okay," the ambulance crew member reassured her.

By the time I got to Sacred Heart Hospital, Antoinette was flat on her back in the intensive care unit. I was allowed to see her for ten minutes.

Striding up to her hospital bed, I was both shocked and relieved. Shocked at her sudden transformation. Relieved because she was alive, if just barely alive.

"Hey, sweetheart, I'm so sorry," I said. "I love you. You're going to be better. Hang in there."

The accident had wrought a wicked blow. Antoinette's head was wrapped in bandages. Her broken jaw was wired shut. Six-inch pins stuck out of her right arm and right leg, both broken. An IV bag filled with a clear liquid emptied into a six-foot tube inserted into her left hand. A heart monitor emitted a steady beep, beep, beep.

Antoinette smiled and tried to say something, but I motioned for her to be quiet by putting my finger to my lips. Through the wires, she mouthed, "I love you," and I quietly returned those words. I clasped her hand and kissed her on her forehead. I just stood there until a nurse came in and escorted me out of the ICU unit.

I sat in the waiting room, staring straight ahead for what must have been a full half hour. First my parents' passing, then Reggie, and now this, I thought. "So where is your God now?" I muttered, just loud enough that other visitors looked in my direction.

Instantly, I regretted my words. At least Antoinette wasn't killed, and if there was a God, I didn't want him to complete the job he had started.

I spent half hour in the waiting room, waiting for a doctor or nurse to come out and inform me of Antoinette's condition. At long last, a doctor came out.

"Given the accident, your wife is extremely lucky," Dr. Hanson said. "In most cases like this, the accident is fatal. But Antoinette is going to make it. We'll need to keep her here for a week or so, just to establish her recovery."

"Is there any permanent injury?" I said.

"I don't think so, but we're not sure," the doctor said. "Her head was pretty banged up, so there may be a permanent scar. But again, given the circumstances, she is a very lucky woman."

"Can I see her?" I said.

"We've given her a sedative, and so she's asleep," Dr. Hanson said. "You can peek in, but only for moment, and don't try and wake her. So it's best if you go home afterward and come back in the morning."

I looked in for the promised minute, and headed for the lobby. Once there, it took me twenty minutes to compose myself enough to hazard walking to my car.

When I walked into Antoinette's room the following day, my lovely bride was sitting halfway up in bed. She was eating breakfast, that is, if you can call being fed through an IV tube eating breakfast.

"Hey, babe, you're looking rather chipper this morning," I said.

Antoinette smiled and whispered through her wired jaw, "You're looking rather handsome yourself."

The police had given me an account of the accident and its aftermath. The young boy who threw the rock and his two companions, all 12 or 13, were taken into custody after one set of parents saw a newspaper report. The parents asked their son about his whereabouts. The youngster made up a story. But his parents, wise in the ways of teenage prevarication, were not fooled, and they contacted the authorities.

"The police told me what happened, Antoinette," I said. "I'm so sorry."

Antoinette shuttered, but was silent.

I sat at Antoinette's bedside for about twenty minutes, not saying a further word. All that time, the unanswered question, unspoken but whispering to each of us, hung in the air.

I broke the silence.

"Antoinette, I'm so grateful that you were not killed," I said. "But where was ..."

"Where was my God, Harry?" Antoinette said, her facial muscles moving against the wires in her jaw. She spoke slowly and quietly, yet audibly, loud enough for me to hear clearly. "Where was my God?" she repeated. "Right there beside me, protecting me, his child, from fatal harm!"

I was silent.

"Harry, this accident was God's grace. It's got his fingerprints all over it. Jesus demonstrated, in the most vivid way imaginable, that he's watching over me."

The speaking left Antoinette a little breathless.

"How can you say that, Antoinette?" I said. "You were almost killed."

"You've got the operative word right, Harry," Antoinette said. "Almost."

"Yes, almost killed," I said. "And left with a broken leg, a fractured arm, and a head pretty banged up."

"And alive, if not yet kicking," Antoinette said. "And able to tell you that God protected me from a life-threatening injury."

"Maybe," I said.

"Remember Job?" Antoinette said.

"Not really."

"Well, he went through a lot, but he turned out okay, just like I'm going to be okay."

I sat there in silence, unable to respond. Antoinette was likewise silent. Then, minutes later, Antoinette pulled out a trump card.

"Remember when I got my job as a bounty hunter?"

"Yeah?"

"Remember my first skip, the guy I caught, or we caught, in the 7-11?"

"Yeah?"

"Well, just before you got here yesterday, some guy showed up at the ICU nurses' station, claimed to be my brother, and asked to see me. It was only because the nurses got suspicious and called hospital security, that they did not let him in."

"Oh."

"He started storming off, but security stopped him, and demanded to see his driver's license." Antoinette paused, took a deep breath, and continued. "They wrote down his name, and they showed the name to me, asking if I knew him. The last name sounded familiar, and then I remembered. Same last name as that first skip I captured, the guy in the 7-11. Turns out that this guy was that skip's brother."

I sat there for a moment, stunned.

"God's grace, Harry, God's grace."

"God's grace," I repeated, not out of belief, but simply repeating Antoinette's affirmation.

"Think about it, Harry," Antoinette said. "I love you, and I want so much for us to be in this together."

"Okay, I'll think about it," I said.

"And pray about it," Antoinette added.

"I'll think about it."

We just looked at each other for the next five minutes. Then the nurse came in, holding out a pill and a cup of water. "Time to give our young lady some needed rest," the nurse said.

I gave Antoinette a goodbye kiss on her forehead and told her I would come back at suppertime. On my way out, I thanked the nursing staff for alerting security about the skip's brother. "The other nurses told us that he just didn't look quite right," one nurse said.

Some weeks later, I found out what happened to the three boys who did the rock throwing. When confronted by the authorities, the teenagers told police that they were just horsing around, and that they didn't mean to harm anyone.

The three boys suffered three very different fates. One boy, who threw several stones at passing motorists but not the rock that struck Antoinette's car, was remanded to a juvenile detention facility. As days turned into weeks, he became increasingly bitter and more difficult to control.

The second boy, also remanded to the juvenile detention facility, began attending a Bible study there.

The third boy, the one who had thrown the stone that had struck Antoinette's car, was also incarcerated in a juvenile facility. Sometime later, he was found dead inside his cell, a suicide.

FIFTY-EIGHT: SHERLOCK

Shortly after my wife was safely ensconced, first in the hospital and then recovering at home, I began carrying out my secret detective work.

I pursued my investigation in out-of-sight and in out-of-the-way places. Cafes on the edge of town. Private offices far from curious passersby. Quietly in my basement when I knew Antoinette was safely asleep upstairs.

Yes, I decided to pursue the God that Antoinette was so sure of -- and I was entirely skeptical of -- as a would-be detective might pursue a suspect without alerting neighbors or friends.

Now, I know, God is not a suspect, even for the non-religious. But my pursuit did have, in a metaphorical way, some elements of a cloak-and-dagger mystery.

My reason for keeping this pursuit secret was simple enough. I wanted to discover, in the depths of my soul, whether this "God thing" Antoinette had told me about was true. But I wanted to know out of genuine conviction, not because adopting Antoinette's belief would be something that would simply please Antoinette.

This was thus my pursuit strategy, the premature discovery of which would bring on unwanted consequences. And so I began my campaign, careful not to leave any evidence that Antoinette might pick up on.

"Are you thinking about what you said you would think about?" Antoinette asked during my next visit to the hospital.

"Oh, that," I said. "Yes, I'm thinking about it."

"Any thoughts you'd care to share."

"Not really."

My next visit. "Any progress on thinking what we talked about?"

"What was that again?"

"Progress on what we talked about?"

"Uh, who knows?"

Meanwhile I was dogged in my pursuit.

When Antoinette came home, I was careful to give her as much attention as possible, sandwiched between my funeral duties. Antoinette took a temporary respite from her bounty hunter activities. So she spent a lot of time very visibly resting in a very prominent place in our house. When she would read the Bible, I would pretend not to notice what she was reading.

Every so often, I mentioned to Antoinette that I needed to take a drive just to take a break, to "get out of the house."

Once out of sight, I pondered. Where to start on this, my secret pursuit?

First of all, I wanted to hear an objective account of what this religion thing was all about. Antoinette had told me in great detail what "faith in Christ" meant, but that was Antoinette. I loved her and respected her views, and she was very engaging. But, with a steely determination,

I did not want to be simply captured by my very strong passion for her.

Where to go? A church visit would be too soon discovered, so that's out.

Aha! I've got it. And so, I stopped by a nearby college, and dropped by the religion department.

The assistant professor I spoke with was intrigued. "It's not often that people stop by to ask about religion," he said. "We appreciate your interest."

So what did he think about what Antoinette said? Was Antoinette onto something, or was it just a passing fancy?

"People experience God in different ways," Dr. Jones said. "So, for Antoinette, it's a wonderful thing that she's undergone a spiritual awakening."

"But is she right?" I said. "Is this something we all should do?" I did not spell out that I was trying to figure out if "this" was something that I, myself, needed to do.

"It's all up to the individual," the assistant professor said. "God is a loving God and very tolerant. We each select our own paths, and God, however you conceive of him or her, respects that."

Even I, with no religious background, could detect equine manure when I smelled it. I thanked the assistant professor for his time and left.

I drove home and made supper for Antoinette and myself. She described her progress in recovering from her broken arm and leg, which was proceeding apace.

"So, did you go anyplace special on your drive?"

"Oh, I stopped by the local branch of the state university," I said. "I thought maybe we should take some classes."

"Any special classes in mind?"

"No, not really."

A few days later, I ventured out again. I wanted to find a place where I could pray, to fulfill my promise to Antoinette. But it would have to be someplace where I would not be detected.

And yes, to fulfill the promise in an honorable way, it would have to be a sincere prayer, not just going through the motions. I thus needed to find someplace where I could pray at some length, without anybody noticing.

And so, after checking out several lunch spots I assumed were mostly empty late one afternoon, I found a café that was dead empty except for one couple at the far end of a large dining area. I brought in a newspaper, which I set before me to deflect any suspicion that my real purpose for being there was prayer.

I sat there for an hour, casually flipping the pages of the newspaper but never reading a word. I just started talking to God, if there was one, as I would talk to an older person I respected. I spoke, moving my lips, but careful to not let any suspicious sound emerge.

I've never been shy of speech, so keeping up this one-sided conversation was not that difficult. I had brought a pen and notebook, so I wrote out my attempt to start the conversation.

"Hello, God, if you're there. How are you today?"

No answer.

"Anything you'd like to tell me today?"

I listened quietly. But again, no answer.

"Antoinette says you're really there," I continued. "But, to be honest, I'm really not so sure. Any help you want to give me on this?"

All I could hear was a faraway clock quietly ticking.

"Okay, God, I really would like to know if you're real. I'm listening."

And I did listen. Real hard. But again, nothing.

An hour passed. During the entire hour, I felt okay, if a little disappointed. This wasn't going to be as easy as I expected.

It was only when I was finished that I felt somewhat foolish. To cover my tracks, I bought an apple pie, the café's specialty, and brought it home to Antoinette.

"Pretty long drive, Harry," Antoinette said.

"I wanted to get you a special dessert, and I looked high and low," I said. "And here it is, thanks to the deli on Fifth and Market."

I wondered if my long and varied absences were becoming suspicious.

And so, I waited two weeks before venturing out again. I did say a few prayers during those two weeks, mostly while taking extended time in the shower. Still, exactly nothing happened during those two weeks. If there was a God, he was surely taking an extended sabbatical.

When I decided to venture out again, I couldn't think of what else to do, since talking with a religion prof and some prayer didn't seem to work. Then it struck me. Let me do a quick Bible read-through.

I had never actually thumbed through a Bible, much less read through one. I had never even owned a Bible. I did not want to go to a church to get one, because showing up on a Sunday to pick up a Bible would give the game away.

Maybe Barnes & Noble has one, I thought. After all, they do have all sorts of books. For me, buying a Bible seemed rather strange, but whatever.

I snuck into the store, trying to not look suspicious. My usual habit in finding a book was to ask a clerk for directions to this or that section, but now I was too embarrassed to ask. Fortunately, there was posted sign listing history, classics, bestseller fiction, religion, etc.

Browsing, I had no idea which Bible to select. Most of the Bibles looked super long, so I settled for a New Testament. Better a close look at a shorter text than a cursory look through something that went on forever.

Overcoming my embarrassment, I approached a clerk. "Give me a copy that's easy to read," I told the clerk. He seemed happy to comply.

I hid my purchase of a New Testament by also buying a popular novel, just in case Antoinette found out about my trip to B&N. I paid cash and tossed the receipt, lest Antoinette ask about a second book I might have bought.

I didn't actually crack open my purchase until about three days later. Fortunately, Antoinette's recovery caused her to sleep extra hours, which gave me a chance to head downstairs and open the New Testament. I took along the novel I had purchased at the same time just in case Antoinette ventured into the room.

But now. Where to start reading?

With the first big chunk of the Bible dropped out altogether, the New Testament seemed reasonably doable. Not familiar with the book, I looked up the table of contents. "Chapter headings," I thought.

I was in luck. I knew enough to know that many Jewish people go for the Old Testament, even though they give it a different name. And here, to my amazement, right there in the middle of the New Testament was a summary of the Old Testament, boiled down to the basics in less than twenty pages.

"Hebrews."

I started reading. It made absolutely no sense at all. I had good intentions, but by about the middle of the second chapter, I was starting to fade. Until …

Until I was stopped dead in my tracks by a pair of sentences that jumped out at me. No, jumped out at me doesn't quite capture what those sentences did. The sentences, quite literally, grabbed me by the throat and would not let go.

I took my pen and notebook and wrote down the stunning words.

"Because God's children are human beings -- made of flesh and blood – the Son also became flesh and blood. For only as a human being could he die, and only by dying could he break the power of the devil, who had the power of death. Only in this way could he set free all who have lived their lives as slaves to the fear of dying."

I sat there, for a long time, simply reading and rereading the words.

"Only in this way could he set free all who have lived their lives as slaves to the fear of dying."

Suddenly, the memory of my grandfather's death came flooding in. Followed by the fire and brimstone preacher man in college. My college friend's sudden motorcycle accident. Reggie. And then, in rapid succession, a flash of every recent funeral I had supervised.

FIFTY-NINE: JOSIAH

Sitting in my basement, I reread the words yet once more.

"Only in this way,' the sentence stated, "could he set free all who have lived their lives as slaves to the fear of dying."

Yes, just as I read that, the memory of my grandfather's death, like an unwanted guest, barged into my mind. Despite the decades gone by, I once again saw the back of my grandfather's motionless head. I felt, once again, my childhood confusion as my mother walked me back from his chair.

Once again, I remembered the shock and fear I felt when death without warning struck down my high school classmates.

And suddenly, battered by those memories, I was utterly exhausted. It was already late. I went upstairs, to bed. Despite being dead tired, I could not sleep for hours. I tossed and turned, the memories repeating themselves like a pair of schoolyard bullies who wouldn't quit. Shortly before dawn, I managed to fall asleep, dead to the world until I abruptly awoke at mid-morning.

"How's my Rip van Winkle?" Antoinette said cheerfully as she brought me coffee.

"Sorry about the over-sleep," I said. "Must have been too much late-night coffee with my reading."

As I sipped my brew, I decided that I needed to figure this out with someone who could both keep a confidence and who might know something about the sentence that had so disturbed me.

Inspiration struck. Chaplain Josiah Smithson.

Chaplain Smithson was the guest pastor who had taught at the prison where my good friend, Reggie, had been incarcerated. Chaplain Smithson had also officiated at the funeral we had held for Reggie after he was murdered in prison.

Getting to see Josiah Smithson involved jumping through a few hoops. After telling Antoinette that I had to do a few unspecified chores, I showed up at the prison's intake desk. Told he would not be in until the afternoon, I went to lunch, impatiently.

"How's my good friend?" Chaplain Smithson said, warmly, as I returned. I remembered his outgoing nature during the funeral. His generous greeting erased any inconvenience I felt during the lunch wait.

Chaplain Smithson, an African-American in his 40s, seemed the perfect fit for his behind-the-walls work. He had a muscular build and tattoos on both arms, tattoos that his shirt did not entirely cover. He had been incarcerated himself, a very long time ago.

"So what brings you here?" he said. "By the way, don't call me chaplain. Too formal. Just Josiah is better."

"Okay, Josiah. Not sure," I said, hedging my bets. "You spoke at my friend Reggie's funeral, very movingly as I recall."

"I remember. Reggie was a great brother."

"Yes he was. But now, I have a question," I said. "I was reading something the other day, and I was wondering if you could explain it to me."

At this, Josiah laughed. "I'll try."

I was more than a little embarrassed, and for a moment considered bluffing my way through the next half hour. But then, steeling myself, I decided to not waste the opportunity before me.

"I was reading a sentence in, what's it called, Hebrews," I said. "And it intrigues me."

Josiah nodded.

I decided to fess up. "No," I said. "Actually, it terrifies me."

Josiah waited patiently as I opened the New Testament I had brought to our meeting. I had placed a folded-up piece of paper to mark the page, and had underlined the sentence that so troubled me.

"Only in this way," I read out loud, "could he set free all who have lived their lives as slaves to the fear of dying."

"Yes, Hebrews," Josiah said.

"It's the 'slaves to the fear of dying' that bothers me," I said. "Have I been a slave to the fear of dying?"

"The fear of dying is something many people experience," Josiah said. "It comes from our inborn sense that we will, at death, stand before God and give an account of our lives."

"But that could be a long time from now," I said. "Why would I have that fear if death is so far away?"

"It's not always far away," Josiah said. "Death can sometimes sneak up on us quite suddenly, quite unexpectedly."

I was suddenly choked up, as if a pair of iron hands had grabbed my throat. My jaw tightened. My palms got sweaty, even as I wiped them on my pants. I was silent for so long that Josiah said, a few minutes later, "Harry?"

Finally recovering my ability to speak, I laid out my tragic death count. "Reggie died in the middle of our good friendship," I said. "Earlier, my parents died, rather unexpectedly. A friend of mine in college died."

"I'm so sorry," Josiah said.

I struggled to finish the account.

"And when I was a young boy," I began, speaking slowly, "my grandfather died." I described to Josiah how it was so unexpected, how I came upon his still warm body, and how my mother had broken the news to me.

"I loved him so much," I said. "After he died, I swore that even if there was a God, he was at fault for taking my grandfather, and that I would never have anything to do with that God."

"What happened then?" Josiah said.

"Well, as the years rolled out, I did have nothing to do with God," I said. "But my fear of death kept getting stronger and stronger. I've tried to shove that fear of death into a closet someplace in my mind, but it keeps escaping."

Adding to its cruelty, I said, was that death was never satisfied. My grandfather. But then, my parents. My friend in college. And now, not so long ago, Reggie.

"And, of course, sometime soon," I said. "Me."

A pause.

"And, of course," I added, "death uses my job to whisper its threat against me day in and day out."

Another pause.

"Perhaps you might like to reread the verse, out loud," Josiah said. "Actually, start with 'Because God's children are human beings …' I think it's verse 14."

I did as Josiah suggested.

"Because God's children are human beings, made of flesh and blood," the sentence read, "the Son also became flesh and blood."

The sentence jumped out at me. "Christians believe that Jesus is both God and a human being, don't they?" I said.

"Yes. But go on."

"The Son also became flesh and blood," I read. "For only as a human being could he die." There, quietly, the more I thought about this, the stranger it became.

"Why a human being and why a human being, only to die?" I said.

"Read on," the chaplain said.

I read, slowly. "And only by dying," the next sentence read, "could he break the power of the devil, who had the power of death. Only in this way could he set free all who have lived their lives as slaves to the fear of dying."

"The fear of dying," Josiah said, "comes because we all know that we all have that appointment with God, that appointment that death summons us to."

I listened intently.

"It's like standing before a judge, knowing in our heart of hearts that we're guilty of the charges," Josiah said. "We dread that appointment. Why do we dread that appointment? Because we know that we're guilty of breaking God's law, and we know that the judge is going to pronounce sentence."

Suddenly, the play that Antoinette and I had seen in the park together so long ago flashed into my mind. Unlike then, when I thought the whole idea was nonsense, or worse, the picture raised by that drama now rattled me.

And now, suddenly, some of my own dishonorable behavior, long forgotten, snuck into my mind. Like how nasty I had been to the first-ever girl I had sex with. Like the time I punched a guy in a wheelchair. (When confronted by my teacher, I denied everything.) And the many times I had mouthed off to my parents when they caught me coming home too late at night.

Seeing I was thinking, Josiah paused before he continued.

"That's why Jesus became a human being, and why he died on the cross," Josiah said. "To take the penalty for guilty sinners like you and me."

Again, a pause.

"And that's why, when we turn away from bad behavior and come to Jesus," Josiah said, "when we receive his forgiveness based on that Jesus paid the penalty for our bad behavior, we no longer need to fear death."

"In the same way an acquitted man no longer needs to fear the judge," I said.

"Exactly," Josiah said. "With no longer a case against us, we no longer experience a fear of death."

Suddenly, and with the passion of a condemned man who hears that the governor is on the line, I wanted that freedom. I desired that pardon with all my being.

"I want that," I said. "Josiah, I want that forgiveness very much."

I began to pray. "Yes, Jesus, this is what I want," I said. "I want that you've paid the penalty for all the wicked things I've done. I want your forgiveness. I want to have this new life."

I was so excited about this new kind of praying that I probably went on for a half hour, alternately laughing and crying.

"Sorry about the long prayer, I said.

"It was a wonderful prayer," Josiah said. "Welcome to the family." He encouraged me to find a Bible believing church, and suggested that we meet again in a few days to talk about how to continue walking as a Christian.

"Lord Jesus, I am so grateful," I said in a loud voice as I got into the car.

I was excited about telling Antoinette what had just happened, but I wondered just how I might do so. I needn't have worried. She knew just by looking at me.

"Hey, babe," she said.

"Hey, sweetheart," I said.

"Hey, babe, praise God?" she ventured.

"Yes, sweetheart, praise God," I replied.

Antoinette started cheering, screaming, a huge smile on her face.

"Yes! Yes! Yes!"

A few minutes later, Antoinette said she had long suspected that my sudden flurry of out-of-the-house activities were part of an investigation into the truth of the gospel.

"But I wanted to give you lots of room," she said.

"I appreciate it," I said. I described to her in detail how I came to faith in Christ.

"God is awesome, isn't he?" Antoinette said.

"He is indeed."

SIXTY: FRIENDS, FRIENDS

In the days after I got converted, my moderately extroverted personality, ordinarily operating in second gear, went into overdrive.

"Have I told you that Jesus is God?" I asked the gas jockey as he handed back my credit card. "Okay," he said, and shrugged.

"God loves you," I told the barista as she gave me change for my double latte. "He loves everybody," she replied.

"I found Jesus," I told a distant neighbor as he walked his dog near our house. "I didn't know he was lost," he replied, stopping only briefly as he and his German shepherd made their routine rounds.

After Antoinette's enthusiastic response when I told her of my encounter with Jesus, I simply assumed others would be equally enthusiastic. What's not to be excited about? I figured. Genuine forgiveness! Assurance of God's love for you, yes, you! Reconciliation with your Creator! The answer to life's puzzle revealed! And heaven thrown into the bargain!

And for me, perhaps the greatest benefit of all. My lifelong fear of death erased.

Okay, maybe these people I didn't really know might be skeptical of what must have come across as religious fanaticism. So, I decided to focus my attention on people I really cared about. Family and friends.

Target number one, obviously, would be Randy, my brother and diehard gun nut. I took a day off to drive down to meet with him. Over lunch at a favorite pancake spot, I poured out my excitement over having become a Christian.

"Jesus is real, Randy," I said. "The Bible is true, it's all true. I've given my heart to Jesus. I've become a Christian."

"But of course it's true," Randy said. "What's the big deal? Hey, pass me the maple syrup."

I reached over to my right side, grabbed the syrup bottle, and passed it to my brother. He tried to pour the syrup onto his pancakes, but the nozzle seemed to be glued shut.

"Hey, they need to fix these syrup containers," Randy said.

"So, I've started reading through the Bible," I said. "It's super exciting, reading God's love letter to us."

"They really do need to fix these syrup bottles," Randy said. "Hey, Harry, maybe you could flag our waitress."

"I never thought I would become a Christian," I said. As I said these words, my long standing fear, after my grandfather's death, together with its recent resolution flashed through my mind. I wasn't ready to share that most personal unveiling, though. "But I did, exactly eight days ago."

"Eight days, huh?" Randy said. Then, having spotted the waitress, he addressed her. "Miss, can we have a syrup bottle that works?"

Randy returned his attention to me. "So, you're reading the Bible these days?" he said.

"Yes, I've read through some of the New Testament, and I'm hoping to tackle the Old Testament after that."

"Did you read the part about where Jesus tells his disciples to take up their guns?"

"Not sure."

"Just before he got arrested," Randy said. "He tells them to take up their guns, but then changes his mind and tells them to put those weapons aside."

"I did not know that."

"It's in the Bible, I forget where."

"So you're a Christian, too?" I said.

"Always been a Christian, you know," Randy said. "Mattie and I go to a big church about forty minutes from our house."

"What are they teaching these days?"

"Not quite sure," Randy said. "We've missed the last couple of Sundays. Anyway, would you like to see my new equalizer? It's a beaut." Randy lifted up the edge of his shirt, revealing a handle sticking out from a holster.

Out of sheer politeness, I looked.

"Once you take the safety off, you can squeeze out bullets with a minimum of recoil."

"Oh."

"It's accurate to hundreds of yards."

"Sounds great."

"Best of all, I got it for a song, a very reasonable price."

"That's nice."

The remainder of our conversation turned to politics, both national and local. "I do think the Republicans are going to trounce those woke libs in November," Randy said. "Here, let me get that," he added as the waitress placed our check on the table.

In the parking lot we said our goodbyes. "Harry, always good to see you," Randy said. "Give my regards to Antoinette."

Oh well. Next, up to bat, Sal. If anyone can relate to my resolving my fear of death, certainly Sal can.

It turned out that Sal was tied up for the next week, so I went for my doctor. I invited him for lunch, explaining him that it was to be a social occasion, not a doctor-patient appointment.

We met at the local IHOP. Upon meeting, I addressed him by his first name, Mark, to establish that we were meeting as equals, not as caregiver and client.

As a patient, I had revealed to Mark some very personal information. Even my closest friends did not know about my ingrown toenails. Still, I didn't know anything halfway personal about Mark. What his hobbies were, or even what sports teams he followed, things like that.

So, I wondered, how to establish a personal bond, a friendship that would serve as a foundation for talking about that most personal of topics, the giving of your heart to Jesus.

Mark beat me to the punch. "So, Harry, have you thought about what I said about Darwin and Voltaire? I remember, the last time we got together, in my office, you seemed pretty interested in those giants of science."

"Actually, I have," I said. "But I'm not sure they were right about things."

"Not right?" Mark said. "Thus sayeth one of the unbelievers of our benighted century."

"Actually, I AM a believer," I said. "But a different kind of believer. I've become a believer in Jesus. He's forgiven my sins, and I'm going to heaven when I die."

"You've not become one of those born-agains, have you?"

"If that's how you want to put it," I said. "But can I explain to you how it works? How a person becomes a Christian?"

"Come on, Harry, don't go Jesus freak on me. If you want to throw science to the winds, that's your choice. But I prefer to stick to reason."

"How about I just give you the basic outline of how a person becomes a Christian. I promise it will only take about two minutes to explain it."

"Come on, Harry. Get real."

"Two minutes, Mark. Two minutes?"

"Okay," Mark said. "Two minutes. No, wait a second. Why are we even wasting time on this topic? You're not going to convince me, and I'm not going to convince you. This topic can only lead to hard feelings between us. I respect you as a friend, and so let's just keep it friendly. So, next topic?"

I gave up. For the next half hour, Mark talked cheerfully about his passion for the Boston Red Sox. It seems he had once had a girlfriend who was all things Red Sox. They broke up a very long time ago. These days, she was a distant memory, but he remained a Boston fan.

We parted on friendly terms, with no further mention of anything Bible related. "We should do this more often," he said, shaking my hand. I wasn't exactly sure he would want to.

When I finally sat down for lunch with Sal, my fellow funeral director and good friend, he looked noticeably thinner.

"They worked us to the bone," Sal said.

I wasn't too thrilled about hearing the good doctor talk about Darwin and Voltaire, but I genuinely wanted to get Sal's take on his recent experience with funerals in Haiti.

"It was horrible beyond belief," Sal said. "Bodies piled up. A stench that ripped through your nose. Families wailing so loud that the sound tore your insides."

"I'm sorry."

Sal continued for about ten minutes, but then fell silent, letting his words sink in.

"I appreciate your sharing this with me," I said. "You did a good work, Sal."

"Thanks for listening, Harry, and sorry to hog all the conversation. So what's new with you?"

This sounded like a good opening.

"Sal, something wonderful has happened," I said. "I've become a Christian. I've given my heart to Jesus. I've become born again."

"You've become a Bible thumper?"

"You could say that," I said. "But it's more than that. Remember how I asked you, off the cuff, if you were afraid of death?"

"Vaguely."

"Well, I've always been afraid of death, ever since I was a kid."

"That's a bad sign for a funeral director."

"Yes it is, but true nonetheless," I said. "But Jesus showed me that I no longer needed to fear death because Jesus paid for everybody's sins, including mine."

"Maybe yours, but I'm not a sinner, Harry. You said so yourself."

"But everyone ..."

"Come on, Harry, be rational. If what you're saying is true, why did I even bother going overseas? Enough already. Let's tell some of our old funeral stories. We can end with a laugh."

And so we did. Alas, sometimes laughter hides a sadness.

SIXTY-ONE: DAUGHTER

For years, I had simply assumed that my fear of dying was the result of having many of my closest family and friends suddenly struck down by death.

That was certainly part of it. But as Josiah explained, there was a deeper root cause. The fear of dying came from knowing, instinctively, that I would be required, at death, to give an account of my behavior to the God who gave me life.

That's why the news about Jesus taking the rap in my place was so appealing. And certainly, I reckoned, if I explained this clearly to others, who wouldn't want to take advantage of the offer.

And so, despite my first three failed attempts, I wasn't about to give up. Hey, my own history was that of a longstanding knucklehead, forever slow on the uptake.

Next up, then, was Jeff Cotton, my tax advisor. Recall, Jeff was one smart cookie when it came to tax law. He was also one lucky devil when it came to beating the rap on accusations of tax fraud and financial irregularities.

"So, how's my beat-the-rap buddy this fine morning?" I said.

"Couldn't be better," Jeff replied as we sat down to lunch at Michelle's. No IHOP or generic pancake place for Jeff. Tastefully arranged chandeliers, a heavy white tablecloth, and uniformed wait staff fairly dripped money. Jeff insisted, in advance, that he was treating.

Jeff's victory in court was now months old, but he was still basking in its warm aftermath.

"Imagine, Harry, the feds went after me and all they got was egg on their faces. Justice may be blind, but in my case, she was seeing with twenty-twenty vision."

"It is quite remarkable that you beat the rap," I said. "The accusations were pretty serious, and the government had some remarkable top tier attorneys."

"You're right about that," Jeff said. "Top tier, but out-hustled like a losing Super Bowl contender." He continued to gloat for about twenty minutes. And he was, truth be told, quite the lucky guy. Very few people expected him to come out on top.

"Especially the reporters covering the trial," I suggested.

"I saved all the newspaper articles and put them in a scrapbook," Jeff said. "If I ever have any grandkids, I'll regale them all."

"I have no doubt about that," I said.

"So, what's new with you?" Jeff said after our waitress left with our order. "I heard rumors that you've gotten religion."

"Not really religion," I said. "I've given my heart to Jesus. I've become a Christian."

"Sounds like religion to me," Jeff said.

"No, not really religion," I said. "Walking with Jesus."

Hearing myself say this, I fully expected Jeff to give me the same brush-off that my three previous friend and family members had responded with. But, no, Jeff seemed genuinely interested. So I decided to tailor my message to something Jeff could relate to.

"You know how your lawyers got you acquitted of all charges in your supposed financial hijinks case?" I said.

"Do I ever," Jeff said. "Best lawyers ever."

"Well, Jesus is an even better lawyer," I said. "He will get you acquitted before God of all the bad stuff you've ever done."

"What do I need a better lawyer for?" Jeff said. "Like I said, and as you know, I've already got the best lawyers ever. And together, we beat a rap when everybody thought I was going to go down for the count."

"Jeff, it's not the same."

"Even if they were rather pricey."

"Jeff, my friend, it's not the same thing."

"Admit it, Harry, you've been out maneuvered, just like those fancy pants government lawyers were."

"Oh, man."

"Hey, Harry, enough of this legal back and forth. Here comes our lunch. So, how's the rest of your life going? How's the missis?"

"Things are going great," I said in a cheerful voice. I decided that there would be no point in letting Jeff know that Antoinette had also found Jesus. And so for about 45 minutes, we talked about baseball, the weather and some other things I can't remember, before parting amicably.

Four at-bats, four strike-outs. It was mid-afternoon when I drove back to my office. Since my conversion, I had developed a habit of shooting up a short prayer or listening to praise music on the radio while driving. Not now, though. I drove in utter silence.

When I got back to my office, my assistant informed me that there was a woman waiting for me in my office.

It turned out to be Alice Anderson, the sister who refused to be reconciled with her brother.

Despite the weeks gone by, I recognized her immediately. She nodded as I greeted her, but sat silent for a few moments.

"How can I help you?" I said, deliberately adopting a friendly but neutral tone, to give her as much emotional room as possible.

"I've been thinking about what I said about my brother," she said. "I've been thinking that maybe I've been unfair to him."

"Okay."

"I've been thinking about it because, much to my surprise, I actually miss him."

I remained silent, giving her room.

"I do miss him, I'm embarrassed to say," she said. "They say that blood is thicker than water, and I think that maybe it's true."

"I am so sorry for your loss," I said, in the gentlest tone I could manage.

At this, Mrs. Anderson began sobbing uncontrollably. She continued to do so for a full fifteen minutes. I handed her a few tissues from a nearby box.

"He was a jerk, but I miss him terribly," she said. And then, a smile amidst her tears added, "But we're all jerks, aren't we?"

I nodded.

"You know, I was reading my Bible the other day," she said. "I hadn't read it since Alex died. I didn't want to read it, but somehow I needed to start reading it again."

I just listened.

"I opened it at random, and just started reading slowly," she said. "It was the story about the prodigal son. I had read the story before, of course. But as I was reading, it dawned on me. It wasn't a story about the prodigal son. As I read it, as tears welled up in my eyes, it became the story of the prodigal daughter."

She paused.

"I was that prodigal daughter."

I remained silent.

"I haven't spoken with my remaining brothers since the funeral," Mrs. Anderson said. "I don't think they even know that I was at the funeral, sitting in the back. But I think that it's way past time that we were all reconciled."

"I think that would be wise," I said.

"Yes, that would be wise," Mrs. Anderson said, suddenly cheerful.

Another pause.

"Yes, I think God would want us to be reconciled," she said. "Me and my brothers. Way past time."

SIXTY-TWO: TEN DAYS

Mrs. Dooley was sitting in my office for the second time this month. I had performed the service for her father. And now, less than two weeks after the first parent's passing, her mother had passed away.

"I'm so sorry for your loss," I said. "I'm sure losing both parents in such a short time must be very difficult."

Like most people, I had heard of such cases in which an elderly couple, married for a long lifetime, passes away, one shortly after the other. It says something about how deeply they were devoted to one another. But having both parents die so close together is extremely hard on their children and extended family.

Following so shortly after the first service, there were still plenty of details to work out for the second funeral in Mrs. Dooley's family. But ironing out those details could wait. Mrs. Dooley, like many grieving family members, simply wanted to talk.

"Can I tell you how my parents met?"

Given the unusual way in which I had met Antoinette, I've always been fascinated with how other married couples met. If those encounters occurred a very long time ago, the tales promised to be even more interesting.

"It all started with a blind date, a blind date that went," and here, Mrs. Dooley paused for effect, "that went, in an unusual direction."

Mrs. Dooley's father, Herbert Knight, was enrolled as a second-year engineering student at Lafayette College, a prestigious private college a few hours north of Philadelphia.

Mr. Knight's father, Alfred, had worked steadily as a machinist, and the son grew up in an environment that produced both a respect for hard work and a desire to move up the professional ladder.

"My father's college days were filled with books, labs, and not much else," Mrs. Dooley said. And then, with a sly smile, she added, "Until he met my mom."

One of her father's college buddies, Larry, an economics student, took pity on her father, Mrs. Dooley continued. Or, more accurately, he took pity on both her father and Nelson, a friend they had in common, also an engineering student. A friend who, like her father, was wholly engrossed in his professional preparation studies.

"'We've got to get you both out a bit,' Larry told them," Mrs. Dooley said.

The proposed solution? A double blind date. Larry had two sisters, Ann and Irene, both nursing students in their early 20s. The four would meet at the Star Diner, an off-campus family-style restaurant.

"Ann was to be my father's date," Mrs. Dooley said. "And Irene was to be paired up with Nelson, my father's engineering friend." After a little coaxing, both engineering bachelors agreed to go.

The four met at the Star Diner. After introductions and the ordering of sodas all around, the four began to get to know each other. There was some conversation in which each engineering student talked with his assigned date, but mostly it was a group discussion. The talk ranged from school and homework assignments to the relative virtues of Caesar salads, fried chicken and steak sandwiches.

Ann was a redhead, and Irene was a blond, a real blond, Mrs. Dooley continued. About thirty minutes in, both girls decided that they needed to go to the ladies' room.

"The girls said they wanted to freshen up," Mrs. Dooley said, a twinkle in her eye. "But I think it was to compare notes."

Meanwhile, the young men who remained seated at the table were also exchanging observations.

"I know that the blond is your date," Mrs. Dooley father, Herbert, told his friend, Nelson. "But she's gorgeous."

"I like the redhead better," Nelson replied. "Blonds, they're always okay. But give me a hot-blooded redhead any old day."

The funny thing, Mrs. Dooley added, was that neither engineering student had much experience with either blonds or redheads, or any other women, for that matter.

"Meanwhile, Aphrodite was working her special magic in the ladies room as well," Mrs. Dooley continued. "My mom, well, she wasn't my mom yet, my mom said she liked her date's young man better than her assigned paramour."

"Okay."

"He just seemed nicer, my mother would always tell me," Mrs. Dooley said. "My mother's friend liked them both, so she was willing to switch partners as a courtesy to her friend."

The big announcement came just as both women emerged from the ladies' room.

"'Boys, time for the big switcheroo,' my mother told the seated engineering students," Mrs. Dooley said. "Pointing to my father, my mother said, 'I want that one.' And then, pointing first to her friend and then to my father's friend, she added, 'And she gets him.'"

"Big smiles broke out all around," Mrs. Dooley said.

"'These girls are geniuses,'" my father whispered to his friend, out of earshot."

"'What was that?' my mother said."

"'Oh, nothing,' my father replied."

For the rest of the evening, the engineering students spoke mostly with their reassigned dates. Herbert with the blond, and Nelson with the redhead.

A good time was had all around.

For Nelson and the redhead, things didn't go much past that evening. They had one additional date, a few weeks later, but any initial spark failed to ignite a romantic fire.

For Herbert Knight and his future spouse, things turned out differently. They began to see each other, in between homework assignments, engineering labs and hospital floor assignments. They didn't so much date, as the phrasing goes, as just get together whenever their busy schedules made room for it.

"Over time, they became best friends," Mrs. Dooley said.

Despite his engineering personality, her father was the more outgoing of the two, Mrs. Dooley continued. Her mother, even as a nurse, was always more reserved.

Mrs. Dooley's father was scheduled to graduate a year before his future wife, and they began to talk about the possibility that they might get married. "It was a delicate topic," Mrs. Dooley said.

"My father brought it up more often than my mother did, and she was always a bit reserved when the conversation went in that direction," Mrs. Dooley added. "I think she had some relatives with poor marital histories, so I think she was a bit wary when the subject came up."

"At long last, my father popped the question," Mrs. Dooley said.

"It was at the most unexpected moment," she added. "Right in the middle of both of them preparing for midterm exams. The timing of the proposal was so unusual, my father was an 'everything in proper order' kind of guy, and the place was so out of the ordinary, the library, if you can believe it, that my mother just blanked."

"Just blanked?" I said.

"Yes," said Mrs. Dooley, "Just blanked. She hardly said anything for the rest of the study session. Then, just before they left for their separate ways, she mumbled, 'Let me think about it.'"

Mrs. Dooley continued.

"That, needless to say, was not exactly what my father expected. But my mother did think about it. She thought about it for a full ten days. My father was a true gentleman throughout the long wait. You can imagine what was going through his mind. But on the evening of the tenth day, she told my father, 'Yes.'"

A pause, and Mrs. Dooley continued her story.

"The wedding was a small and intimate affair, a few family members from each side. After they got married, he worked full time, as did my mother, until my big sister came along. Afterward, my mother worked part-time when it was possible to do so while raising my sister, my older brother, and me."

"Ten days on the way to a marvelous life together," I said.

"Just a little more," Mrs. Dooley added. "When I was in my teenage years, my father got an offer for a fantastic promotion, a job in the Denver area. Always the gentleman, he ran it by my mother before deciding whether or not to take the position."

"And?"

"And so, when he asked my mother, my mother said the move would be a big adjustment, what with us kids being in school. She said she would like to think about it."

"Let me guess."

"Yes, exactly ten days later, my mother, after a bit of prayer I might add, told my father that she was excited about making such a move. We stayed there a few years before coming back to this area."

"I so much appreciate you sharing your story with me," I said. "And I appreciate your willingness to allow me the honor of doing the service for both your father, and now, your mother."

"Did you notice something?" Mrs. Dooley said.

"No, did I miss something?"

"My father died twelve days ago," Mrs. Dooley said. "My mother, two days ago."

"Ten days," I said, hitting my forehead.

"It always took Mom ten days," Mrs. Dooley said, "to follow Dad into whatever he ventured into."

SIXTY-THREE: RETURN

"She looks very peaceful."

Mrs. Anderson was laid out in a tasteful outfit in her open casket. A line of family members and friends stretched from the coffin to the back of the room. Gospel music played softly.

Six weeks after making her surprise visit to my office, Mrs. Anderson had suffered a massive heart attack. She died after spending three days in a hospital's cardiac unit.

Mrs. Anderson's final weeks were a flurry of activity. After she came to see me, a visit that found her broken and sorrowful over how she had never reconciled with her suddenly deceased bother, Mrs. Anderson had striven mightily to make right what remained.

"We were utterly surprised when she called us up and told us she wanted to talk about Alex," Paul, her youngest brother, told me as I supervised the ceremony from the back of the room. Mrs. Anderson's husband, Mark, stood silent as her brothers spoke.

"It was a compete change in attitude," Greg, her oldest brother, added. "Instead of Mrs. High-on-her-Horse, Alice was devastated that she had for years never spoken to Alex before he died."

Mrs. Anderson, the brothers told me, had planned how to reconcile with her brothers very carefully. One by one, she had invited each of the brothers to her house.

"Each of us was under the impression that it was a one-on-one invite," Dan, the middle brother, said. "She told each of us to not tell any of the rest of us, because it was just going to be the two of us."

"I've got to admit," he added, "when she said 'don't tell anybody,' I got a little suspicious, thinking that she was up to something."

"It turns out she was up to something," Greg said. "What she was up to was inviting each of the brothers."

"And each of us was given the same day and time to show up," Paul said.

"What happened then?" I said.

"Having everybody show up at the same time wasn't the only surprise," Greg said. "Dan, tell Harry the first surprise."

"The first surprise was that Alice had set up a huge table, and laid it out with, surprise, surprise, a Russian foodie theme."

"Russian?" I said. "Why Russian?"

"It's what she had studied in college," Dan said. "She had also been to Russia a few times, you know, after the Commies got out and the place opened up."

"So what kind of food?" I said.

"Gosh, what a table," Dan said. "Russian meat pies. Salads. Special cakes. Borscht. You name it."

"She even handed out special index cards with the names of all the foods, so we could name them," Greg said. "For starters, piroshky."

As Alice sat around the table with her remaining brothers, she told them how she regretted her stubborn attitude. "She asked forgiveness from each one of us," Greg said.

"Did your sister give a reason for her change of heart?" I said.

"She said it wasn't easy," Dan said. "But she said that she finally realized that the conflict between her and Alex wasn't just Alex's fault, or even mostly Alex's fault."

"She described herself, and this was really a jaw dropper," Dan said, "that she was, as she put it, the 'chief of sinners.'"

I kept Mrs. Anderson's confidence and did not disclose that she had spoken with me in my office some weeks before her meeting with them. Still, I was struck by how Dan characterized her speech.

"What else did she say?" I said.

"Well, we talked about how our father had played favorites," Dan added. "You remember how we mentioned that when we spoke with you at Alex's funeral."

"I remember."

"Well, when it came up at this reunion, Alice had a different take on it," Dan continued. "Actually, several takes."

A pause.

"First of all," Dan began again, "Alice said that the whole thing about our father playing favorites, and that Alex was somehow the favorite, was all wrong."

"Because …" I said.

"Because, she said, it wasn't really fair to say that our father played favorites," Dan said. "It might seem that way, she said, because he did certain things with certain of his children, and certain other things with certain other of his children. But he loved us all equally, even if in different ways."

"Her saying that really cleared the air," Greg said. "When she said that, you could see everybody relax."

"You mentioned that there was something else, a second thing," I said.

"The second thing was just as liberating," Dan said. "Alice said that even if our father did favor one of his children over another, not that he did, but even if he did, it did not make sense to let the feelings or actions of someone long gone to dictate how the rest of us treated one another."

"That was the real liberation," Greg said. "The deceased, as loved as they were, do not rule the living."

"Yes," I agreed. "The deceased do not rule the living."

"And one other thing, which we should mention," Greg said. "Our sister was a Christian. She made a profession of faith a long time ago, but hers was a rocky road."

I was listening intently.

"Yes, Alice was a Christian, as are each of us," Dan said. "It's been a slow process, but over the years, all of us have put our faith in Jesus. For some of us, it's been pretty easy. For others, not so much."

My heart was warmed.

"For Alice, it was especially difficult," Greg said. "Alice had a lot of personal issues to overcome. Recently, and for a long time, it almost seemed like her faith wasn't registering, especially in her refusal to reconcile with Alex. But at this meeting that she had invited us to, she told us that Jesus had prompted her to call the meeting, to tell us that she had repented of her stubbornness."

"She actually used that word, 'repented,'" Paul said.

My heart was strangely warmed.

"But it was a bittersweet moment, of course," Paul added. "All this clearing and reconciliation happened when Alex was not able to hear it."

"I suspect Alex may be hearing about it just now," I said. "I suspect they may be enjoying a tearful reunion right about now."

"You're a believer?" Greg said.

"Yes, a believer," I said. "And like your sister, someone who struggled to get there."

"Awesome," they said. They returned to the viewing line.

At just this moment, Antoinette came up and gave me a kiss on the cheek.

"Hey, babe," she said.

"Hey, babe, yourself," I said.

I was struck by just how gorgeous Antoinette looked. Not a surprise, but still, wow. We always wear our "Sunday best" when officiating at funerals. But somehow, Antoinette was always a special rose among the flowers.

"These brothers were just giving me a special update on God's grace," I said.

"That's awesome," Antoinette said. "And I have yet another example of God's grace, special delivery to you."

"And what might that be?"

"I'm pregnant."

A graduate of Columbia University, George Berkin is a former newspaper reporter and blogger. He has taught English to native Russian speakers in Moscow, Ukraine, and Philadelphia. As the pandemic recedes, Mr. Berkin hopes to return to a Philadelphia prison, where he taught a Bible study for several years. Mr. Berkin's family and friends prefer to remain anonymous, for reasons that will become obvious to readers.

The author would like to thank those who gave their time, effort, and skills to bring this project to completion.